LOVE ALWAYS,

Bailey

SAMANTHA COOKE

World Castle Publishing, LLC
Pensacola, Florida
Copyright © 2023 Samantha Cooke
Paperback ISBN: 9798891260955
eBook ISBN: 9798891260962
First Edition World Castle Publishing, LLC, November 13, 2023
http://www.worldcastlepublishing.com
Licensing Notes
Editor: Karen Fuller

Table of Contents

Chapter 1

Me, 9:15 a.m.: You're coming, right, Bails?
Me, 9:17 a.m.: Please tell me you're riding with us.

It had been seven months since I last heard from my best friend, Bailey.

That was all I could think as I glanced into my duffel bag one final time, making sure I had packed enough bathing suits and sunscreen to last the week.

"Morgan, Noah's here!" my mom yelled from where she stood out on the front deck.

My bag weighed heavily on my shoulder as I walked out of my bedroom and down the hall to the front door. The screen door closed slowly behind me with a groan, the sound of my childhood home doing its best.

I heard my cousin's blue Honda before I saw it. Noah had the windows down and the stereo turned up, blasting a top-forty radio station. He climbed out of the driver's seat and ran up to the porch to meet me, reaching for my duffel bag with a smile. Earlier that morning, he had texted me one simple line: Remember the plan.

"Are you sure you're ready for this?" my mom asked. "There's no rush to get back to school." She placed her hands on my shoulders and stared at me, the wrinkles around her eyes defined as worry washed over her face.

I instantly felt guilty.

"It's just a week," Noah chimed in. "Plus, the professor leading the class is one of my favorites."

He must have thought I was going to blow our story.

"Well, take care of each other," my mom said.

She looked at the car and waved to Ethan, who sat in the passenger seat. He smiled and waved back, which my mom took as an invitation to walk over and chat.

Once she was out of earshot, Noah nodded to me. "Good job."

"I hate lying to my mom."

He smiled and placed his hand on my forearm. "The guilt will go away as soon as we're at The Highview."

He walked down the porch steps with my duffel bag slung over his shoulder and out to his SUV. He threw the bag in the trunk and sat in the driver's seat. My mom waved goodbye to Ethan and Noah and met me on the walkway.

"I think this will be good for you." She brushed a strand of straight brown hair behind my ear and placed her hand against my cheek. Then she wrapped me in a hug, and I took a deep breath, exhaling against her neck. When I pulled away, she had tears in her eyes.

"Mom, it's just a week." I tried my best to give her an encouraging smile, but all I could think about was the lie that lingered over me.

She nodded, and I took that as my cue to get in the car as fast as I could.

"I'll call your dad and tell him you're heading out," my mom yelled to Noah.

"Nah, I'll just text him," Noah answered quickly.

"All right, well, not while you're driving. And be safe. I know you think you're adults now because you've gotten a year of college under your belt, but—"

Noah assured my mom we'd be just fine and spoke of the imaginary classes he swore we were enrolled in. An extended semester, he had told his dad. Morgan should do it too, he'd suggested to my mom. It was a simple lie to get us where we really wanted to be: toes covered with sand, hair dried with salt. We wanted The Highview, and if we had to lie to get there, so be it.

The Highview was where we had grown up. Uncle Daniel had bought the house when we were kids, and Noah and I had shadowed him throughout the summer as he renovated it, adding a deck that led straight to the beach and a spiral staircase that led up to the top of the house. The Highview was ours, and though a rotation of strangers vacationed in it most of the year, it had always felt like home.

I got into the back seat behind Ethan, who was scrolling through a playlist of songs. He kept his eyes on his phone for a brief second before turning around in his seat to look at me. He had cut his blond hair, and his sunglasses had left a tan line around his blue eyes. In many ways, he still looked like the seventh-grade boy who had been Noah's first friend in middle school, but something seemed different about him. I just couldn't tell what.

"Hi, Morg."

"Hey."

Noah pulled out of the driveway and drove down my street. When he turned left at the stop sign, his eyes caught mine in the rearview mirror.

"You really didn't tell your dad we were going to The Highview?" I asked.

Noah shook his head. "No way."

Today's journey had started back in May with a simple text message from Noah. Meet at The Highview, July 1. The text message had gone unanswered in the group thread, and the lack of response had made me sick with the belief that they were all texting without me.

As Noah drove down my street and turned toward the interstate, I thought of the last night he had visited me before sending the text. I had been sitting in the living room, empty cans of Diet Dr. Pepper littered around me, and the television turned to some new reality show about friends with a marriage pact.

"Will they end up together?" Noah had asked as he leaned back against the couch cushions.

"Hard to tell, but I'm rooting for them."

"Well, I hate to be the one to ruin your good time, but I have bad news." Noah handed me his phone. On screen was a website with a list of houses for sale. I noticed what he was trying to show me instantly.

The Highview.

"What the hell? He's selling the house?"

"My dad thinks it will sell by the end of summer, so we aren't going in July." Noah shook his head. "But I have a plan." He looked around the living room to make sure my mom wasn't around, then leaned closer to me.

"University of Central Florida offers mini semesters in the

summer. We can tell our parents we're all taking summer classes. We'll tell your mom that you're going to try UCF out to see what you think. Then we'll go to The Highview. All of us."

"Bailey, too?" I asked.

Noah looked at me. "We can make it all right, Morgan."

Last night, Noah had texted me again to confirm he would pick me up in the morning and to remind me for the tenth time not to tell my mom the truth.

Now, we blazed forward to The Highview, three hours away in Englewood Beach, in Noah's SUV. My anxiety settled as the excitement hit me. I would see Bailey today. We would have a chance to make it right.

In the front seat, Ethan rambled on to Noah about a class they had both taken last semester.

"I can't believe you passed," Noah said. "You did none of the reading."

Ethan shrugged. "I'm made for college, man."

Noah turned and glared at him, and Ethan shook his head. "Oh, damn. I'm sorry, Morgan." He flashed me the same pitying smile everyone gave me.

"It's all good. A lot of people take a semester off."

"That's true," Noah said.

"But, hey," Ethan said, "this extended semester could really be a game changer, huh?" He put air quotes around extended semester, and Noah laughed.

I chose to focus on the music that was playing, the only thing that felt normal about our trip this morning.

~*~

The Highview looked the same as always: The beautifully landscaped yard lined with seashells plucked straight from the beach. The gravel walkway leading to a large staircase and wrap-around deck. The red front door framed by potted plants, which somehow drew attention away from the bright orange staircase at the front of the house that led up to the house's top deck. The top deck gave a full view of the entire backyard beach. We could see the sand and ocean go on for miles from up there, and each night, the top deck would be waiting for us at sunset.

Us.

I thought it with such ease as if I would walk through the front door, and everything would be back to normal: Uncle Daniel asleep on the couch, a bowl of melted ice cream on the coffee table. Noah constantly checking the forecast. Ethan fighting to figure out the smart TV. Allie pulling at strands of her perfect blonde hair in the hallway mirror. Ryder watching clips of the Miami Dolphins at training camp. And Bailey—her long legs stretched out and a book in her hands.

Us.

It was such a small word. Yet, in this case, it carried so much weight that if a hurricane the year before hadn't already knocked down the huge palm tree in the back, me walking through the front door right now and saying, "The deck is ready for us tonight," would have.

It wasn't until Noah turned off the car that I noticed it: planted directly in front of the house was a For Sale sign bearing a few obnoxious lines of catchy slogans, such as Ready for some fun under the sun? and A flip-flop's throw to the beach! and my personal favorite, It's sun o'clock somewhere. The specifics of the house were plastered on the sign as well: Open concept! Three bedrooms! New roof!

"You should see the pictures my dad took to give to the realtor," Noah said.

We all got out of the car and stood in the driveway.

"We're in deep shit if anything happens to the house while we're here," Noah added.

Ethan opened the trunk and pulled out our bags. "Don't worry, dude. We'll keep destruction to a minimum."

Memories of previous summers flashed through my mind, all decorated with images of us growing up. We had experienced so much in that house, from first loves to first losses, and being back felt like we had unlocked a time capsule.

Ethan stared up at the house. Noah walked over to him and patted his shoulder. Noah said something, and Ethan cracked a smile before nodding.

My stomach hurt. My heart sank. I was home, and it was familiar, but at the same time, it was so far away. I couldn't explain the feeling, but it was almost like The Highview didn't want us there.

Noah took out his copy of the key and unlocked the door. The three of us barreled inside as though racing to find which room we wanted to sleep in, even though it was an unspoken rule that the sleeping arrangements never changed. Three extra keys sat on the kitchen counter. Ethan picked one up and attached it to his keyring. Beside it, right next to his car key and apartment key, hung a frayed and weathered pink string.

Bailey's anklet from last summer.

Ethan opened the sliding glass door that faced the beach, letting the breeze flow inside. Other families in the houses around us were already staking claim to the sand, reapplying sunblock, and drinking from cold water bottles pulled from coolers. The back deck that led to the beach still had five chairs on it, forming a circle. It was as if we'd never left.

Ethan walked down the hall and opened the door to the room he, Noah, and Ryder always shared. Noah picked up my bag and followed, stopping one door earlier, where Bailey, Allie, and I always slept. Part of me wondered if they were already here, fighting over who had to sleep on the top bunk. Another part of me wasn't surprised to find the bedroom empty when I walked in.

One twin bed was pressed against the wall opposite the bunk bed. The closet, once used to hide a stolen six pack of beer, was closed. A flat-screen television that we never turned on sat in one corner, next to a lamp with a light bulb that had been broken since I could remember. The window, cracked open despite the heat, soaked up sunlight and air.

I didn't realize I was holding my breath until Noah spoke. "I'll leave you to unpack."

The familiarity of the room stirred my thoughts. In the last year, a handful of strangers had slept there. Bodies drained from the sun curled up underneath soft blankets, laughter filling the space between here and the living room, the smell of burnt toast wafting from the kitchen in the morning. These lives intersected, yet they didn't even know it.

By the time I was done unpacking, Ethan had changed into running sneakers and shorts, slipped in his earbuds, and walked out the sliding glass door. Noah and I watched from the top deck as he broke into a jog down the beach and, with every pounding footstep on the sand, disappeared farther into the setting sun. Noah had brought up his portable speaker and was playing a shuffled playlist of all our favorite summer songs from over the years. A cover of "The Boys of Summer" by The Ataris was playing now, the only cover song Uncle Daniel had told us "could hold a flame to the original."

"Morgan," Noah said suddenly, "Ryder texted me today. He's coming."

I thought back to that simple text message that Noah had sent. Meet at The Highview, July 1.

Though no one had responded in the group thread, Noah had assured me we were still on. He had told me he would pick me up with Ethan and dodged my questions when I asked why he hadn't included Bailey in the original text.

"No one ever responded. I didn't think he'd come."

Noah nodded. "He wasn't going to. But he changed his mind last minute. He'll be here tomorrow morning."

The Highview had been home for so many people over the years, including Ryder, who had been the last to join our group of friends in eighth grade. Ethan and Noah had welcomed him into their friendship with open arms and without question, and as they bonded over surfing, it became the six of us: Noah, Ethan, and Ryder with Allie, Bailey, and me. Our week at The Highview was the highlight of our summer vacation every year and something we would spend the rest of the year talking about. Ryder would always have a countdown going on his phone until the second week of July when we'd usually go. He'd pack for the week the morning of, just throwing in swim trunks and the bare necessities. He'd show up at the house with a backpack while we lugged duffel bags and suitcases up the stairs. He would always tease Bailey because she usually forgot her toothbrush.

We had the best memories all together in the house, but I wasn't ready to see Ryder.

Noah and I fell into silence as Ethan ran back down the beach and up to the deck. He took his earbuds out and checked the time on his watch.

"My best mile time yet. He's back, everyone." He grabbed a water bottle from the table where he'd left it. Leaning against the railing, he pulled his phone out of the armband he was wearing, disconnected his music, and then looked back up at us.

His sweat-soaked brow furrowed. "Did you see Ryder's text, Noah?"

Noah nodded. "That's what we were just talking about." He looked back at me, and Ethan followed suit.

"Morgan, when was the last time you saw Ryder?" Ethan asked. "When you dumped him back in April?"

"Really, Ethan?" Noah asked.

"That's right," I said.

Ethan laughed. "Man, you date a girl for two years, claim she's the one, and even though you're only eighteen, prepare to give your life to her. Then she just leaves you in the dust."

"Can you not?" I asked.

He was right, though. Ryder and I had had the perfect love story. For two years, we'd made plans for the beach houses we'd own and the stamps we'd collect in our nonexistent passports. Best friends first, we'd shared a giggly first kiss, followed by late-night phone calls and Friday-night dates at Cobb Theatre. Even when we were accepted into different colleges, we swore we'd make it work. The drive from Orlando, where he would be, to St. Augustine, where I would be, was a quick one, straight down I-95. We'd agreed it would work, and it had.

Until it hadn't.

Chapter 2

Me, 6:23 a.m.: There's a new Dunkin' Donuts on McCall.
Me, 6:23 a.m.: I bet they'll still mess up my order. So annoying.

I woke with the sun the next morning and immediately made my way to the back deck. Thankfully, Noah went to the grocery store last night and bought what he deemed as necessities: bread, eggs, lunch meat, four bags of Lay's chips, and, for me, coffee and coffee creamer. With a coffee mug in hand, I sat in my favorite Adirondack chair that gave me the perfect view of the ocean and breathed in the salt air.

The houses that surrounded The Highview were all vacation rentals as well. Peak visiting times were during the summer season, and there was always a revolving door of new guests for us to mingle with each year. As I looked to the house to the left of us — the only one on the street with a swimming pool — I wondered who would be there this year. It was notoriously known for being rented to families, except for the one time two summers ago when a fraternity rented it out. They'd spent their days doing clean up on the beach for their time giving back to the community and their nights in full on party mode. The house to the right of us was smaller, with a slab on concrete as the back deck and a pull-out couch as the sleeping accommodations. The selling point for this entire row of houses was the private beach access, only available to residents of Shoreview Drive.

I looked out at a sailboat in the distance as it floated along the ocean. The water looked still, the orange sky a backdrop to what the day would bring. It had started raining last night around nine and stopped this morning around four. I'd spent the night tossing and turning, listening to the sound the rain made as it hit the window in my room. When I'd gotten bored of that, I moved to the living room and listened to the sound it made as it hit the roof.

I'd lain awake all night wondering how it would feel to hear Ryder's Honda Civic revving down the street with its windows down, Queen playing on the classic rock station we all secretly loved. His musical taste had always been as eclectic as everything else about him. He'd get out of his car and tell me it was okay and that we could work on it. He'd bring a tray of fountain drinks because he always laughed at me for needing an iced coffee or a Dr. Pepper in hand at all times. He'd tell me he still loved me.

But, when I really thought about it, I guess I didn't have the right to wish for all of that. After all, I had been the one to call it quits. He'd been willing to fight for us at a time when I had nothing left to give.

My history with Ryder was like a story out of a rom-com. We'd spent years becoming best friends, and one night, during the summer after ninth grade, Ryder had asked me what would happen if he kissed me.

I shrugged. "Only one way to find out."

He held out one fist in the palm of his other hand.

"Rock paper scissors? Really?" I giggled harder than the

joke warranted. Leaning forward, he pushed a strand of light-brown hair out of my eyes.

"If I win, we kiss. If you win, we kiss," he said, instantly setting butterflies loose in the pit of my stomach. He won, best two out of three, and kissed me on the back deck, right where I now sat.

We'd fallen in love so fast that no one even had a chance to say the words, "I never saw that coming!" He'd made me feel safe, always, and with him, I'd felt that we could take on anything together. I'd always scoffed at the idea of a person being your home, but with Ryder, I was home.

I'd loved Ryder. I probably still loved him, with part of my heart, but so much had changed since that first summer, I didn't know if he could still love who I had become. With everything that had happened in the last few months, the bigger part of my heart was now empty, and I felt like he would have spent the rest of our relationship trying to do the impossible: fill it.

There was just something so special about him, though. I'd spent countless summer nights with my head under his arm as we laid on a blanket on the beach, staring up at the sky. And what a treat it was for both of us to see that our relationship could withstand life outside of summers at The Highview. We'd been in a bubble here, for sure, but going back to AP classes and after school jobs at the grocery store, we'd learned that it wasn't just the magic of a summer romance. We did some serious growing up together. Ryder always joked that when he was with Ethan and Noah, he had to act cool. They had a running joke that since he was the last to join our friend group, he'd be the first to get voted off the island. With them, he always joked and goofed around, but with me, he was inquisitive and sensitive. He'd told me once that I had every part of him.

Ending it had made sense. We'd left for different colleges, and we had grown distant in the miles that separated us. We texted each other less throughout the day, we made fewer plans to visit; our endless flow of conversation was replaced with bouts of silence. But it wasn't just that. When I'd decided to drop out of Flagler, he had worried I was being rash. I told him he didn't care about us anymore. At the time, walking away from not only our past but our future had seemed nearly impossible, but it had to be done.

In the days that followed our breakup, I'd close my eyes and pretend I was back with him. We were together at our lunch table back at Space Coast High. We were sitting next to each other in Spanish, with Senora Marti lecturing us about verb conjugations. Ryder had been everywhere and everything to me for a long time, and as the days ticked by, he'd slipped away from me more and more. I struggled to remember the things that I'd known so well about him, like how his mom used basil scented laundry detergent on his t-shirts.

It had been 173 days since I'd last seen Ryder. And yes, I was definitely keeping track.

As if I'd conjured him, I heard a car pull into the driveway. The windows must have been down because I could hear the music perfectly until the engine was cut, and two car doors slammed, one right after the other. Noah told me that Bailey wouldn't be here, but what if Ryder had convinced her to come? I stood up just as Noah opened the sliding glass door and poked his head out.

"Ryder's here."

I turned around and nodded. "Did he come alone?"

Noah nodded and raised his eyebrows at me, "Who would be here with him?"

I brushed it off, struggled some more as I confessed to Noah, "We haven't talked since we broke up."

"I know, Morg."

I couldn't look at Noah. My cousin had been around me my entire life. If I looked at him just once, I knew I'd start to come undone, and I had a rule about no crying until after my first cup of coffee.

From inside, I heard the front door open and close, and Noah, Ethan, and Ryder exchanged greetings as if they hadn't seen each other in years. Now or never. I walked toward the open sliding glass door.

"How is she?" Ryder asked. He was holding a large McDonald's cup that surely contained sweet tea and a Nike backpack. He wore his staple outfit: a tank top and shorts, complemented by the flip-flops I had bought him for his birthday last year. His right shoulder bore a quarter-sleeve tattoo he had gotten on his eighteenth birthday, a scene of a surfboard and the ocean. I felt sick to my stomach as I realized he had added to it since I'd last seen him.

"She's fine," Noah said quietly, his eyes darting toward the floor.

"And Bailey?" Ryder asked.

"She hasn't mentioned her yet." Noah looked at Ethan. "Has she said anything to you?"

Ethan shook his head.

I turned, trying to leave the scene, and bumped against the doorframe on the way out, making more noise than I would have liked. All eyes were suddenly on me.

Ryder gave me a tight-lipped smile. "Hi, Morgan."

"Hey, Ryder."

Ethan stared back down at his phone and pressed play

on whatever video he had been watching. Ryder grabbed his backpack and walked past me. For a moment, he lingered beside me; in the past, he would have taken the moment to push a strand of hair out of my eyes or gently touch the side of my face with his thumb. If he was in a silly mood, he'd swat at my butt or point to an invisible stain on my shirt to try to get me to look down. I held my breath, waiting for something, anything. When he continued walking without touching me, I tried my best not to be surprised.

Ryder walked down the hallway, Noah behind him, and pushed open the bedroom door with his foot. He and Noah walked in, letting the door swing mostly closed behind them. I stood in the middle of the living room and stared at the cracked-open door, straining to hear their hushed conversation.

"Is Allie coming?" Ryder asked.

"Doubtful," Noah said. "She never answered."

As if I hadn't already felt the absence of something or someone, the reminder that Allie had elected to keep away buzzed around my head.

I looked around the living room, hoping for something to catch my attention.

Ethan stood up. "Let's go down to the water."

"Yeah, okay." I paused. "What are they talking about?"

"Don't worry about it, Morgan. It's time to move on." He didn't even bother to look over his shoulder as he walked toward the back door.

Needing to change, I walked down the hallway, but I passed my door and paused in front of theirs.

"She was doing fine in April, but I think my dad's announcement about selling the house set back any progress she'd been making with the therapist."

"What can I do?" Ryder asked.

Behind me, Ethan cleared his throat. "You coming?" I nodded and turned back to my own room, where I put on my bathing suit.

~*~

Ethan had dragged a beach chair and an umbrella down to the beach and stood staring at the water by the time I joined him minutes later. Families and other vacationers were slowly setting up shop. Tourists were easy to spot based on what they brought down to the beach with them. Baskets and baskets full of beach toys and extra towels usually got in the way of kids who would rather bury their legs in the sand, laughter exploding from them whenever a wave came in and washed the sand away. The waves had picked up and were now crashing against the shore as they broke. The blueness of the water stretched on for miles, the end nowhere in sight, and for the first time in my life that scared me a little.

Ethan walked over to his beach chair as I sat down next to him.

"What do you think Ryder and Noah were talking about?" I asked.

Ethan looked at me. Sadness—and anger?—washed over his face as he exhaled. Though he had sunglasses on, I could see the furrow of his brow. His sudden coldness caused me to look down at my freshly painted toenails. The polish color—The Fuchsia Is Bright—was one Allie had discovered two summers ago. Before Noah, Ethan, and I had left, I'd applied a coat for good measure. I'd hoped it would bring us good luck.

Ethan finally spoke. "Doesn't that get exhausting? The constant worry?"

"And what am I supposed to do? Just sit back and relax, huh?"

Ethan shook his head, "What I don't understand is how you, of all people, can pretend nothing happened. You were there, Morgan."

"Is that why you've been so distant with me? You're still mad about winter break when I told Bailey she shouldn't date you."

Ethan stood up and walked down to the water. His shoulders rose as he took deep breaths before he turned around and stared at me.

"That's what you think this is about?"

"Well, why else wouldn't she be here? She would never miss a week at The Highview. I keep texting her, but she hasn't answered me since January, and she's my best friend."

Ethan stared at me, then turned away and shook his head. "What do you mean, you keep texting her?"

Behind me, footsteps announced Noah and Ryder's arrival. Noah tossed his portable speaker onto the sand a few feet away from me, and when I looked up, I found that Ryder was already drinking a soda. Noah sat down in the sand next to his portable speaker.

"You couldn't bring us down some chairs?"

Ignoring the question, Ethan turned back to me, his jaw tight. "Morgan, you're texting Bailey?"

"What's going on?" Ryder asked.

My stomach dropped in the face of Ethan's sudden anger. Standing up, I walked back toward the house.

"Morgan, come on. Where are you going?" Noah called after me.

"Away from here."

I kept my eyes down as I walked toward the house. Behind me, I could hear their voices blending together, surely trying to figure out what had just happened.

I made it to the back door and noticed my hand was shaking as I slid it open. I walked inside the living room and was stunned by the silence. The house looked empty, and as I looked around, I realized why, for the first time: Uncle Daniel must have packed up the majority of the ocean themed decorations. Where there were once seashells and wooden boats on every shelf surface, now, the selves were empty. There were still blown-up sized photographs of the sea, but that was it. All of the decorations that made The Highview more than a vacation destination were gone. I remembered what Noah said: you should see the pictures my dad gave the realtor.

Damn. He was actually going to sell the house.

Behind me, the door slid back open. I turned around, and Ethan stood in the doorway.

"Noah told me I have to apologize. I'm sorry," he said.

"Gosh, Ethan, that's so genuine."

"You don't even know what I'm apologizing for," he said.

I looked at him and realized it didn't matter. It didn't matter why he was stuffing a half-assed apology down my throat, only because Noah surely guilted him for losing his temper with me. It didn't matter now. For some reason, he felt a trace of guilt. None of that mattered because the house was still getting sold, and Allie and Bailey were nowhere to be found. I sat on the arm of the couch and looked around the room again.

"It's so empty," Ethan observed. He walked inside and sat on a wicker chair — one that we all always used to fight over who had to sit in it because it was so uncomfortable — and stared at me.

"I haven't talked to Bailey either, in case you were wondering," he said.

And I knew then and there that we had a lot to figure out this week. I just hoped I didn't have to do it alone.

Chapter 3

Last Summer

Bailey, 12:04 PM: Tell me how we graduate tomorrow, and I've never once stepped inside the 600 building?? What the hell is even there?

Me, 12:04 PM: We had homeroom there in 9th grade
Ryder, 12:05 PM: And Geometry 10th grade
Bailey, 12:05 PM: Oh…

I reached across the cafeteria table and grabbed a handful of chips from the bag Bailey was offering me. Next to her, her black purse balanced on the cafeteria bench. We had just spent the last five minutes discussing whether the drama department should keep a picture of her as Roxane from Cyrano de Bergerac as their marketing photo now that she was graduating.

She had insisted that it was someone else's turn. I'd pointed out that she had worked hard in her four years in the department, ending as the troupe's president this last year. Plus, the picture was beautiful. In it, her light-brown hair was braided on both sides into a bun at the nape of her neck. She had worn just enough stage makeup that up close, she had looked like a twelve-year-old playing with eyeshadow for the first time, but from the audience, she had looked radiant. Natural. She deserved the recognition.

Allie sauntered over from the cafeteria entrance and slid onto the bench next to me. She grinned at Bailey. "Bailey and Ethan sitting in a tree, am I right?"

"What are you talking about?" Bailey asked.

"Did you not see Ethan's quote on the senior superlative page in the yearbook?" Allie unzipped her backpack and pulled out her yearbook. I bit my tongue to keep from laughing; she had to be the only senior still bringing a backpack to school. We would be graduating tomorrow.

She flipped through pages of pictures until she got to the last half of the yearbook, which was reserved for the graduating class. She stopped on the page titled Senior Superlatives, which listed everything from Most Athletic to Most Likely to be Famous, including the category that Ethan and Bailey had won together: Most Unforgettable. In their picture, Bailey's hair was pulled back in a messy ponytail, and she stood shoulder to shoulder with a grinning Ethan. It was a stark contrast to Bailey as Roxane but somehow still elegant.

Allie handed Bailey the yearbook, pointing to the page. A small paragraph sat under the picture. "Here it is. Read what Ethan said about you."

Bailey scanned the page for a moment before looking back up. "So?"

I took the yearbook from her and read the same paragraph. In it, Ethan shared that he and Bailey had a marriage pact that said if they were both unmarried when they turned thirty-five, they'd end up together. I read the last sentence aloud and started laughing: "It wouldn't be the worst thing if that happened; Bailey's a cool girl."

Bailey crossed her arms over her chest and looked between Allie and me as we laughed. "Yeah, so? You guys have known about that marriage pact."

"There's a difference between us knowing about a marriage pact and him announcing it to the world that he hopes it happens," Allie said. "Come on, Bails, he's so obsessed with you. I wish he'd just admit it."

"It's not like that at all. We're just friends."

Noah walked over from the senior section of the cafeteria, where he had been organizing the last hoorah for our graduating class. "Guys, it's time to throw your trash away. There's only ten minutes left for us to go add our handprints to the senior wall. Don't you want to live forever? Where's everyone else? I want our handprints all next to each other."

Noah had been active in the student government for the last two years, and this year, he was the head of the senior committee, meaning that every school dance, spirit day, and graduation festivity had been organized and led by him. He'd spent the entire year roping us in to work carnivals, help sell prom tickets, and, worst of all, run a kissing booth.

He pointed to the senior section, an area with fifteen or so tables reserved for seniors to eat at during lunch. Today, it was blocked off with red and gold paint—our school colors—for seniors to go leave their painted handprints on the wall. The tradition had started years ago, and one of the only benefits of living in a small town was that there was still enough wall space for our graduating class.

"Okay, we're coming." Allie gathered the trash off our table and walked it over to the garbage can a few feet away.

Bailey and I stood and followed suit, and the four of us walked toward the senior section.

"Hey, Bailey, where's that husband of yours?" Noah burst out laughing.

"Real funny, Noah."

Just as Noah was going to say something else, Ryder ran up to meet us, his phone in his hand. He stood in front of us, forcing us to stop walking, and flashed his phone at us.

"We've got the dates for The Highview."

"How do you have them and not me?" Noah asked. "He's my father."

Ryder looked up from his phone and pushed his curls out of his eyes. "Doesn't mean I'm not his favorite," he joked. "Anyway, it's a group text. Check your phones." We all pulled our phones from our pockets and opened the text.

"Are you guys seeing this?" Ethan ran up to join us in the middle of the cafeteria. The six of us stood in a circle, our faces buried in our phones. It was a good thing we were graduating the next day; we obviously didn't care about the no cell phones on campus rule.

Allie gasped. "Wait. We have The Highview for the entire month of July?"

"This is going to be legendary, you guys," Bailey said.

"Legendary enough for a...wedding?" Ryder looked between Bailey and Ethan before exploding into laughter.

"Very funny," Ethan and Bailey said at the same time, which only caused the rest of us to laugh. We walked over to the senior section, where we were handed palettes of paint.

"If anyone should have a marriage pact, it's Morgan and Ryder," Allie said as she dipped her hand in red paint. She pressed it against the spot on the wall that Noah had reserved for us and handed the paint to Ryder. He dropped his hand in the gold paint and stared at me with a smile. My heart instantly beat faster.

Ethan interrupted the moment as he grabbed the paint from Ryder. "Guys, you're missing something very important here. We graduate tomorrow, and then we only have to get through two more weeks before we can spend an entire month at The Highview."

Ryder and Ethan both pressed their hands against the wall. Their hands looked comically big compared to Allie's handprint. Allie handed them each a wipe from the table as Bailey and I dipped our hands.

Ryder threw his wipe into the garbage can while Bailey and I added our handprints to the wall. "Yeah, that's a good point, dude. Why aren't we freaking out about this more?"

"Because Noah has been breathing down our necks to paint our hands," I said. Noah squinted and gave a sarcastic laugh. He pressed his painted hand against the wall, cementing the six of us to live forever on the cafeteria wall of Space Coast High. We stood back and stared.

Bailey sighed. "One last summer before we all go our separate ways."

"Stop being dramatic," Ethan said. "We'll see each other during the breaks."

Noah wiped his hand and looked around the senior section, nodding at the handprints. "Finally."

"You act as if you just went to war, dude," Ethan said.

"Trying to plan anything with you guys is my own personal war," Noah said.

I went to grab another wipe off the table. Just as I was going to clean the last of the paint off my hand, I paused and instead turned and quickly wiped the paint on Ryder's face.

He raised his eyebrows at me with a smile and then laughed. "Really, Morgan?" I gave him my best innocent smile just before he wrapped his arms around my shoulders. I exploded into laughter as he yelled to Bailey for backup. "Hand me the paint."

Bailey grabbed a paintbrush coated in gold paint and handed it to Ryder. As I laughed against Ryder, he painted a thick line across my forehead. Allie lifted her phone to take a picture of us, but I snatched up a paintbrush with red paint and flicked it at her.

She gasped, her jaw dropping as red paint streaked her blonde hair. "I hate you."

The rest of us laughed obnoxiously. Even Noah, who knew this would require much more cleanup than he had planned for.

"Oh, come on, Allie," Bailey said with a smug smile. "Red is a great color on you."

Allie and I looked at each other and didn't miss a beat; we smeared our hands in paint and ran them across Bailey's face. Ethan tried to hand Bailey a wipe but was caught in the crossfire as Bailey retaliated against Allie and me.

"That's it. You're going down." Ethan grabbed the bottle of acrylic paint from the main table. Walking over to us, he squeezed the bottle over the three of us. We were falling down with laughter, tears streaming down our cheeks as we fought to speak.

"Stop!" I gasped out between giggles.

By the time we'd finally regained our composure, we were all covered in paint.

Noah pulled out his phone. "At least you didn't get any on my wall." The six of us stood in front of our handprints and grinned for the picture Noah wanted to take. Noah positioned the phone to get all of us in the shot and smiled. "Happy last day of high school, you assholes."

"Speaking of," Ryder said once the picture had been taken, "are we meeting anywhere before graduation tomorrow?" He grabbed an entire package of wipes off the table and started handing them around. We tried our best to clean up the paint that was quickly drying on our skin.

Allie closed the pocket mirror she had been staring into. "Can't. My grandparents are coming in. But after, we should."

"Agreed," I said. "Bailey, want me to swing by and get you so we can ride together?" Bailey nodded.

When the bell rang a few minutes later, we walked out of the cafeteria to finish our last afternoon as high schoolers, covered in paint and feeling exhausted after how hard we had just laughed. Ryder squeezed my hand before he walked down the hall from the group. He stopped a few feet away and turned around.

"Hey, Morgan. You've got something on your face."

Chapter 4

Me, 3:20 p.m.: Ryder's here.
Me, 4:01 p.m.: Come on, we always said we'd never have to go through the hard stuff alone.
Me, 4:03 p.m.: This is the hard stuff.

I tossed the knife into the sink and watched as the running water tried to wash the peanut butter off. My shoulders felt sensitive with sunburn beneath the straps of my tank top, even though I had barely been down at the beach. Besides the irritation from the burn, I was still reeling from my conversation with Ethan. There was no way I'd ever called him one of my best friends. How did Bailey always see the good in people? No, not just people. Ethan. She'd always seen the good in Ethan. Though he apologized, it was half-hearted and weak. Plus, he didn't understand what I was going through.

I pulled out my phone and opened the text message thread with Bailey and Allie. I scrolled through months of unanswered messages, landing back in January — the last time anyone had responded.

Allie, December 31, 10:23 p.m.: I can't believe you guys are partying at The Highview, and I'm on a cruise with my mom. She's already asleep.
Bailey, December 31, 10:25 p.m.: Ethan says you should go to the bar and try to get free drinks.
Allie, December 31, 10:28 p.m.: That might be the only good idea Ethan's ever had.
Allie, January 1, 12:03 a.m.: HAPPY NEW YEAR! This is going to be the best year yet. Love you guys!!!!

I stared at the words and thought about New Year's Eve. After everything that had happened, I'd obviously expected Bailey to go silent on me for a little while. We'd all gone back to school after Christmas break, and the start of any new semester was crazy. Plus, she'd been pissed at Ethan. Mad and hurt—because she was Bailey and felt everything on a nuclear level. In the months that followed New Year's, I always wondered if Allie and Bailey were texting without me. I'd expected Bailey to not respond to me, but Allie? What did Allie care? She hadn't even been there, plus she'd been glad that Bailey and Ethan…

"You know what sucks about not having my dad here?" Noah walked into the kitchen and opened the fridge. He didn't wait for me to respond as he shut the fridge door and stared at me. "We have to not only figure out our own dinner but pay for it too."

Ethan joined us from the back deck. "Gone are the days of free meals." He wiped water droplets off his face. I noticed he had forgotten to put sunscreen on his chest.

"Don't worry, though. I've been planning for this." Noah took a wad of cash out of his wallet and explained that he had saved money from leftover school scholarships. Plus, he had worked a few nights a week at the café on campus. "Apparently, girls love a guy who can make a decent iced latte."

"So, you pimped yourself out for this?" Ethan asked.

"Those tips were earned through steamed milk and pumpkin spice."

Ethan laughed. After a moment, he looked at me. "Come on, Morgan, that was funny." I just stared back at him.

"Dude, whatever." Ethan grabbed his phone off the counter and walked toward the bathroom.

Noah looked as if he were going to start lecturing me, but all he said was, "He's missed you, you know." Then he walked to the back deck, where Ryder was. Noah sat down next to him, and they started in on whatever conversation they easily flowed into, leaving me alone to stare at the peanut butter still stuck to the knife.

~*~

That evening, I sat on the top deck watching pinks, oranges, blues, and reds streak across the sky, a book I'd already read on my lap. Next door, a young couple laughed loudly together while eating hamburgers off flimsy paper plates. Across the street, three young sisters chased each other in the front yard, their giggles turning to screams when something happened that they deemed "No fair!"

But the loudest noises came from directly below me as Ethan repeated for the third time, "Are you ready?"

Noah skated around in circles on his longboard, pushing across the pavement with one leg. Ryder straddled a bicycle, his feet firmly on the ground as Ethan tied a rope to the bike's rear reflector.

"So, hold onto this, and when I say go, Ryder will ride as

fast as he can. Then we can put my phone in slow motion mode and make the world's most viral video." Ethan spoke with the same energy we used to see from him whenever we'd attend his soccer games in high school, as if this were the most important game of the season and he was about to lead his team to victory.

"This is going to be pretty dope," Ryder said.

Noah grabbed the rope trailing from Ryder's bike with both hands. After confirming they were all ready, Ryder pedaled slowly to the end of the road. As soon as Ethan gave them the go-ahead, Ryder pedaled full force down the road. Noah swayed from side to side, not giving mosquitos a chance to land on his freshly sunburnt skin as the three of them propelled forward at full speed.

Ethan ran backward, his phone still up and filming as Ryder and Noah drew closer to him. All three laughed wildly as if this were the most fun they'd had in a very long time. Just as Ryder began to slow down, a car turned the corner, its headlights flashing across their faces.

Ethan saw the car first and yelled for Ryder and Noah to pay attention, causing Ryder to swerve his handlebars. The bike turned to the left, flipping him over the handlebars to land in the grass. Noah shot right past him, rolling straight into a bank of mailboxes. The familiar black Ford Focus that had caused them such distress came to a screeching halt in the middle of the road.

"You guys are idiots!" a faceless voice yelled from the driver's side.

I knew the voice, and I'd definitely heard it say that sentence before…especially to the boys. I stared down at the car as it pulled into the driveway and watched Allie open the door and climb out. She stood in the driveway and stared up at me, her once-long blonde hair now cut into a shorter hairstyle she'd always wanted to try but never had. She wore a maxi dress, which I had never heard her even entertain the idea of before and strappy sandals. She put her hands on her hips and blinked hard, almost as if she were willing me to disappear.

I waited for her to say something and wondered if maybe I should say something first. We stood in a tortured silence, her standing in the driveway below and me leaning against the deck railing, the last six months culminating in this moment.

Just as it seemed like we were both going to talk, Ethan ran over. Ryder and Noah trailed behind him, both somehow unharmed, laughing and begging Ethan to show them the video. Noah gave Allie a bear hug, Ethan offered to grab her bag, and then laughed when she thought he was serious, and she and Ryder smiled at each other. I stood on the top deck, watching the reunion I'd hoped would be mine unravel before me, and I'd never felt so far away in my entire life. Besides Noah, no one had talked to me in months. And now, I had to stand here and watch them all celebrate their reunion, grown-up, and a year of college under their belts. I was so out of place. When did that happen? We'd all promised we'd be best friends forever, but now, it looked like their timeline had changed. Or at least, their forever timeline excluded me.

Everyone wandered inside, their voices colliding with each other as the front door opened and shut. I stayed where I was, needing the comfort of the stillness outside before I even began to think about approaching the hurricane inside.

I heard footsteps coming up the spiral staircase. "Allie's here," Noah said, pausing at the top of the stairs.

"Oh, really?"

"Come inside and say hi," Noah started, "We're going to order pizza. We can get garlic bread if you want."

"Yeah, just let me finish this chapter."

"Come on, Morgan," he quietly urged.

I wanted to hate my cousin. I wanted to scream at him, remind him that my so-called friends had ditched me in my time of need. I wanted to tell him, through angry tears, that he just didn't understand. He hadn't lost anything, while I had lost everything. Bailey probably still talked to him.

Instead, I stood up and followed him down the spiral staircase, feeling each step echo the beat of my heart. Why was I so nervous? It was Allie! I'd known her since she was eight years old and still wetting the bed. I had been there when she got her first kiss and had been the one to teach her that toothpaste on a pimple was the quickest solution to make it disappear.

But this was a different Allie. That Allie had been on my team. From what I could already tell of this Allie, she wanted nothing but to see me crumble.

I walked into the living room, where she stood with her back to the front door, and I could feel that everything (yet nothing) had changed. She still commanded the room, her energy a teetering scale of over the top and not enough. She shifted her weight from foot to foot, something she did when she was uncomfortable in social situations. She was all bark and no bite, always putting on a front that she was a lot tougher than she actually was. She had mastered the angsty teenage art of the "I don't care" attitude early on and had never outgrown it.

"Hey."

"Hi, Morgan," she said, already a little bit softer than ten minutes earlier when she'd stood outside and shot daggers at me.

"How was the drive?"

She shrugged. "The usual."

I'd never understood the sentiment of being able to cut

tension with a knife, but the way the living room felt then, I could have cut the tension with a toothpick. Noah raised his eyebrows at Ryder. Ethan busied himself with his phone, surely waiting for the video of Ryder and Noah to upload onto social media.

"I like your hair like that."

"Thanks. You look good, Morgan. I see you avoided the Freshman Fifteen. But I guess you didn't finish the whole school year, so that probably helped."

"It was just temporary," I said, the same thing I told anyone who asked me how school was going.

But that was the thing: Allie wasn't just anyone. Allie was my best friend—maybe?—so why were we dancing around each other like strangers in a dorm room on their first night together? I should have been able to tell her that I hadn't been able to go to class at Flagler because I would have panic attacks in the hallways, thinking she and Bailey were replacing me. I should have been able to tell her that my mornings were consumed with anxiety when I woke up to no messages from her and Bailey. I should have been able to tell her that, above everything else, all I needed was a friend. Allie was here for a reason, and if we were going to even think about trying to fix what had once seemed broken beyond repair, we needed to be honest with each other. She wouldn't have wasted her time coming for the week if she didn't think the same thing.

"Where should I put my stuff?" she asked suddenly, looking from person to person.

"The normal room," Ethan offered. She looked at me.

"Do you need help?" I pointed to the two bags at her feet.

"No."

She picked them up, threw one over her shoulder, and dragged the other behind her down the hall. Out of habit, I followed. She pushed open the bedroom door and smiled.

"It looks the same."

She inhaled deeply and exhaled slowly, her shoulders rising as she did. She hoisted both bags onto her bed. I wondered if she saw the same memories I did: Midnight sleepovers when Bailey would whisper to us to see if we were still awake. Sitting on the beds across from each other, seeing if we could throw Skittles into each other's mouths. Sneaking back in two summers ago after attending a party at the house across the street, which had been rented by a fraternity who had thought we were way older than we actually were.

Allie turned and looked at me, and we both opened our mouths to speak at the same time. I laughed nervously.

"You first," I said. I hoped what she was about to say would be along the same lines as what I wanted to say, a proclamation of "I missed you" and "Let's go back to normal."

"I'm only here because Noah begged me. I didn't want to come back here, just so you know. We both said some things we probably didn't mean, but I'm mad, and I hate this house. I'm only staying for a couple of days, maybe three tops. I really just came to make sure you haven't completely lost it."

It was as if Allie had slapped me. It was one thing to wonder how she could say those things, but it was another to wonder how she could say them and actually mean them. And I knew Allie. She meant them.

She started to unpack, hanging up tank tops and folding linen shorts as if it were the most important thing in the world, completely disregarding what she'd just done. By not answering my calls, by not being on my side to try to help make things right with Bailey, by just announcing to me that she didn't care—she'd ruined any chance we had at being better.

~*~

The house felt emptier than usual despite the loud music Ryder was playing on the back deck as Noah told a story from the semester before.

"And then, after a night downtown, Ethan threw up so much that we actually considered taking him to the ER." Noah laughed.

"That's what happens when Lazy Moon opens up a new restaurant right by campus, okay? I can't help it if they make the best pizza in the city of Orlando, and I can't control myself."

"Control yourself?" Ryder interjected. "Dude, you ate two large pizzas and an order of breadsticks by yourself."

"So, wait, were you sick from drinking or eating?" Allie asked.

"Oh, eating all the way," Ethan said.

I stood alone in the kitchen, staring out at the back deck and pulling frayed strings off my shorts while the others sat around catching up. Earlier in the evening, my greatest fear had been confirmed. Allie had visited the boys a few times over the last semester, and from the sounds of it, they had seen each other over spring break. I had been right. They were moving on without me. Despite the silence in our group text, this reunion, though, was something all four of them had been looking forward to. I, on the other hand, was still trying to wrap my head around basic human interaction or social greetings.

"Morgan, get out here! I need your opinion!" Ethan yelled.

I walked out onto the deck and leaned against the doorframe.

"Your desert island meal: Lazy Moon's cheese pizza or Frankie's number five wings?"

"Frankie's, most definitely."

"Told you."

"Sit down." Noah kicked a chair toward me. Allie reached into the cooler and handed me a beer from a case the neighbors had dropped off for Uncle Daniel, who Noah had said, expertly lying, would be here at the end of the week.

"I prefer spiked seltzers now," Allie said, "but hey, beggars can't be choosers." I assumed she was talking to me, but she still wouldn't look at me.

Since January, I had tried to keep tabs on Allie, logging into social media accounts for the first time in months just to see what she had been up to. She'd posted pictures of herself cheek-to-cheek with a group of new friends at the beach, each picture showing her a shade darker and exponentially happier than before. She'd won a scholarship for sophomore year, which I'd learned through a post her mother had tagged her in, praising her. She and her roommate had also decided to live off campus next year. The second I'd seen that, I deleted my Instagram account and let my phone's battery die.

I took the beer from Allie and stood cautiously. Around the deck, Noah, Ryder, Ethan, and Allie looked like they were having the time of their lives. Two stark differences from the summers before wrapped around my brain. First, they were fine without Bailey. Second, they were fine without me.

"I was just coming out to say good night," I said.

I walked back inside to the bedroom and sat on the bottom bunk.

If Bailey were here, she'd know exactly how to handle Allie's mood. She'd do whatever it took to make things feel right. In a few minutes, Allie would be sleeping in the bed across from mine, in a room she had purposely stayed away from.

With that in mind, I pulled Allie's favorite blanket down

from the closet and placed it at the end of the bed she always claimed. I closed the curtains so that when the sun began to rise, no natural light would come in. I thought of other particulars Allie had for sleeping, like how she needed the ceiling fan on or how she slept with her phone in airplane mode, convinced that any sound would cause her to shoot up in the middle of the night. So many little things we had learned about each other over the years had eventually become ingrained in my nightly routine.

Now that the room was Allie-fied, I wondered if it was a step in the right direction.

Allie walked into the room shortly afterward. If she noticed what I'd done, she said nothing. If she hadn't noticed, then she really was out of it.

Allie took a pair of socks out of her drawer and put them on. She braided her newly cut hair into a single braid. She rubbed moisturizer on her face and took her contacts out.

Months ago, I had swallowed the pain of my heart breaking over leaving Ryder, but I never thought I'd have to look my best friend in the eye as she broke what was left.

Allie turned off the light and crawled into bed. The old bed frame, which was on wheels, creaked. In the past, we would laugh whenever she got into bed, and the entire thing moved. Whoever slept in that bed would spend the majority of the night waking up and pulling pillows out from between the bed and the wall as the mobile bed moved just enough for the pillows to jump ship.

"Morgan," Allie whispered. "I miss Bailey too."

Chapter 5

Me, 7:57 a.m.: Ryder and I have barely said a word to each other. So awkward.
Me, 7:58 a.m.: Allie said she misses you, Bails.

Early the next morning, armed with SPF 50, a cooler of water bottles, and a cloud of confusion from Allie's attitude the night before, I walked down to the beach as soon as I'd finished my last sip of coffee. The beach was surprisingly empty for it being so close to Independence Day, but with a quick glance at the clock, I realized why. It wasn't even nine in the morning on my third day at The Highview, and I was already adjusted to being up before the masses.

I pushed my beach chair into the sand and pulled off my sundress. Tossing it over the top of the chair, I faced the ocean. The smell of salt water, a scent I had grown up around, still took me by surprise on quiet mornings like this. It was as if I were being rocked to sleep by the waves, the smell of salt water, an essential oil that relaxed my mind.

Usually, it helped, but not today. No matter how I tried to

relax, I could not shake Allie's voice from my head. One minute, she was looking me in the eye and telling me, "Thanks, but no thanks," and the next, she was trying to bond with me over Bailey.

And she was so different. We were growing up, we weren't kids anymore...but she had changed. It wasn't just her haircut or that she wore dresses now; it was something deeper. Something in her eyes had changed. The way she spoke to us had changed.

Well, not us. Me. The way she spoke to me had changed.

"You should still put sunscreen on, even if it's early."

I turned around to see Ethan jogging down from the house. Dressed in running shorts, sunglasses, and headphones, he slowed as he approached me.

"Going for a run?" I asked.

He nodded. "I couldn't sleep with Noah's snoring."

Ethan had been an athlete in high school, running track and playing soccer. Every year, he'd beg us to wake up with him and go for a run on the beach. We had all agreed once. We'd woken up early, thrown together some semblance of workout attire, and joined him on the beach. After a few steps, I realized I hated running. Allie sat down in the sand, and Ryder and Noah went for a dive in the ocean. Bailey had stuck next to Ethan, though, her competitive nature whirling as we watched her run shoulder to shoulder with him until they'd disappeared down the shore.

"Do you still run every morning?"

"Most of the time," he said. "I miss soccer, though."

I smiled. "Flagler had these teams you could join and play for fun. My roommate was on a volleyball team; she met a lot of friends that way."

Ethan raised his eyebrows. "Yeah, maybe. I don't need friends, though."

"Well, I just wondered if you missed being on a team, that's all."

"I miss a lot of things, Morgan."

I shifted uncomfortably and wanted to tell Ethan that I knew the feeling, but instead, I just told him to enjoy his run. He nodded and pressed play on his music. I watched as he ran off, down by the water, gaining momentum until he reached a steady pace, running through the sand like it was the easiest thing in the world.

I sat back down in my chair and pulled out my cell phone from the side pocket. I stared at the green messaging icon that had no notifications and put the phone away out of embarrassment. I had nothing to occupy my brain except my own thoughts and that kind of stillness scared me. I thought back to how Ryder and Allie both acted when they saw me. Both were distant and while it wasn't explicitly stated, it felt like they wanted to be anywhere but near me. I didn't know how to fix that, but as I sat alone on the beach, I realized I wanted to try.

Within the hour, Ethan finished his run, Ryder and Noah stumbled down to the beach with kayaks, and Allie came down to join me. She offered a nod and a "Hey" before spreading her towel out and lying on her stomach, her phone in her hand as she endlessly scrolled. Watching her with her phone confirmed that she did, in fact, know how to use it. She had just been ignoring me all these months.

In the ocean, Noah attempted a front flip off his kayak, failing miserably and hitting both ankles on the edge as he dove headfirst into the water. Ryder and Ethan reacted loudly, causing Allie to crane her neck to see what had happened.

"Noah tried to flip off the kayak," I offered.

She squinted through her sunglasses and murmured

"Idiot" under her breath. After a beat, she sat up and reached for the sunscreen, spraying more across her shoulders. She reached for the portable speaker next to Ethan's chair, which was currently turned off, and went through the motions of pairing her phone to it. After she tapped on her phone screen, the speaker made a quick tune as the speaker and her phone synced up. Allie scrolled through her music, but in the end, it looked like she just hit shuffle. She put her head back down on her towel as the speakers began to play a Blake Shelton song from the summer we were obsessed with country music.

"Love this," we said simultaneously. She laughed lightly, but her laughter stopped almost immediately after it started. She sat back up and looked at me.

"I meant when I said that we can't go back to normal."

I nodded. "I figured."

"And I brought up Bailey last night because you're not the only person who misses her. I think you forget that. She might have been your best friend, but—"

"What do you mean, my best friend?" I asked. "We were all best friends, Allie."

She tilted her head to the side and gave me the look.

"Come on, Morgan. It was always you and Bailey against the world. You brought me along for the ride, but it was never the three of us. That's how we got here. If we had all been together on New Year's Eve, this wouldn't have happened."

"What does New Year's Eve have to do with any of this? Are you talking about us figuring out that Ethan and Bailey were secretly hooking up? Because who cares? Sure, I was pissed at first, but I would've gotten over it if Bailey had just given me a chance."

Allie stared at me.

"I hoped that Noah was exaggerating, but he wasn't."

She stood up with a dramatic roll of her eyes and walked toward the water. Over the sound of Blake Shelton singing about naming the dogs, I heard the collision of laughter from my friends and wondered if they noticed that something — someone — was missing.

Chapter 6

Last Summer

Me, 9:42 PM: I swear if you guys ditch and make me endure this lock-in with just the boys, I'll kill you.

Noah, 9:43 PM: Gee, Morgan, thanks.

Me, 9:43 PM: Oops. Didn't realize the boys were on this group text.

Bailey, 9:43 PM: Busted.

I tapped my foot against the sidewalk and craned my neck to see the front of the line. Classmates that we graduated with hours before stood in front of us, the excitement in the air. We stood outside Seaside Health Center, a 24-hour gym that shut its doors on graduation night for a senior class lock-in. Noah paced the line, chatting up now fellow classmates and reminding people to have their tickets out.

"This is going to be so lame," Ethan whispered as he leaned over to me.

"I'm telling Noah," I replied.

The lock-in happened every year, a hope that it would deter drinking and driving on graduation night, and as Noah's final duty as senior class president, he had put blood, sweat, and tears into making sure it would be the best one yet.

Ryder looked up from his phone, "Oh come on, don't you want to paint your face and eat stale Domino's Pizza?"

I checked my phone for the time and looked around the full parking lot to see if I'd see Allie's car. She and Bailey had less than ten minutes to get here before they missed the cut-off to get in.

At graduation practice this morning, Noah made it clear to the senior class that if you weren't at the front door of Seaside Gym by ten PM, you would be turned away. Though he was talking to the entire senior class, he looked directly at where Allie, Bailey, Ryder, Ethan, and I sat in the auditorium. He knew us too well.

After that, Noah looked out at the senior class, "Any questions?" he asked.

"What if I show up at 10:03?" Bailey asked with a raised hand.

Mrs. Patrick, our principal, ducked her head and snickered.

"Then you won't be let in," Noah said.

Ethan chimed in, "We all know how crowded Grissom gets on game days. I can only imagine what the traffic will be like on graduation night."

Noah sighed, "Anyone else?"

At that point, my hand shot up, and I didn't wait for Noah to acknowledge me before I called out, "What if we're eating dinner with our family at Frankie's Wings, and they're really busy. If we promise to bring you a ten-piece of the buffalo wings—"

Noah cut me off, "Just get there by ten PM."

So, with loyalty towards my cousin, Ethan, Ryder, and I

arrived at 9:30. Now, at 9:55, Bailey and Allie were nowhere to be found. I scrolled to Bailey's name on my phone, knowing she was more likely to answer than Allie, and pressed the phone icon. Just as it started to ring, I saw them running up to us in line. They ignored the groans from the people they were cutting in front of. Bailey just flashed a smile and an innocent wave and stopped next to me.

"You almost missed it," I said.

"That wouldn't have been the worst thing," Allie mumbled.

The line began to move forward, and there was a buzz of excitement in the air. Maybe this would be fun. I reached into the back pocket of my shorts and pulled out my ticket.

"Bails, can you send me the pictures from graduation?" Allie asked.

"Sure," Bailey said and dug in her purse for her phone. "Oh, by the way, I think I know what tattoo we can get."

She scrolled through some pictures and flashed the screen to Allie and me.

The three of us had been planning on getting matching tattoos for years. We debated back and forth, thinking about different designs or even a song lyric from our favorite Taylor Swift song, but we could never agree. Allie and I looked at the picture. It was a hand drawn picture of a seashell with blues, greens, and purples filling it in. It was beautiful.

"Did you draw that?" Allie asked.

Bailey just shrugged like it was no big deal and popped a piece of gum in her mouth.

"Bails, it's amazing," I said.

In front of us, Ryder and Ethan were busied now, talking to one of Ethan's soccer teammates. I looked at them and back at Allie and Bailey as the line moved forward again. It seemed too convenient that just down the road, there was a tattoo shop. Convenient, or just good luck? Noah continued pacing the line, yelling out to everyone to have their tickets out and that the doors were opening up.

I kicked Allie's foot to get her attention and signaled with my head to get out of line. Bailey noticed and smirked at us.

"We'll be right back," I said to Ryder, touching his shoulder. He turned and nodded at me before he continued talking with Ethan and the soccer team.

I tapped the top of my thighs as Allie and Bailey sat down next to me. Brett, the artist who introduced himself to us as we walked through the tattoo parlor doors just minutes before, washed his hands at the sink in the corner of the room. It had taken him just ten minutes to print the seashell picture from Bailey's phone and set up his station. After careful consideration and understanding that I would probably faint if I had to sit around and wait, we decided that I would go first. Now, I sat with my tank top strap pulled down and my hair tied up in a ponytail, my shoulder exposed, and my heart racing.

"I can't believe we're finally doing it," Bailey said.

"My mom is going to kill me," Allie laughed.

Bailey shrugged, "You're eighteen now."

Brett walked over and looked at me with a smile.

"You ready?" he asked, and all I did was nod.

He laughed lightly, probably sensing my nerves. I heard the machine power on and the buzz of the needle turn up. I squeezed my eyes shut as I felt the needle pressed against my shoulder. I tried not to hold my breath, as in a quick Google search on the car ride here, I read aloud an article about how to survive your first tattoo. It advised against it.

"The guys are texting us to see where we are," Bailey said. She stood in front of me and held up her phone. "Say cheese," she said. I smiled, and Bailey took the picture and sent it in our group text thread.

We stood in front of the full-length mirror, all next to each other, craning to see our shoulders in the reflection.

"It looks amazing," Allie said.

I caught our eyes in the mirror as we all looked at each other and then again at our matching seashells. Brett had taken an 'artistic liberty' and added tiny swirls of white around the shell, and it made it even more beautiful.

"Hopefully, we don't hate each other in a year," Bailey said. I laughed.

"Great idea, Morg," Allie said. Brett approached us and bandaged over the tattoo, handed us a complimentary bottle of cleaning solution, and instructed us to go to CVS and buy unscented lotion to use three times a day.

We walked out of the tattoo parlor. I looked at my phone and laughed.

In all caps, Noah let us know that just because we were his friends didn't mean he would let us in. Underneath it, Ryder and Ethan had sent a picture of themselves with an expressionless face that said: you gals are missing all the fun. ☺

"Well, damn, looks like we won't be able to get in," Allie said and sighed a long exhale.

Bailey and I laughed.

"Junk food and a sleepover?" I asked.

After stopping by CVS for unscented lotion, three different flavors of Lay's potato chips, and a bag of chocolate chips, we pulled into Bailey's driveway. Her parents were the least likely to grill us about why we skipped out on the lock-in and would maybe even encourage our "stick it to the man" attitude about all of it. We walked through the front door, where Joe and Sarah, her parents, were sitting on the couch. In one motion, they both looked at the large wall clock, noted the time, then looked back at us.

"This is a pleasant surprise," Joe said.

Allie sat down on the loveseat diagonal to them, "We decided the lock-in wasn't for us. Why spend any more hours pretending that we liked our classmates?"

They both laughed, "Well, Allie, we can always count on you to tell us like it is, huh?" Sarah said. She patted the spot next to her for Bailey as I sat on the other loveseat in the room.

"Please tell me that's a photo album," I said.

Joe smiled, "I'm surprised you know what a photo album is. I assumed everyone's photos were digital now. We were feeling a little nostalgic. Our only baby graduating high school, heading off to college soon."

Any other teenager would have rolled their eyes, but Bailey just smiled. She rested her head on her mom's shoulder. I felt a stab in my chest. Everyone was so excited about talking about graduating and moving on, but all I wanted was to enjoy one final summer before everything got flipped upside down. I had been ignoring the WELCOME TO FLAGLER COLLEGE emails I'd been receiving since getting accepted back in March. The guys were all accepted into UCF and didn't even think twice about whether or not they'd live together, and Bailey and Allie were always good at doing their own thing. Me, though, I was really struggling, and it felt like this would be something I'd have to struggle through alone. I didn't know how to even bring it up, and when I mentioned it to my mom, she said she was almost certain that everyone was feeling how I was feeling. But still, I didn't want to show my weakness. I didn't want my friends to know that the thought of being alone and away from them was terrifying.

After crashing Joe and Sarah's trip down memory lane for ten minutes or so, Bailey, Allie, and I walked down the hallway to Bailey's bedroom. She flipped on the light switch and tossed her purse on her fabric desk chair. Allie sat down on the bed and opened up a bag of sour cream and onion chips, and I popped the tabs off the three Dr. Peppers that Bailey had grabbed from the fridge before we came in here.

"I'm probably in the minority, but man, I'm going to miss my parents," Bailey said. She sat down next to Allie and stuck her hand in the bag of chips. Allie, Bailey, and I all had no siblings, probably another thing that brought us together early on. We desperately craved the companionship of a sister, but we learned quickly that a best friend was the next best thing. And that was another thing: what the hell was my mom going to do in an empty house? She'd joked before that she'd sell it and buy an apartment on the beach with Uncle Daniel, but I think that she was scared to let go of the last thing tying me to my childhood. At least, I hoped, anyway.

"Don't think about it too much," Allie started, "your parents will be happy to get rid of us."

"At least my parents didn't make me pose for a graduation picture with my ex-boyfriend," Bailey said. Allie rolled her eyes.

"Yeah, what the hell was that?" I asked. Allie pulled up a picture on her phone and showed it to us.

"Do you know how awkward it was to go up to Grant and say, 'Hey, I know we broke up, but my parents want a picture of us'?" Allie said. In this picture, she showed us she was standing next to her senior year boyfriend, Grant, who she broke up with the second they got accepted to different colleges.

"Grant was so nice," I said.

"Too nice for Allie," Bailey joked.

Allie gave a tight-lipped smile. Bailey and I were convinced that the break-up hurt her a little bit more than she led onto, something we confirmed when we caught wind of Allie making playlists on Spotify filled with depressing songs that she added us to collaborate on.

"Anyway, not all of us can be indestructible like Morgan and Ryder," Allie said.

I didn't respond. Instead, I focused my attention on sipping my soda can.

"Okay, something's up," Bailey said. I looked up at them and huffed out a sigh.

"I hate that you can tell when something is wrong," I said.

In reality, Ryder and I didn't feel indestructible these days. He was so focused on making sure that everything was set up for his first semester at UCF that he didn't notice that I was slinking into myself, scared and lonely, even though I was still surrounded by my group. He never asked me how I was feeling, and most days, it felt like the majority of our conversations were about how excited he was and never about whether or not he noticed that not only was I not on the same page as him, but I wasn't even in the same book.

"What if Ryder and I don't make it?" I asked.

Bailey crossed from her desk chair to the bed and sat down next to Allie. I walked to the bed, and Allie wordlessly scooted over to make room. I laid down, and Allie and Bailey laid down next to me. We all stared at the ceiling until Allie rolled over and propped herself on her elbow.

"If you and Ryder don't make it, then there's something wrong in the universe," she said.

I shook my head, "But it takes work, and we don't know how to have to make it work. We've been so simple since we started dating."

"What does that even mean?" Bailey asked.

It meant that if I had a bad day, Ryder knew all I needed to cheer up was a bag of Sour Punch Straws. It meant that when Ryder had to get an after-school job to pay for the dent he got on his car when he hit Ethan's mailbox, we moved our date night to Wednesday instead of Tuesday. It meant that any problem we'd had this far was small, but being two hours away from each other meant that if we were having an off day, it couldn't be fixed with candy and ice cream.

To Allie and Bailey, I shrugged. "What if this was just high school love, and it's run its course?" I asked.

Allie and Bailey both looked at me. Bailey rubbed my arm, and Allie laid back down flat on her back.

"Well," Bailey started, "We can't promise that you and Ryder will be forever, but how about this: we'll be forever."

"Ah, yes, another marriage pact for Bailey," Allie joked, "Don't tell Ethan. I'm pretty sure he'd fight us for you."

Bailey rolled her eyes, "This isn't about Ethan and me!"

I smiled, "Do you guys promise that we'll be friends forever? We'll always be like this?"

"We just got matching tattoos. What more do you need?" Allie asked.

"A blood contract," I joked.

I didn't know how to feel. Ryder had told me the same things that Bailey and Allie were telling me. We'd always have each other; we'd make it work. There was just something that seemed like that wasn't the truth.

Our sleepovers always ended the same way, with Bailey falling asleep too early and Allie following quickly after. As I tossed and turned on the edge of Bailey's bed, surprised that the three of us all still fit in it together, all I could think about was my future with Ryder. Breaking up hadn't even crossed my mind when we got accepted into two different colleges. During the application process, he was dead set on UCF for their Broadcast Journalism program, just as I was sold on Flagler because of the smaller class sizes and beautiful campus. We hadn't even applied to any of the same schools. We both made decisions for our individual futures, and it never occurred to me that we could have made the decision for our future.

I rolled over and grabbed my cell phone off the charger. The clock on my lock screen lit up at 3:37 AM. From what I could tell with Snapchat and Instagram posts from classmates, the lock-in was still going strong. I remembered that Noah had told us time and time again that no one would be allowed to leave until 4 AM on the dot. I scrolled through my messaging app and clicked on Ryder's name.

Me, 3:38 AM: Having fun?
I stared at my screen and waited for the three bubbles to signal that Ryder was replying to show up.
Ryder, 3:39 AM: Tired AF. But, yeah, pretty fun.
Ryder, 3:39 AM: I wish you guys had stayed. I could've used you on my team in air hockey.
Me, 3:40 AM: Maybe I'll study arcade games in college!
Ryder, 3:40 AM: Not a bad idea. Couldn't sleep?

Me, 3:41 AM: Nope. Thinking too much.
Ryder, 3:41 AM: You just wish I was there with you ;)
Me, 3:41 AM: Don't be creepy. Bailey and Allie are sleeping in the same bed as me.
Ryder, 3:42 AM: I missed you tonight.
Me, 3:42 AM: I missed YOU tonight.

I swallowed down the guilt as I sent the last text to Ryder, with a realization that I didn't miss him, not really. I plugged my phone back into the charger and stared at the ceiling, willing myself to fall asleep.

Chapter 7

Me, 12:16 p.m.: Forgot how lethal Allie can be when she's mad.
Me, 12:16 p.m.: You were always the buffer, Bails.

I stared at my phone, aimlessly scrolling between the homepage on my iPhone and my email app, not sure what I was even expecting to find. At the end of my first semester at Flagler, I deleted the social media apps off my phone, a result of pure jealousy in seeing my friends and others that I went to high school with enjoying their newfound college lives. I'd spend my evenings lurking on Instagram, comparing how the majority of my days were spent in my dorm room, not at parties. Bailey and Allie posted pictures of their respective campuses, parties they attended with their roommates, even shots of iced lattes and textbooks. They pressed me to share pictures in our group text, asking if I'd hung up any pictures on my dorm wall yet, but it had always felt temporary.

I opened up the messaging app one final time and saw my thread with Bailey, still unanswered. I've been giving her space for the last month or so, hoping that my silence would make her miss me, but being back at The Highview made me ache for even a simple hello from her. The fact that it was our third day here, and I'd still heard nothing, well, that seemed like a bigger issue than the fact that I'd already blown my shot reconciling with Allie.

I put my phone away as Allie and Noah walked out of the water. Without a word to me, Allie stuffed her clothes and extra towel into her bag, her eyes downcast. Even if I'd wanted to interject an "Allie, wait," there was no way she would have stayed.

Noah sat down next to me and opened a water bottle. He took his time taking a sip, shook his head, and sent water droplets flying. After a few seconds, he cleared his throat.

"Allie told me you guys got into an argument."

I shrugged. "She's being stubborn, as usual. How are we supposed to be friends again if she keeps acting that way?"

"This is hard for her too."

"It doesn't seem like it."

"You know, Allie, she doesn't like to talk about her feelings."

I stared blankly at the water, where it looked like Ethan and Ryder were about to come out.

"I wish we could go back to last summer," I said, hoping Noah would agree with me.

When he didn't, I continued on, "It's just weird being here without our parents."

But the lack of parental supervision was the last thing that I missed about summers before. I'm not even close to who I was before. I miss her.

I don't have time to relax or think about who she was because Ryder and Ethan barreled out of the water and ran up to our spot. Ryder grabbed a towel, and Ethan collapsed into the other chair next to me.

"I gotta be honest," Ethan started, "I really wasn't looking forward to this week. But it's good to be back."

"I cannot believe you pulled this off," Ryder said, "How was The Highview not booked for the week of the Fourth?"

Noah smiled, "You know Jeremy?"

"Our neighbor Jeremy?"

Noah nodded. "He hacks for fun. He hacked the website and blacked out the dates. I don't think my dad thought too much about no one booking it because he's been so preoccupied with the sale."

"And your parents all really believed that we decided, spur of the moment, to take a week-long summer intensive class?"

"Yours didn't?" Ethan questioned.

"I don't lie to my parents," Ryder insisted. "I told them the truth. Even told them y'all were lying to your parents so in case they see them at the store or wherever, they won't blow your cover."

"Live a little," Ethan said. "Tell a lie every now and then."

"I think you've got enough lies for all of us, my dude," Ryder said. Ethan mimed being stabbed in the heart.

Noah and Ethan started packing up their things, talking about what they were going to go make for lunch. Ryder stood in front of me and told them he'd meet up with them in a minute. Ethan promised to have a sandwich ready for him.

I reached into the cooler and grabbed a can of Diet Pepsi, grabbing him a Coke out of habit. "Here."

He turned around and smiled, taking the can. "Thanks, Morgan." Opening the Coke, he took a sip.

"Sit down," I offered, and he sat in the chair next to me.

"The weather looks like it'll be good for fireworks," Ryder said.

I could suddenly feel his presence more strongly than anything I'd ever felt in my life. This was the closest we'd been in a very long time, and I was very aware that one of his hands drummed along to the song while the other gripped his soda can for dear life.

"Don't jinx it." I smiled and wondered if the expression was more for my sake or his. He reclined in the chair and closed his eyes as my phone shuffled to the next song.

The too-familiar opening to our favorite song started. A song about finding love after heartbreak—what did we know about that when we were sixteen and first falling in love? We'd never had our hearts broken nor needed to find someone else to fix the blue that found its way to unpack after years of neglect.

The first time I played the song for Ryder, he'd rolled his eyes when I said, "It's off Taylor Swift's new album!" The second the song started, though, he'd reached over the center console of his car and held my hand, rubbing his thumb gently across the top of mine. We were sixteen and in deep.

Now, I tried not to read into the fact that neither of us made a move to change the song.

"This song always reminds me of junior prom," he said.

"When I spilled ketchup on my yellow dress before we even made it to the dance?"

Ryder laughed, "I had forgotten about that. I was talking more about after prom."

We'd gone to a party at a hotel on the beach thrown by one of Ethan's soccer teammates. The whole party buzzed with excitement. We were so close to senior year, which obviously meant we were so close to graduation. It had been a great night, even when Noah let loose for the first time in his life and threw up in one of the fake planters that lined the hallway of the hotel. After we'd all went our separate ways, Ryder and I stayed on the beach. I'd told my mom I was spending the night at Allie's. He'd told his parents he was staying at Ethan's, and instead, we'd stayed the night wrapped up in blankets as we slept in our prom clothes in the sand.

"The bottle," I said, my voice barely above a whisper as the memory hit me.

We'd found an empty bottle in the sand. Ryder ran into the hotel and came back with a pad of paper and two pens. He'd told me to write down where I hoped to be in five years, and he would do the same. Taking it literally, I'd written down some cool city. When we showed each other the papers, he'd written *wherever you are*. We'd rolled the pieces of paper up, stuffed them in the bottle, and sent them out to sea.

"We used to know everything about each other," he said sadly, looking at me as the song ended. "Now I feel like I can't even ask how you're doing."

Up until this moment, I'd thought that Ryder and I were going to be living in the shadow of our breakup. This moment was different. We weren't on his balcony one random Florida winter night, tears drying on my cheeks. We weren't dropping off boxes of each other's things—his favorite hoodie, my broken phone charger.

We were here. In a moment when I could apologize and put us on track to make things right. Here at The Highview, with memories of our first giggly kiss, laying out blankets on the top deck and watching the clouds move over the moon. We were in the place where it had all started, not the place where it had all ended. I was living in the past: waiting around for a text message that might never come, remembering moments of summers before when things felt good, retracing footprints in the sand that had long been washed away.

Things could've been so different.

"Yeah." My voice echoed his sadness.

I'd believed in everything when I was with Ryder. I'd believed that things could get better. I'd believed that I could get better.

I'd been wrong.

Ryder took another sip of his drink and drummed his thumb against his thigh. His dark-brown hair still dripped water from the ocean, and his cheeks were turning red.

I began to pack up my bag, avoiding eye contact as I did. I knew that moment would be the perfect time to throw everything on the table, to figure out how to say goodbye to what we had been and create a new story for what we were going to become. Romance aside, Ryder was my soulmate — that, I was sure of. He knew everything about me, and I'd given him everything I could — everything I'd had — to make sure he knew that as well. I wanted so badly to sit back down and fix things, but my legs pushed me up, and before I knew it, I was heading up the beach to the house. Ryder cleared his throat, a gentle reminder that he was still there, and it hit me that the major difference between us was that when things got hard, Ryder stayed.

~*~

When I walked inside, Ethan handed me a plate. "I'm making corn dogs," he said, his eyes focused on the oven.

"A watched pot doesn't boil, Ethan, or whatever that saying is," Allie said from the table.

"Are we going to eat any vegetables this week?" I asked. "You know there's no actual corn in corn dogs, right?"

Allie chuckled and then stopped abruptly. She looked over at me. "I'm really trying to stay mad at you."

"I know. I wish I knew why."

"You dropped off the face of the planet, Morg. I needed you."

I shook my head and stood at the kitchen island. "You told me you never wanted to see me again. And I don't even know why."

"I was mad. Sad. I had a lot of feelings going on."

Ethan slammed one of the cabinets closed. "Don't you think it's time you two moved on?"

Everyone kept saying we needed to move on as if moving on was that easy. As if we could all just pretend that nothing had happened. As if it would solve everything. Allie looked away from me and busied herself typing on her phone. Out of the corner of my eye, I could see that it was a text message. My heart raced at the mere thought that it was Bailey. Maybe Allie was complaining about me. Maybe Bailey was responding with her favorite emoji — the laughing face that also had tears rolling — and they were both talking about what a loser I was. Bailey was telling Allie how I was desperately trying to talk to her. Allie was telling Bailey how I wasn't trying hard enough with her.

"Have you talked to Bailey, at least?" I asked.

Ethan picked up a corn dog, plated it for Allie, and handed her the bottle of mustard. Allie made no moves to open it, though, because she was too busy glaring at me.

"What do you mean, have I talked to Bailey?" Allie asked.

"Don't waste your breath with it, Al." Ethan pushed a plated corn dog across the island to me.

"Has anyone talked to her?" I asked. Neither Allie nor Ethan answered. "Because I text her, and she doesn't respond.

The messages don't even get delivered. Is she okay, at least?"

More silence. I continued on.

"I figured she blocked me. Will you just tell me that? Are you both really so immature that we can't talk about it? Seriously? I thought Bailey was one of your best friends. It was a stupid fight, and everyone freaked out." I crossed my arms over my chest. I felt cold. All I wanted to do was stand under the stream of a hot shower and then curl into my bed with blankets. I wanted darkness.

"Whatever." I walked to the bedroom and shut the door behind me. I stripped off my bathing suit and pulled on my favorite sweatpants and tank top, and collapsed onto the bed.

My brain hurt, my heart raced, and my eyes felt heavy. As I pulled a blanket over my head, I heard Allie and Ethan talking in hushed voices.

I wanted my friends back. I wanted Ryder back. But more than that, I wanted who I used to be back.

I stared down at my bright yellow toenail polish.

I'm running. No, sprinting up the stairs. Rain splashed down next to me. I didn't see anything but my toenail polish.

"Morgan, wait."

Bailey's voice. She sounded far away. Then she sounded under water. I saw the beach now, and I realized I'm standing on the top deck. It's raining harder. As I looked over the ledge of the deck, I noticed the house below crumbling. The roof was ripped off, and rain poured into each room. I looked closer and saw Ryder swimming in the flooded house. He reached out a hand and called my name. Someone touched my shoulder, and then I'm falling off the top deck.

Falling into the flood.

Screaming.

Tossing.

The last thing I see before I hit the ground is Bailey standing on the top deck. She called down to me: "Now you know how it felt."

I shot up in bed, panting and shaking. The blanket that was wrapped around my body was soaked with sweat. I looked around the room.

I had to remind myself where I was.

My room at The Highview. A twin-sized bed. Ryder, Ethan, Noah, and Allie were here somewhere. Bailey was not.

I took deep breaths. Each time I exhaled, my shoulders sunk and shook a little bit more. I pushed the blanket off of me. I felt like I was suffocating. No, I was suffocating. And this house was to blame.

I laid back down, rolled over onto my side, and stared at the wall, wondering how long I could lie here. We'd been at The Highview for only three days, and other than a rainstorm, a sunburn, and a headache, I had nothing to show for it.

I reached for my phone and saw a notification for two text messages. My heart raced as I opened the messaging app, hoping more than anything it was finally Bailey. I didn't know why I felt such disappointment when I saw it was just my mom.

Mom, 4:16 PM: Well?? How are the classes going?

Mom, 4:17 PM: Make sure you check out their science department. You loved biology in high school.

I didn't have the energy to lie to my mom right now, so instead, I swiped out of the app and put my phone in the bedside table. Maybe if it was hidden out of sight, I wouldn't feel like a part of me was missing every time I typed in my passcode and saw no notifications.

I got out of bed and walked to the door. I stood near it for a second, waiting to hear voices. I was so used to waking up from a sunburnt nap to voices running over each other in the common spaces, someone begging someone else to put their swimsuit back on and go back down to the beach. But I heard nothing this time.

Another reminder that things were different.

I opened the door and walked into the living room. Both the couch and kitchen were empty. I looked out the back door and saw Noah and Ryder sitting in lounge chairs next to each other while Ethan stood over the grill. Allie was at the large table in the corner of the deck, putting out plates and silverware. They were functioning as a unit, like we always had, except pieces were missing, and they didn't seem to notice. Maybe Allie was carrying the extra weight of making two trips to the kitchen to bring out plates and condiments. Maybe Noah had to cut the onion, even though he hated the smell. Maybe they had to plaster on smiles and pretend they weren't all thinking the same thing: this sucks.

I slid open the door and stepped onto the porch. Ethan looked over his shoulder, acknowledged me with a nod, and turned back to the grill. Ryder looked up with a slight smile while Allie avoided eye contact. Noah jumped to the rescue and pulled a chair up next to him for me to sit in.

Allie turned from the table and looked at all of us.

"Who's going to talk first?" she asked. Noah looked at Ryder, who looked at Ethan, who looked at Allie.

"Oh, really? Fine. I'll go." She paused and took a breath.

"We all get that this summer is different and that this year has been drastically different. Life changing, even." Allie stopped and avoided looking at us as we all stared at her. Once she'd composed herself, she added, "But this is where we are now. We have four days left here before the jig is up. By the way, I am still astounded you told your father you were taking some extended-semester-class bullshit. He believed you?"

"Why is it so unbelievable that I would want to better myself for the summer?" Noah asked.

Allie looked at Noah directly. "You were the one who was so sure that being at the house would help. Now, it's time to stick to your gut. Make it work."

Noah sat up straight and stared at Allie. "It will work. The Highview fixes things."

"More like ruins things," Ethan said.

"How did I know it would be you who started this up?" Allie asked under her breath.

"What's that supposed to mean?" Ethan asked.

Allie tilted her head and stared at him. "Oh, please. We all know you don't want to admit your guilt in all of this."

Ethan's jaw dropped, and he forced out a shocked laugh. "I don't want to admit my guilt? Is no one paying attention to anything that's happening around us? Ryder is so desperately trying to win Morgan back. Noah is trying to be everyone's best friend. Allie, you waltzed in here like the mega bitch you are—"

"Woah!" Allie said, taking a step toward Ethan.

"I'm just saying, you guys all want so desperately to go back to where we were, but that's impossible. And no one is admitting it's impossible because no one will admit what we all want to talk about but aren't. Bailey isn't coming back."

He punctuated every syllable of the sentence: Bailey isn't coming back. How could he say that? I wanted to scream that it had just been a fight, and this just showed that Bailey knew how to hold a grudge. Ethan stared at me before breaking my gaze and shaking his head.

"Come on, Ethan," Ryder started.

"What don't you guys see? We can sit around here all we want, pretending that everything is good, but it's not. If I have to sit here one more day and watch you guys tiptoe around the truth, I might lose it. Did you know that Morgan texts Bailey? Why has no one addressed that? We were all there on New Year's Eve. We know Bailey isn't going to respond. I'm done pretending. I'm done playing along with this bullshit story. I'm just done." He tossed the spatula he'd been holding onto the table and walked down to the beach.

We were left in complete silence because what was there to say? We'd had months to pick up the phone or meet for lunch, and we hadn't. We hadn't even tried.

Noah got up first and walked away without any indication of where he was going or what he was doing, leaving Allie, Ryder, and me on the deck. Allie, who never cried, had red eyes. Ryder, who always knew how to make us all feel better, kept his eyes on the ground. Having felt the ebb and flow of every emotion possible today, I felt tired and drained.

In the background, the waves crashed upon the beach. I heard the last of the families on the beach packing up to go home. Eventually, all there was, was our own silence.

"Should we go get Ethan?" I finally asked.

"No, he sucks." Allie's voice was hoarse and quiet as she got up and walked inside.

Ryder looked up at me from across the deck. He walked over and sat down next to me.

"Do you think I romanticize things?" I asked after a few

seconds.

"What do you mean?"

I shrugged. "I don't know. This week here. The Highview. Our relationship. My friendship with Allie and Bailey. I created this idea in my head that it's perfect. That nothing could go wrong with it."

I stopped and looked at Ryder. He stared down at me.

"And it always goes wrong." The realization hit me hard.

Ryder slowly placed his arm around my shoulders, his hand rubbing my back as I dropped my head onto his shoulder. We sat there until the only thing to be heard was the waves crashing.

Chapter 8

Last Summer

Bailey, 8:27 AM: SHOTGUN!
Me, 8:27 AM: You can't call shotgun before we're at the car.
Bailey, 8:27 AM: Says who???

Allie was on a schedule. She had agreed to drive from Cocoa Beach to Englewood this year after Bailey's VW Bug, which was as old as we were, kept overheating at stoplights. Last week, Bailey had had to hop out and pour an entire bottle of water into who knows where under the hood just to make sure we made it home. Allie had complained — her car was a brand-new graduation gift from her parents — and insisted that if she was going to drive, we were following her rules. That meant leaving right on time, no open containers in the car, and the stereo's volume didn't go above seven.

At eleven on the dot, Allie tossed the last of the suitcases into her car. She turned and stared at Bailey and me as we sat on the front porch of Bailey's house, laughing at a video on my phone screen.

"Yeah, I've got this, thanks," Allie said, hand planted on

her cocked hip.

Bailey stood up and grabbed her large purse. "Sorry, Al. Morgan keeps showing me these stupid videos about graduation-day fails. Man, I thought me almost tripping and falling into Michael McAdams's lap was bad."

I stood, too, following Bailey's lead. "That was bad, Bailey, but not as bad as the fact that he probably would have liked it."

"Gross." Bailey laughed and playfully swatted at my arm. When Allie crossed her arms, still staring at us, Bailey added, "Stop doing that. We're coming."

This had been our routine now for years. Since the start of our friendship, Allie had, admittedly, spent most of the time waiting on Bailey and me because we sometimes moved as if we had all the time in the world. But it was summer, and there was nothing worse than breaking a sweat before lunchtime, especially due to physical labor.

"The boys are going to beat us to The Highview, and we're going to end up doing the supply inventory. Do you want to spend our first afternoon there making sure no guests walked away with a beach chair in the last year?"

Allie opened her car door and climbed in, turned the key in the ignition, and buckled her seat belt. Bailey and I took this as our cue to follow, and Bailey raced to the front passenger door.

"I never did understand why the first car there doesn't do inventory," I said. "It seems like a punishment for driving safe."

Bailey reached back and handed me a stick of gum, a necessary precaution since I always got carsick on long rides. "That's so true. It's not our fault Allie's going to drive ten under the speed limit."

Allie turned and glared at Bailey. "Good one," she said sarcastically, just as Ethan's Jeep pulled into the driveway. Noah sat in the front seat, connecting his phone to the dashboard to provide GPS directions for Ethan. Ryder sat in the back seat with the windows rolled down and his arm hanging out.

"Race you there?" Ethan called from the driver's seat.

"Absolutely not," Allie said. "I'll be going the speed limit the entire time. It's a holiday weekend, dumb ass; the cops will be everywhere."

"She has a point," Noah said.

"Fine. How about the first person that has to pull over to pee buys lunch?"

"No, Ethan," Ryder said.

I often wondered if we'd ever outgrow our competitive nature. Ethan made everything a competition, especially when we were at The Highview. Who could stay up the latest? Who could eat the most Doritos without getting sick? Who could charm the clerk at the liquor store to sell to us? We all liked nothing more than a friendly competition, but Ethan usually pushed it too far.

"Can we just get going?" Bailey asked, dramatically fanning herself with an old road map Allie's mom made her keep in the glove compartment.

I stuck my head out the window. "Are we meeting your dad there?"

Noah nodded, and Ryder smiled.

"Hi, Morgan."

"Hi," I said with a laugh. I was always taken aback by the way Ryder could make me blush just by saying my name.

"Oh, young love."

"You better get used to it, Bailey," Noah said. "We've got an entire month with them."

"A month? You'll have to deal with this for an entire lifetime," Ryder said, eliciting a mixture of "Aws" and "Come on, dudes."

"Are we going?" Ethan asked. "Or are we just going to sit here and chat like we've got nothing better to do?"

Allie put the car in reverse and checked her mirrors. Then she looked over at Ethan's Jeep. "See you there."

~*~

We pulled into The Highview at 3:26 p.m., exactly on time, according to Allie's calculations. The boys were nowhere to be found.

"I think it's actually August, and we spent the entire month of July driving here." Bailey climbed out of the car and stretching her arms.

"Holiday weekend," Allie reminded us as she gathered the trash we had collected in our five-hour drive (which should have been three if not for that same holiday traffic).

"I bet they got lost at the detour." I pulled my phone out to see if Ryder had texted me. Nothing.

As Allie popped the trunk, I stood with my hands on my hips, staring up at the house. The Highview's sign was freshly painted, my uncle's contact information on the bottom in a cool shade of blue. There had been some minor cosmetic work done since last summer, but the most noticeable change was the complete revamp of the top deck — the reason for the name The Highview.

It had once just had a few lounge chairs, perfect for watching the sunset over the ocean. Now, the spiral staircase led up to what would definitely be our hangout spot for the summer: an open space with new outdoor furniture and tea lights lining the rails. Uncle Daniel had had outlets installed and wired so we could plug in our speakers for music. At night, we could push all the chairs to one corner and spread out blankets — perfect for looking at the stars and falling asleep to the waves.

It was crazy; I had stood in front of The Highview so many times, but each time felt like the first.

"I wonder where they are," Bailey said as she grabbed the suitcases out of the trunk.

"I'm telling you: lost."

"Wait," Allie whispered. We all froze on the gravel walkway.

"Why are you whispering?" Bailey asked.

Allie crept to the end of the driveway and pointed. "Look."

Parked three houses down was Ethan's Jeep, doing its best to hide among the cars around it. Then we heard it — the unmistakable sound of footsteps on the metal of the spiral staircase.

"Hey, ladies." Ethan leaned over the edge of the top deck. He smiled — the smile that could get him out of any trouble — and tilted his head.

Instantly, Noah and Ryder popped up with water balloons in hand.

"No..." Allie lowered her head in defeat.

"We decided to cut you some slack," Noah started. "Instead of making you buy lunch, we figured this would do." He tossed a water balloon up and down in his hand, and I wished more than anything that he would drop it and it would pop.

I looked up at Ryder. "Don't you dare."

Ryder looked around. "Who? Me?"

Bailey sighed. "Just get it over with."

"Happy Highview," Ethan said.

They launched the water balloons off the top deck. They continued launching them, one after the other, and soon Allie, Bailey, and I were drenched as the balloons popped at our feet. We ran around the driveway, trying to avoid the popping balloons, but no luck.

One balloon landed by my feet without popping. Picking it up, I hurled it up to the top deck. Allie and Bailey threw their hands up in celebration when it popped and got the boys wet. Through laughter and screams, we held up our hands in a truce, salt water and tap water soaking through our clothes.

~*~

Once inside, we fell into our yearly "summer at The Highview" routine. Bailey, Allie, and I claimed the bedroom with the bunk bed and twin bed. Noah, Ethan, and Ryder fought over who would sleep on the air mattress in the room next to ours, even though there was a whole other room we never used for some reason. I unpacked my suitcase and started the community drawer of bathing suit tops that the three of us could share. Bailey opened a book and snacked on peanuts she'd found buried in her purse. I stifled a laugh as Allie hung up the bathroom schedule she had made; she swore we would thank her for the practice when we weren't surprised by dorm room living.

A few hours later, Uncle Daniel pulled into the driveway. We were spread across the living room when he walked through the front door. He smiled and dropped his duffel bag on the floor by his feet. He kicked off his flip-flops and threw his hat on the counter, revealing disheveled brown hair that matched Noah's. He held up a popped water balloon in one hand, "I hope you knuckleheads know you have to pick up the popped balloons."

"Those were there when we got here," Ethan said.

Uncle Daniel picked up his duffel bag and walked toward his room. "Go clean the balloons up, Ethan."

"Why just me?"

Uncle Daniel paused in his doorway. "Because, Ethan, I

know you well enough to know it was your idea."

~*~

Ethan picked what we hoped was the last of the popped balloons out of the bushes and dropped it into the trash bag he held. After a competitive round of rock paper scissors, it had been decided that I'd help Ethan while the others inventoried the supplies.

"Are you getting nervous about leaving for school?" Ethan asked.

"Of course I am. I won't know anyone. I'm so jealous that you, Ryder, and Noah are going to the same school." I picked up a rogue balloon and tossed it into the garbage bag. We walked through the front gate to the side yard.

Ethan tossed the bag into the garbage can. "You'll meet new people."

"That's easy for you to say. You make friends easily." I'd been friends with the same people for basically my whole life. I didn't even think I knew how to start a conversation with someone, let alone live with a stranger in a single dorm room.

"Morg, everything will work out. Besides, Allie and Bailey will visit."

We went to the back of the house, where the rest were just finishing up, piling the last of the chairs and umbrellas neatly in the shed.

"I'm dripping in sweat," Bailey complained.

"What's the verdict?" I asked. "How many people walked away with chairs?"

"In an unprecedented turn of events, we actually gained two chairs," Ryder said. He placed a gentle hand on my shoulder and squeezed as Noah looked at all of us.

"Beach?"

~*~

We ran down the sand to the water. Ryder and Noah pushed a paddleboard into the water, and I climbed on.

"Ready?" Noah asked and pushed the paddleboard into the water. As I floated away from the shore, I waved a dramatic goodbye to Ethan, Noah, and Ryder and called for Allie and Bailey to come join me. Bailey ran into the water, Allie following in her splashes, and swam up to where I was floating. Bailey placed her hands on the paddleboard to push herself up.

"Hold it steady, Morgan. Please?"

Allie followed suit, and I maneuvered slightly to make room for them. We sat, letting our legs dangle in the water as we stared out at the horizon.

"I'm gonna miss this," Allie said.

"Miss what?" I asked. "It's the first night, Allie. You'll be sick of us by the end of summer."

"Plus, we're not going anywhere," Bailey assured us.

Allie smiled. "Well, I know that. But things will be different."

"Things are supposed to be different," Bailey said. "You aren't supposed to remain the same. You can't live the same day over and over for ninety years and call it a life."

"Please. You think you're going to live to be ninety with the amount of Dr. Pepper you drink?" Allie joked. Bailey leaned forward to splash water on her. The movement caused the paddleboard to rock back and forth until it finally flipped, sending all three of us into the water. Our laughter continued as we came up, our hair now wet, and Allie frantically grabbed for her sunglasses, which were floating away.

"Look!" Uncle Daniel called from the shore. We looked out toward the horizon and saw the sun begin to dip below the horizon.

Uncle Daniel clapped. "The first sunset of the summer. Now we can start to party!"

The house next door to The Highview has a swimming pool. It was a fact that we always brought up at least once a summer as we'd gaze longingly at whoever was staying in the house, wishing we were the ones splashing around in it.

"To be clear," Ethan once said, "The Highview is an exponentially cooler house than that one. But a swimming pool!"

Uncle Daniel had thrown his hands up in the air, "The damn ocean is right there! Better yet, go splash around in the bathtub if you want."

None of us could explain it, though. The feeling of jumping into a swimming pool after spending all afternoon at the beach. The saltwater washing off our skin as we'd race from one end of the pool to the next. Floating on a large pink flamingo as the sun beat down on us. It was the one thing missing about our lazy summer days. So now, as we watched the car next door pull out of their driveway after asking Uncle Daniel for a good dinner recommendation, we all were scheming. We'd been sitting around a fire that Ryder had built, drinking the one beer each that Uncle Daniel had allotted us, "now that we're adults," when Noah stood up and walked to the fence. He looked at the swimming pool and then back at us.

"I'd kill for that pool right now," I said.

"What if I told you that you didn't have to kill anyone? You'd just have to jump a fence," Noah said. We all looked at each other. Bailey was already taking off her swimsuit cover-up.

"I don't know about that," Allie said.

Ethan laughed and stood up, "Didn't realize Allie turned into such a rule follower once high school ended."

Never one to back down from a challenge, Allie exhaled angrily and stood up. She walked to the fence and before anyone could say anything else, put her hands on the top of the waist-high wooden fence that separated the property lines. In one motion, she had her legs over on the other side and jumped into the pool, not even bothering to take her cover-up off. We all clapped and yelled until Noah shushed us, motioning with his head to the house where Uncle Daniel was inside.

We all jumped over the fence and cannonballed into the pool, splashing around.

"They're going to know we were here. The deck is going to be soaked," Ryder said.

"Oh, who cares," I said as I floated on my back.

Allie and Bailey climbed onto a float that was already in the pool and sat side-by-side on it.

"This is heaven," Allie said, "Good thinking, Noah."

Noah tipped a pretend hat as he swam to the edge of the pool and sat on a built-in step. From across the pool, Ethan looked at me and pointed towards where Allie and Bailey were now comfortably floating. I smirked at him and dove underwater. We reached their float at the same time, and both placed our hands underneath and flipped it over. Allie and Bailey screamed as they splashed underwater. When Bailey came back up, she lunged at Ethan, placing both of her hands on his shoulders and pushing him under. Before she could get him all the way under, he wrapped his hands around her waist and threw her underwater again. Allie, who was clearly not amused by this, swam over to where Noah was and huffed as she pressed on the deck with her hands and got out of the pool. Ethan and Bailey continued splashing, laughing as they did so, and Ryder swam over to where I was.

"I thought we were the couple," he joked.

"Ew, gross," I said, not even wanting to entertain the idea of Bailey and Ethan together. Ryder smiled at me and flicked water in my face.

After a close call with the neighbors pulling into the driveway before we'd all made it back to our own yard, we settled back around the fire after changing out of our wet bathing suits. I ran my fingers through my chlorine drenched hair, wincing every time they got stuck in a knot. Ethan dropped two bags of chips on the extra chair and sat down next to me. Noah and Ryder were still inside, and Bailey and Allie both insisted they had to take a shower before putting clean clothes on.

"Look at the couch my mom found for the apartment," Ethan said. He held his phone up to show me a picture of a worn blue couch that was now stored in Ethan's parent's garage.

"That looks so comfy," I said. My friends and I had never talked about things like buying new furniture. What was next? Commentary on buying new health insurance? I made a mental note to go online and look up how to even buy health insurance.

"I feel like I'll really thrive in college," Ethan said.

"Really? Why do you think that?"

He put his phone away and grabbed a bag of Doritos. He shrugged, and, with a mouthful of chips, said, "I just think that it'll be good for me. I charmed my way through high school."

"That's not true. You studied hard," I said.

"I barely did my homework. I depended on my natural abilities. Besides soccer, I didn't really try at anything. I'd like to change that," he said.

I laughed, "Wow, is Mr. Golden Boy saying he wants to grow as a human?"

"Hey now, I'm not that bad," he laughed.

Ryder stuck his head out of the sliding glass door, where he stood with an armful of soda cans and water bottles.

"Does anyone want a drink?" he asked.

Ethan called out for a water, I asked for a Diet Pepsi, and Ryder smiled and walked back inside. Ethan looked over at me.

"Are you and Ryder going to break up?" he asked.

I scoffed, "What makes you ask that?"

"I'm just curious. You've been together for a long time. I didn't know if you were going to follow Allie and dump him just because you're going to different colleges," he said.

"People who do that were never meant to be," I said.

"That's not true. Allie really liked Grant," Ethan said.

I cocked my head, "Allie doesn't really like anyone."

We both laughed and let the few beats of silence settle over us. Truthfully, it hadn't even been a question when Ryder and I got into different colleges. We'd just make it work. Sure, there were days where I was nervous, but I'd never told Ryder that because I didn't want to make him nervous. If I'd never mentioned it to Ryder, I definitely have never mentioned it to Ethan. I'd only ever told Allie and Bailey about my fears, but there was no way that they'd said anything to Ethan. At least, that's what I'd told myself.

"Does Ryder want to break up with me?" I whispered.

I was terrified of the answer. Just because I had doubted every now and then, that didn't mean I wanted it to end.

"Dude, what? No, I didn't say that. I'm just curious," Ethan said.

I swallowed hard just as Ryder and Noah walked out and sat down around the fire with us. Ryder reached over and handed Ethan and me our drinks.

"Everything alright?" Ryder asked.

I nodded, perhaps a little too hard, and plastered a smile on my face.

The next afternoon, Bailey fanned her hand over my toenails and squinted at them. She sat back and closed the bottle of fuchsia nail polish. Next to her was a pile of cotton balls that were covered in polish remover and the remains of my old yellow color. Allie walked out on the back deck and placed a bowl of potato chips in front of us.

I picked up the bottle of nail polish and turned it over in my hand. The sticker on the bottom read, "The Fuschia is Bright."

"Man, this color is the best," Bailey said.

"Will you do mine next?" Allie asked. She sat in the chair next to Bailey and propped her feet up in Bailey's lap. Even though we ate dinner an hour ago, I reached over and grabbed a handful of potato chips. Ryder, Ethan, and Noah were still inside on kitchen duty, scrubbing dishes. Allie leaned over her shoulder to look inside the house, then turned back to me.

"Have you talked to Ryder yet?" she asked.

"Not yet," I said to her. Bailey opened the bottle of nail polish and started painting Allie's toenails.

After hanging around the fire last night, Allie, Bailey, and I stayed up for another hour or so, whispering to each other in the darkness of our bedroom.

"Just tell him what Ethan said," Allie had said.

"Ethan didn't say anything alarming, if you ask me," Bailey countered.

As we whispered to each other, I wanted too badly to ask them the burning question: had either of them said anything to Ethan? On the outside, Ryder and I looked like the perfect couple.

There was no way we were projecting any sort of doubt because all we did was talk about how excited we were for the other or about the playlists we would share with each other for the car drives to visit each other. Only Bailey and Allie knew my true fear. That it wasn't going to work.

"Did he act weird today?" Bailey asked. She didn't look up from the paint job she was doing on Allie's toenails.

"No, he was absolutely normal."

"So then, why stress yourself out by bringing it up?" Allie asked. I didn't say anything. This time, Bailey shot her head up and gasped. Allie flinched at the sound, and the fuchsia nail polish streaked on the top of her big toe. Bailey grabbed a cotton ball and wiped it off, and gave Allie an apologetic smile.

"Sorry, Al, I was just shocked there because now it sounds like our Morgan does want to break up with Ryder," she said.

"Okay, I did not say that," I said.

Allie and Bailey both stared at me. They knew me better than anyone in the world, and they had to know maybe I did.

That's because the minute that Ryder and I got accepted into different colleges, the idea crossed my mind for maybe a millisecond. But once we assured each other that it would be fine, I felt like I had nothing to worry about. The night before, when Ethan asked if we were going to stay together, doubt started entering my mind again.

"Okay, it freaked me out a little bit," I said, putting my hands up in defense, "but that doesn't mean that I want to end everything."

Allie sat back in her chair as Bailey finished her last toenail, "Yeah, you guys will barely be an hour away from each other."

Bailey closed the nail polish bottle again and gathered the used cotton balls. "Allie's right, plus, you love each other. That's enough."

The back door slid open, and Noah walked out. He stood in front of us.

"Crazy idea, ladies. The bridge on Beach Road. We're jumping off of it," he said. I raised my eyebrows at him.

"Hell no," Allie started, "That bridge is at least thirty feet high."

"We've wanted to jump off that thing since the first time we saw it!" Noah practically yelled.

I shook my head, "It's dangerous. We don't even know if the water is deep enough."

Though we rode our bikes over Beach Road Bridge nearly every evening on our way to the ice cream shop or the grocery store, that was totally different from jumping off of it. Sure, each time we rode over it, we joked about jumping off, but we always laughed it off and kept riding. "We'd never," we always said, but we all wondered what it would be like to fly through the air, waiting for the seconds following as our feet would break the surface of the water.

Noah sat at the edge of Allie's lounge chair, "So? I'll go first! Worst case, I sprain my ankle. It's not like we're going to die," he said.

I looked at Bailey and Allie.

Bailey shrugged, "Yeah, okay," she said. Obviously, she would do it. She'd always been more of a daredevil than Allie and me.

"Compromise," I started, "You guys jump, and Allie and I will stand guard at the top."

"No way. If we go down, we go down together."

Minutes later, and with some gentle coaxing from Ryder, I ended up with my toes hanging over the edge of the cement railing of the bridge. For the first time in her life, Allie may have been wrong: there's no way this bridge was only thirty feet high. As I stared down at the water, I couldn't see the bottom. I'd been over the bridge hundreds of times, but I never thought about looking over the edge. I reasoned with myself that boats were off in the distance, and if they were able to safely float by, the water had to be deep enough for us to land. I looked to the left of me and saw the low bank of sand, though, which was our hypothetical exit route once we hit the water. Over there, the water looked shallow and barely waist deep. To my left, Ryder clapped his hands. To his left, Ethan and Noah were making jokes about calling a lawyer to write up their will.

On my right, Allie looked at Bailey and asked, "Is it going to hurt?"

Allie had been the last to agree, but Ethan had finally worn her down after telling her that she "probably couldn't handle it anyway."

"No. It's just like jumping into a pool," Ryder said.

"Except we're a little higher, and we have no clue what awaits us at the bottom," Bailey said. She grabbed Allie's hand.

"But what about the sign that says not to do it. If we get caught, we could get in major trouble," Allie said.

"Then don't get caught," Noah said. Noah, the ringleader of this adventure, looked at each of us.

"If we survive the bridge, then we survive anything," Bailey said.

"Way dramatic, Bails," I said, but my palms felt sticky with sweat, and my heart felt like it was dropping into my stomach as Ryder reached for my hand. It caused me to grab Allie's and hold on for dear life.

"Ouch, Morgan," Allie said as I squeezed.

"Ready?" Ryder asked.

"I can't believe I agreed to this."

Ethan, who was at the end, looked down the line at all of us. "Let's do it."

Noah counted us off to three, and without thinking, I closed my eyes and jumped.

We flew through the air with the sun setting in the distance, and in that moment, I had no fear. No fear of what would happen between Ryder and me, no fear as to what college would bring, not even fear about what was waiting for us in that water. Flying through the air, I had the comfort of knowing that as long as I jumped with the people beside me, everything else would work its way out.

Chapter 9

Me, 4:04 p.m.: I really need you, you know.
Me, 4:57 p.m.: Alright, Bailey, whatever.

Noah and I drove in silence down Shoreview Drive to A Better Scoop Ice Cream. We pulled into the ice cream shoppe and got out. Noah walked ahead of me and held the door open. There was a line that snaked from the register to the door. I stared at the menu with its endless combinations. Ryder did the math once, and there were nearly 2,000 combinations that could be created, a fact that Allie refuted with detailed equations. In the years that we'd been at The Highview, we probably could have collectively tried all of those combinations, but ice cream was the one area where we all agreed that there was no reason to be adventurous. Why mess with perfection? I'd been eating cookie dough ice cream with rainbow sprinkles since I could remember, and Noah gravitated towards chocolate ice cream with a half spoonful of peanuts. So, when he ordered a bowl instead of a cone and strawberry instead of chocolate, I knew something was up.

    I have very few memories of Noah's mom because his

parents divorced when we were four, and she left. Had Noah left with his mom, his life would be notably different: suit jackets instead of swim trunks, winter houses instead of summer houses- that sort of thing. The one memory that really sticks about Noah's life when his mom was around was whenever one of us was upset, she would give us strawberry ice cream. Early on, she had found out that the pink color always made us laugh. With no explanation, it became our thing- feeling blue? A bowl of pink. Noah and I sat down at a table in the corner of the dining area, and he took a bite and closed his eyes.

"They should package this stuff and sell it. I'd bulk order to have it for the year," Noah said.

I dug around in my bowl, pushing clumps of cookie dough to the side to save for last. An hour earlier, just as the sun was setting, Noah came back from hunting for Ethan. They walked up the beach, and Ethan crossed the deck to the inside of the house without a word to me.

To me, Noah said, "Let's go get ice cream," as he shook the sand off his legs.

I agreed with a simple okay and didn't question when he said, "Just us, let everyone else do their thing."

Noah and I sat now, him enjoying his ice cream after successfully avoiding any questions I asked on the drive over about what was going on with Ethan and me, trying to ignore the sickness I was feeling in my stomach.

"This was a good idea. I needed to get out of the house for a little bit," Noah said.

"It was your idea," I reminded him. I paused, "What's going on, Noah?"

He looked up from his strawberry cup and shrugged.

"You tell me, Morgan."

Sitting across from Noah now reminded me of the Intro to Theatre class I took during my first (and only) semester at Flagler. The professor, a man in his early 30s who insisted we call him Mike, spent an entire lecture weighing the pros and cons of having two characters sit at a table and talk. He argued that it looked stagnant and the audience would be bored out of their mind, but on the other hand, it was a little more realistic to have the characters that intimately close. Not every conversation involved prancing around the room and lamp throwing. Sometimes, two people figuring out a problem required stillness. This was demonstrated perfectly now with Noah and me. I couldn't help that I was imagining storming out of the small ice cream shop after throwing my cup in Noah's face, slamming the front door, and storming through the perfectly timed rain after Noah answered my question. Instead, I let the uncomfortableness of the stillness settle.

I traced the swirly logo on the napkin in front of me, and it wasn't until three traces that I realized it was an ice cream cone with a seashell perched on top of the cone. Clever. I looked over to my right and stared out the window at the covered picnic tables that were crowded with teenagers not much younger than Noah and I were, and I felt a tug at my chest. I looked at the laughing girl that was closest to the window, with her curly blonde hair framing her face and her tan lines sticking out of her strapless dress, and imagined that just last summer, that was us. I tried to avoid my own reflection in the window, my own hair hanging lifelessly down my back, my skin flushed red from my burn. It was my eyes that scared me the most, though: deep circles underneath them gave away my sleepless nights that should have been equalized by my afternoon naps but weren't.

"I feel as lost as I must look," I said, turning back to Noah.

In my minutes of observing the outside, he'd finished his ice cream. He folded his napkin and clasped his hands.

"Where's Bailey?" he asked. I shrugged.

"Do you know what happened?" Noah asked. I nodded.

Noah looked out the window, his glance now following the outside group as they all got on their bikes, some sitting on the handlebars of others, some opting for a skateboard instead. Noah gave a simple nod of his head and pushed his chair back. He stood up and threw his empty cup away. He paused at the garbage can before walking back over to me.

"Are you playing a game here with me, Morgan?" he started, "I can understand why you'd be mad at everyone else, so you think that this is getting back at them, but I did nothing."

"I'm not sure I know what you mean," I said.

"Morgan, do you know where Bailey is?" he asked again.

"I just said yes."

"I miss her too, okay? But she's gone. And she's not going to text you back," he said gently. I focused back down at my ice cream and pushed the little bit that was left around in the cup. I thought about the last time I saw Bailey on New Year's Eve. Her black jumper, her waved brown hair, how we giggled in the sand but didn't make it to midnight. I hadn't realized it then, but Bailey was gone the minute we'd all left for college. She had made a new life for herself, complete with new friends and new hobbies. New Year's Eve was her goodbye party, complete with a blowout fight to cement that she didn't want me around anymore.

"Do you think she's okay, at least?" I asked. Noah gave me a sad smile, the corners of his mouth turned down as he shrugged. I placed my hand against my cheek and rested on my elbow. I concentrated on Noah's sad smile that he gave me. I imagine Bailey in her dorm room at FSU.

"Why is your dad selling the house?" I asked.

"Your guess is as good as mine. We've been fighting about it since the day he called me and told me."

"Do you think you could convince him not to?" I asked.

"I've tried everything. I even told him how I'd always planned on bringing my future kids there. Didn't work. That's why I wanted us to come here. I wanted one last summer here together, even if it feels different." Noah paused, "I know you miss Bailey, Morg. We all do. But please, let's enjoy the rest of this week, okay?"

I shook my head no and stabbed at the last of the cookie dough in my cup. I wished he would stop bringing Bailey up. I couldn't help but feel a stab of embarrassment whenever he did. Just like I knew why Noah ate strawberry ice cream, he knew my tell-all signs as well. I wished he would think about the fact that I was embarrassed that my supposed best friend didn't answer my phone calls and didn't even read my text messages.

"I don't really feel like talking about Bailey," I said and scooped the last of my ice cream out of the bowl. Noah said nothing, just got up and walked outside.

It wasn't until five minutes later, as Noah and I were stopped at a red light, that I realized how different I felt. Noah turned the volume up on the car radio as one of our favorite songs from childhood played. Normally, we would have rolled the windows down and sang along loudly, taking turns singing the different verses like we did when we were younger. Now, I stared out the window at the passing houses and clasped my hands together in my lap. In my head, I counted breaths to slow my heartbeat. I didn't remember where I learned this, but it helped. Even though Noah tried to make me talk about Bailey, I was thankful for him. I did feel a pang of sadness for him, though.

He thought The Highview was enough to save us.

When Noah and I pulled into the driveway, we both heard the fight before we saw it. Ryder stood on the back deck on the opposite end from Ethan. Ryder had a bag of frozen fruit pressed to his lip, and Ethan sat in a chair with Allie bandaging his swollen knuckle.

"What the hell?" Noah asked.

"Why didn't you answer your phone?" Allie yelled, throwing the last of the fabric bandage on the table next to Ethan. He squeezed his fingers in and out, just like they did on movies, to make sure they didn't break a bone. Ryder didn't look at anyone. His gaze cemented so hard on the sandy porch that he looked more like a fixture of the house. It was déjà vu right now, us in a tight circle with anger pulsing through the air.

Ethan pulled his hand away from Allie, "You know what? If I have to hear about New Year's Eve one more time, I'm going to lose it," he said.

"That's what started them in on it," Allie started, "Arguing about what happened on New Year's Eve-"

"Yeah, and then Ethan fucking punched me," Ryder said. Ethan looked over at him.

"And dude, I am sorry about that, but this is ridiculous. Why doesn't anyone see what's going on here? Morgan's back. Ask her for yourself."

Ryder turned and stared at me. "You've really been texting Bailey?" he asked.

I didn't respond.

"That's what Ethan said earlier," Ryder said, "And I didn't want to admit it, but when you and Noah were getting ice cream, I saw your texts on your laptop. You've been texting her since January...Almost every day."

"Almost," I said.

No one said anything.

Ryder looked at Noah, "She needs more than a house to help her."

"Listen, I know everyone thinks I'm crazy," I started, "but if I can just get Bailey to answer her phone, we could talk it out."

Across the deck, Ryder turned away from me. Noah stood next to me and gently placed his hand on my forearm. I continued.

"Ethan, I could tell her that you really did care about her," I stopped, noticed that Ethan looked away immediately, "And I could tell her about Flagler, and hating college, and wanting to go travel for a year. I could tell her how lonely I'd felt and how I had hoped that New Year's Eve would have changed that. You know, none of you ever asked me if I was okay. And I wasn't. I was struggling so hard at Flagler, and I was so lonely, and you guys all just forgot about us. You all adjusted fine, and I was so scared of how sad I was."

There was silence on the deck. Allie walked over to me and pulled me into a hug. She rubbed my back, but it didn't last. She froze against me and quietly asked, "Do you even remember what happened?"

Of course, I remembered. I remembered New Year's Eve and how Bailey looked when she yelled at me. How it felt to call her a liar. Ryder's face when I stormed past him. Ethan and Noah sitting off to the side, helpless. I remembered running up the bridge. I remembered Bailey following. To Allie, I just shrugged. Allie pulled out of our embrace and stood in front of me. She was the only one looking at me now. When Ryder did look at me, he practically spit in my face as he told me that what I was doing was cruel.

"You were there, Morgan," he said, as he walked past me

and through the back door.

We ate dinner in silence, tip-toeing around each other in the kitchen as we scooped spoonfuls of macaroni and cheese that Noah had made. Ethan said nothing as he took his bowl and walked outside, climbing up the spiral staircase to the top deck. Allie walked out of the kitchen and onto the back porch, not even looking at anyone. Noah stood with me in the kitchen, and Ryder sat by himself at the kitchen island.

"Do you want more?" Noah asked. I shook my head and pushed the food around in my bowl.

Noah looked out the window at Allie.

"I haven't seen her cry since..." He stopped his sentence short. Looked at me and slumped his shoulders.

He walked out of the kitchen, and I felt a stab in my stomach. Noah just wanted us all together. He wanted us talking and laughing. He wanted us back to where we were last summer when the biggest fight we had was over what movie to watch. Our lives were so different now.

Ryder looked up from his phone as Ethan sat down at the kitchen island next to him.

"The landlord emailed us about signing a new lease," Ryder said.

Noah nodded, "I saw it."

"If we don't kill each other by the weekend, I'd like to live with you again."

Noah laughed and clasped his hand on Ryder's shoulder. I looked at them as they talked about apartment leases and excitement about starting their sophomore year. They talked about the broadcast journalism class Ryder hoped he would get into. They were talking about a life I didn't know anything about.

It only confirmed my fears: my friends were paces and paces ahead of me and had no intention of waiting for me to catch up. But were they even my friends anymore? I thought back to our first semester away from each other when the boys still had each other and Allie and Bailey forged new friendships. I thought of sitting alone on my dorm room bed, physically aching from loneliness, and how it felt in the days when all I wanted was Bailey or Allie to text me and tell me they missed me.

But they never did.

And now, I was going through it again.

While Ryder and Noah continued talking, I pulled my phone out of my back pocket and scrolled through unanswered text messages, all the way back to January.

Allie is unbearable. I'd sent to Bailey after Allie and I got into an argument.

Unanswered.

World History is kicking my ass this semester. I'd shared with Allie and Bailey.

No response.

I think Ryder has a thing for their neighbor across the hall. I'd lamented to them.

Silence.

Months and months of other unanswered text messages until a single message appeared from Allie in April.

Come on, Morgan, just stop.

Then, it was my turn to ignore her.

I looked up at Noah and Ryder, who had made their way

into the kitchen and were cleaning the counters and eating the rest of the macaroni and cheese straight from the pot.

"We've gotta make sure the house is spotless when we leave," Noah said, "My dad absolutely cannot know we were here."

"Yeah, yeah, yeah. We know," Ryder said. He opened the dishwasher and reached for my untouched bowl.

"Are you going to eat that?" he asked.

I shook my head. He took it and emptied it back into the pot, and placed my bowl in the dishwasher. I stood against the counter and stared out the window at Allie. She was sitting in one of the Adirondack chairs, her legs crossed and her bowl in her lap. Noah walked out the back door and sat down next to Allie. I looked at how her smile lit up when he said something, probably trying to make her laugh. He leaned closer to her and showed her something on his phone, which made her drop her head back and laugh even louder, a laugh that I could hear echo inside to the house.

I heard footsteps outside the front door, and as it opened and Ethan walked in, he paused in the doorway. He looked away from me as he crossed to the dishwasher and put his bowl in. He washed his hands. He cleared his throat. He looked over at Ryder.

"You have a black eye," he said.

"You fucking punched me," Ryder replied. Ethan opened the freezer and pulled out an ice pack that we usually reserved for the coolers. He handed it to Ryder.

"I'm sorry," he said.

Ryder snatched the ice pack and placed it against his eye. It was slightly swollen but not very noticeable.

"I'm just mad, okay?" Ethan started, "I'm mad that we're

all fighting. I'm mad that it's my fault that we're even here."

Ryder shook his head, "I keep telling you, man, it's not your fault."

Ethan looked over at me.

"I'm actually jealous of you," he said, "I wish I was in denial."

I stood in the kitchen in the middle of Ethan and Ryder. I nervously ran my hand through my hair and tied it into a ponytail.

"I'm not in denial," I whispered.

I started to remember more, but it still didn't make sense. The sound of rain. The water bottle in the sand. Beer pong. The music. The framed picture of us and our handprints. The bridge.

Chapter 10

Last Summer

Ethan, 2:45 PM: If you guys stop at 7-11, will you bring back slurpees?
Me, 2:46 PM: How are we supposed to bike with slurpees?
Bailey, 2:46 PM: Sure, what flavor?

I parked my bike on the side of The Barefoot Trader and turned around to see Allie and Bailey riding up.

"What the hell, how did you pedal so fast?" Allie asked.

"Ya'll are just slow," I said.

Bailey hopped off her bike, and the three of us walked inside the store. The inside of The Barefoot Trader was crowded with others who were staying in the area, all of them sifting through t-shirt racks and beach toys. We wandered aimlessly around the store for a moment, each of us picking up shot glasses or keychains that had ENGLEWOOD, FL, stamped on the front. I walked over to where Bailey was looking through postcards.

"I think I'll buy one for Marissa," Bailey said.

I was jealous she was on a first-name basis with her future roommate at Florida State when I didn't even know who my roommate would be yet. Bailey picked up a card that had the coordinates for Englewood Beach plastered across a picture of a beautiful sunset.

"Do you think those are the real coordinates?" I asked.

Bailey looked at me and laughed, "Why would they lie about that?" she asked and started to walk away. I followed her through the aisles until we eventually met up with Allie, who was spinning a tall rack that was filled with an assortment of jewelry. Each year, we always bought matching anklets. Though we usually picked different colors, we always got the same style. Bailey bent down and picked up a gaudy anklet filled with seashells and dangling turtle charms. She looked at us and laughed, "Please?" she begged.

Allie mimed, throwing up, "Hell no."

"I'll do anything if you let me get this anklet," Bailey said.

"Absolutely not. That thing is hideous," Allie said. Bailey pouted and crossed her arms over her chest.

"I'll make you a deal," Allie started, "We can get that anklet next year."

Bailey smiled, "I'll remember this."

Allie held up our usual go-to: a thinly braided anklet with colored beads through the braids. Bailey took it from Allie, apparently satisfied with the pink coloring of the beads.

"I think I want an orange one," Allie said. It was no secret that she was decking herself out with her future school colors of orange and blue. Bailey turned the rack around until she found an orange one and handed it to Allie.

"What about you, Morg?" she asked.

"Surprise me," I smiled.

"I'll get you gray to match your soul," Bailey said.

"What's that supposed to mean? I'm sunny," I said.

Allie scoffed, "Oh, please. You've been acting like doomsday is coming up."

"Well, I'm sorry, I'm not excited to be leaving my friends behind," I said.

Bailey handed me an anklet with an emerald green bead.

"We aren't excited either, but what are you going to do?" Allie said, "We have to grow up. We have to go to college."

Bailey shook her head, "Technically, we don't have to go to college. We could just move here to Englewood Beach and take over management at The Barefoot Trader and sell anklets all day,"

"Yeah, and smoke pot in the back alley like all of these employees do," I added.

"Oh, good call. And drink slurpees from 7-11 next door!" Bailey said. She smiled at me, and Allie laughed. Instantly, I was comforted. We walked to the cash register to pay for our anklets.

"Really, though, Morgan, we're all scared too," Bailey said.

"But…"

"I didn't say but," Bailey argued.

"Sure, I could hear it coming, though," I said.

"Allie, tell her there's no 'but,'" Bailey said. She placed her anklet on the counter. Allie squinted at us both.

"I don't know, it sounded like there should be a but," Allie said. Bailey sighed as she slid a five-dollar bill to the cashier.

"Owen, help me out here," Bailey said to the cashier after a quick glance at his name tag. He looked to be around our age, if not younger, and did not look amused by Bailey's sudden interaction with a stranger to get him on her side.

"With?" he asked.

"Tell my beautiful friend Morgan here that we will be just

fine when we all go to college, and we will still see each other on breaks and birthdays and holidays," Bailey said.

Owen handed her the change, "I don't know about that. My brother went to college a few years ago, and he doesn't talk to any of his friends from high school."

Bailey stared at him with a blank expression. "You aren't helping, Owen," she said, and he just shrugged.

After we all paid, we walked out of the store (definitely to Owen's excitement) and went over to our bikes. We only had a few days left at the house, and we were using up every free minute of the day. Bailey, Allie, and I all got on the bikes and took the longer way back to the house, looping around the block a few times before ultimately biking straight onto the beach. We dropped the bikes in the sand and went and sat down near the water. Bailey pulled our anklets out of the bag and ripped the tags off of them. She stuck her left ankle out to Allie, who was the only one of us who ever got the complicated knot needed to keep the anklet secure for longer than a week, and Allie worked her magic. She held her hand out for me to hand her my anklet and tied mine on before tying hers on as well. We held our ankles next to each other, and the sight of our tanned ankles decorated in such a simple piece of string made my throat constrict. Allie snapped a picture on her phone and then perked up.

"I got added to a group on Facebook about incoming UF freshmen, and there are so many cute guys," she said. She turned her phone around to show us a picture of some blond guy with dimples who posted about being excited to meet everyone at orientation.

"You'll probably never see that dude," Bailey said.

"Way to be negative," Allie said, and she kicked a little bit of sand at Bailey.

"I'm just saying, what a waste to be thinking about guys you're going to meet."

Allie rolled her eyes, "Okay, Ms. Perfect, calm down."

Bailey looked away from us out at the water.

"What's going on?" I asked. She turned and looked at me and shook her head.

"Nothing, I'm just not concerned over guys to meet," Bailey said.

"Okay, someone's acting weird," Allie said.

Bailey smiled, her usual version of a white flag when things got weird between us, and shook her head.

"Everything is wonderful," she said with such a forced sense of positivity that neither Allie nor I wanted to address it.

With just two days left at The Highview, we were starting to get sick of each other. In theory, an entire month spent at the house sounded great: we would spend every morning at the beach, hang out each afternoon, and enjoy our last nights together before we all left for college. But it had been three weeks of that. It wasn't that we weren't enjoying each other's company, but it felt like we were living in a fantasy world of endless beach days and endless shrimp to escape the looming reminder that in a few short weeks, we would be college freshmen.

It was nearing midnight when Noah and I decided to get some fresh air on the top deck. We were the only ones who had not fallen asleep while being forced to watch Uncle Daniel's favorite movie, The Princess Bride. The two of us were used to the film's quirkiness; the others, not so much.

I considered how, in one month, we would all be starting a new life. I'd known I would miss my friends and I'd miss Ryder, but for some reason, it hadn't hit me until that moment that I'd have Noah to miss as well. Before I could share the sentiment, a piece of popcorn kernel landed on my thigh. I looked over at Noah.

He smiled. "I picked that one out of my teeth."

"You're disgusting, Noah."

He laughed. "The ladies love it."

He fell silent as hushed voices drifted from down below. We stood up and looked around the empty beach. Since it was sea turtle hatching season, the only illumination we had this close to the beach was from the moon, so we could barely see anything as we leaned forward. I didn't need my vision to recognize who it was, though. The same laughter that always answered my bad jokes was muffled only slightly by the crashing waves.

"Stop!" I heard through a giggle.

"Is that Bailey?" Noah asked. We leaned further forward.

"Do you have my shirt?" another voice asked.

"And...Ethan?" I asked.

"You don't need a shirt. Everyone is asleep. Just get back inside," Bailey said.

Noah looked at me. "Should we go down there?" he whispered. I shrugged.

"Come here," Ethan said just as he and Bailey entered a patch of moonlight on the deck below. There, in the moonlight, Ethan wrapped his arms around Bailey's waist and kissed her.

~*~

The next morning, Noah and I sat at the kitchen counter in silence, only speaking when necessary. We glanced at each other every few seconds, willing the other to say something. Last night, when Noah and I waited for Bailey and Ethan to get inside the house, we decided we'd figure out what to do about what we'd seen. Our silence now surely was distracting to Ryder, who had been staring at us from across the kitchen island, but I didn't care.

"Pass the butter," he said. I handed it to him.

Ryder looked between the two of us, took a bite of his waffle, and looked at us again.

"Okay, what is going on?" he asked. Noah looked at me.

"Tell him," I said.

"No, you," Noah said.

"Rock, paper, scissors?" I suggested.

Noah placed one hand in the palm of the other, but we were interrupted by Allie, who walked out of the bedroom with her beach bag over one shoulder.

"Tell him what?" she asked.

"These two are being really weird," Ryder answered. "They have been all morning. Great way to spend our last day at The Highview." He eyed my uneaten waffle, and I pushed it across the counter to him.

"Don't say anything," I said in a hushed voice, "but we saw Ethan and Bailey kiss last night."

"Wait, what?" Allie asked. Ryder tilted his head.

"I think it might have been something more than kissing, honestly. Ethan didn't have a shirt on, and Bailey looked like she'd just spent the entire night laying in the sand."

"Gross, Morgan," Allie said. I shrugged.

"She's right, actually," Noah said. "And it wasn't the kiss you give Nanny on Christmas Eve."

Allie sat down on the barstool next to me and grabbed the last piece of Ryder's waffle. Noah walked to the fridge and tossed Allie a water bottle from within, to which she nodded in thanks.

"You know that Bailey would tell us if she was hooking up with Ethan," Allie said.

"Well, that's what I thought, too," I replied.

"She really hasn't said anything?" Ryder asked.

"No. Did Ethan?"

Noah and Ryder both shook their heads. I heard one of the bedroom doors open, and Allie jerked her head toward the hallway and mouthed, "Shut up" to us as Bailey walked into the room.

She reached over me and grabbed an apple off the counter. Taking a bite, she noticed some sand on her shirt — the same shirt she'd worn last night — and wiped it off. "Man, I feel like I should just sleep on the beach. There's so much sand everywhere in here."

We all let out a nervous chuckle that she didn't catch on to. Instead, she grabbed a towel that hung over the back of a kitchen chair and walked outside. When she was out of sight, Ryder turned and looked at the group.

"Are you going to say anything to her?" he asked me.

"Should I?"

"No. Definitely not," Noah interjected. "Just wait and see if she brings it up. Maybe it was just a one-time thing."

"Why do we have to say something? You guys should ask Ethan," Allie suggested.

Ryder shook his head, "We don't talk about that stuff."

"Yeah, right, so you didn't tell them the instant you and Morgan slept together for the first time?"

Ryder looked at Noah, then back at Allie, "Noah would've kicked my ass if I tried to talk about that."

Bailey stuck her head back inside. "Are we going down to the beach, or what? It's our last day here."

We all mumbled a collection of "Yeah," "Definitely," and "I'm gonna go change."

Minutes later, I was sitting next to Bailey on the shore. She rubbed sunscreen on her face, moved down to her shoulders, and then rubbed a small amount on the tops of her feet before handing me the bottle. I took it and held onto it, too distracted to think about skincare in a time like this. I looked toward the water, where Ryder, Noah, and Allie were floating on paddleboards, and silently glared daggers at them for leaving me here to be the one to bring up the kiss.

"Can you believe we're going to be college freshmen soon?" Bailey asked.

I shrugged. I hated talking about leaving with her. She was so excited to go to Florida State and start a new life. Two nights ago, I'd walked in on her video chatting with her new roommate, Marissa, and the jealousy I'd felt over her excitement to move on was something I'd never experienced before.

"I haven't thought too much about it," I lied.

"It's all I can think about. When we get back home, we're basically going to pack up and move."

"Yeah, it's crazy." I opened the sunscreen and absentmindedly rubbed some on my face.

Bailey was quiet for a moment, and then she looked at me. "Okay, what is going on, Morgan?"

"You tell me."

She shifted in her chair and looked out over the water, where Noah and Ryder were now timing to see who could stand the longest on the paddleboard while the other one shook it. "Are you seeing this? Is everything a competition with them?"

"Where's Ethan?" I asked.

At first, Bailey said nothing, just adjusted her sunglasses and tapped her fingernails against the chair. When she did finally speak, her voice was quiet. "What do you know?"

"Noah and I were on the top deck last night."

Bailey's eyes dropped, and she stared at her feet. When she looked at me again, she asked, "What do you want me to say?"

"An explanation would be cool."

"I don't have to tell you everything, you know."

"No, Bailey, you don't, but this is huge. And since when do we keep secrets from each other? Was that the only time you guys hooked up? What—"

"Morgan, shut up. It's none of your business, okay?" Her tone held a casualness that broke my heart. "God, this is why I didn't tell you when it first happened because I knew you'd make a huge freaking deal of it like you do with everything."

"Sorry, I care about you, Bailey."

"He kissed me graduation night before we all met up. We've been casual ever since. There. Are you happy?"

"Did you—you know?" I asked.

"You really wanna know?"

"You lost your virginity to Ethan? And you didn't tell us?" I was more hurt by this than I wanted to admit to, but it was a huge deal. That was something you told your best friend.

She just sighed and stared at me again.

"I thought you wanted to wait until college to lose your virginity."

"Well, things change, Morgan. Something that you literally cannot seem to accept." Bailey stood up and walked toward the water.

I stood and followed. "Stop pouting."

She whipped around and glared at me. I'd never seen her look so angry. "Let me guess. You already told everybody?"

I looked away. I couldn't hide the fact that I had.

Bailey stormed off and dove into the water, swimming

away from where everyone else was. Allie must have noticed because she was soon walking out of the water. She stood next to me on the shore and wrung the excess water out of her hair.

"Did she tell you what's going on?" Allie asked.

"They've been hooking up all summer. She's going to get her heart broken." I shook my head. "Remember Mason?"

Allie nodded. "Oh God, she didn't leave her bed for an entire weekend after he picked April to be his lab partner instead of her."

"Exactly. If she's been serious with Ethan, then you know this is going to be worse. They've known each other forever. You can't just go hooking up with your friends; it doesn't work that way."

Allie and I walked over to our beach chairs. She sat down in one and wrapped herself in a towel. "That doesn't seem fair. No one said that when you and Ryder started dating."

"That's not the same," I argued.

Allie laughed. "I know you don't want to hear this, but it might be." She shrugged. "Who knows. Maybe this will work for them."

I was surprised by how casual Allie was being about this. Bailey, Allie, and I had told each other everything about our lives from the very beginning. This was huge, and for both of them to look at me like I was overreacting was a huge slap in the face. What was next? Would Allie confess her love for Noah?

Allie turned the music on through the portable speaker and sang along quietly to the song that was playing. In the water, Bailey swam next to Noah and Ryder. We weren't thirteen anymore. I understood that. I knew that things had to change, like going off to college and trying new sports, but why did that mean that our friendships had to change as well? There had to be a world where everything could change except for us, and I would do whatever it took to find that world.

Allie nudged me and pointed to the water, where Ethan had joined the group. Ryder, Noah, Bailey, and Ethan stood in a circle talking, the waves crashing around their stomachs. Allie got up and walked toward the water. Suddenly, she stopped, glanced at the sky, and then turned back toward me. "We need to get inside before it starts raining." Turning back to the others, who were still in the ocean, she waved her arms and pointed to the sky.

Noah squinted at her. "What?" he yelled.

Allie pointed to the sky again and made a huge sweeping motion with her hands. "It's going to rain!" she yelled. In return, Ryder and Ethan began mocking her by making exaggerated movements with their arms as well, including their own version of the YMCA. In the water, Bailey, Ryder, Ethan, and Noah were cracking up.

"Well, whatever." Allie walked back toward me. At the same time, thunder cracked in the distance. She quickly turned and pointed to the water., "Ha! Told you."

Allie folded her chair. "If they want to get struck by lightning, so be it." We finished packing our things and walked across the sand up to the back deck. We sat down in the Adirondack chairs that faced the ocean, where we saw the others now getting out of the water.

"Don't tell Bailey I told you," I said. Down on the beach, Noah folded a chair.

"Do you think she'll admit it to me?" Allie asked.

"I don't know, Al. She didn't really want to talk about it. I wouldn't take it personally, though." Allie sometimes got jealous if she felt left out of something. And this was definitely something.

Minutes later, the others came up and dropped their things next to ours.

"Anyone want a sandwich?" Ethan asked.

"Yeah, man, I'll help," Ryder said.

As Ryder walked by my chair, he leaned down and kissed the top of my head. I knew he would want a report later of what I'd learned. Noah sat down on the other side of Allie after grabbing a bottle of water from the cooler that lived on the back deck. Bailey was washing off her legs in the outdoor shower and picking at her anklet.

"If you keep messing with that, it's going to—"

The string broke, sending pink beads rolling across the deck.

"Guess we'll need to go buy new anklets today," Allie said.

Bailey turned the water off and wrapped herself in a towel. She walked inside, toward the garbage can to throw it away but was intercepted by Ethan. From where I sat on the deck, I could see her walk to the corner of the kitchen. Ethan smiled at her. They exchanged words. Bailey held up her anklet to show him, and he took hold of it. He grabbed his keys off the counter and tied the broken anklet onto the key ring. Bailey laughed and headed back outside. Ethan watched her every move as she returned to the back deck and sat down next to me like nothing had happened.

Chapter 11

Me, 7:46 PM: Everyone is mad at each other.

After suffering through an awkward dinner, I'd gone into my room, shut the door, and opened the book I'd stuffed into my purse. I stared at the words on each page for minutes too long and made it halfway through the book before realizing I had no clue what was going on. After tossing the book back into my purse, I paced around the room. It had always felt small when three of us were staying in it, but now, even with just myself standing in the middle of the room, I felt suffocated. I walked to the closet and opened it up, and reached for my favorite hoodie. As I took it off the hanger, I noticed something that sparkled against the light gray carpet. I picked it up and held an earring between my pointer finger and thumb. It took me less than a second to place where I'd seen the earring before: it was Bailey's.

I walked out of the bedroom with the earring still in hand and placed it on the counter. Looking around the living space, I saw that it was empty. I hadn't heard any noise for the last hour or so and just assumed that everyone had gone to their own rooms, except for Allie, who'd never shown up to our room. I sat down at the kitchen island and pushed the earring back and forth. The fake diamond sparkled on the stud, and there were tiny pieces of carpet fibers stuck between the post and the backing of it. I pulled the pieces off. When I tried to think back to when Bailey had lost it, I drew a blank. Had she wanted to wear it on New Year's Eve?

The front door opened, and Allie came in. She had her car keys and a grocery bag in her hand. She unpacked her groceries, a variety of unsalted crackers, a block of cheese, and a huge produce bag filled with peppers, and started to walk by me without saying anything.

"I found Bailey's earring," I said.

She paused and faced me. I held up the earring for her to see.

"Bailey was not the only person to ever own a diamond earring," Allie said.

I shook my head, "No, this is hers. I remember her losing it."

"Should I wear the black jumper or jeans?" Bailey asked.

"Who cares? It's just us."

"Come on, I still want to look cute at midnight! Have you seen my other earring?"

I shook my head.

"Damn, why do I always lose things?" she asked.

Now, Allie put the earring back on the counter and sat down on the couch. She grabbed the remote and turned the television on. She flipped through channels before landing on a reality show. I looked over my shoulder at the TV. I'd been addicted to this very show. It challenged singles around the country to try to find their perfect match within the house. At the end of ten weeks, if they were able to guess who their perfect match was, the whole house would win one million dollars to split.

I tried my best not to tell Allie that they never figure out everyone's perfect match. Instead of focusing on the television, though, Allie stared at her phone and aimlessly scrolled. I always hated that she did that. In fact, when we were all together, I hated when anyone would be preoccupied with their phones. It always made me feel like I was second rate to whatever fancy technological life they seemed to prefer.

It made unanswered text messages even worse. I knew my friends constantly had their phones, they were basically an extension of their hands, but during our first semester at college, messages would go unanswered for hours. It wasn't that they were just busy. Now, looking at Allie, I knew that it was a purposeful decision to not respond.

"I never told you guys that I hated Flagler," I said.

Allie looked up from her phone. Though her eyes were on me, she still held her phone as if it were her life preserver. I shrugged.

"Everyone had such a fun time at college, and I was fucking miserable," I continued, "But worse than that, you guys had to have known that I was depressed. And no one did anything about it."

Allie shifted uncomfortably. She looked as if she was playing with words in her head, trying her best to sound compassionate. Empathy had never been Allie's strong suit.

She looked away from me, "What were we supposed to do? I love you, but it's not my job to make sure you're taking care of yourself."

I raised my eyebrows at her, "I didn't say it was your job, but you just never checked in on me. You knew I was lonely."

Allie and I had never been able to have the difficult conversations. We were too similar in conflict. We both always instantly went on the defense. Allie raised the defensiveness up a notch and crossed her arms over her chest.

"You could have told us you were lonely. I'm not a mind reader."

"No, but you were supposed to be my best friend. That should account for something."

Allie rolled her eyes, "So, what? You want an apology?"

"I'm not asking for anything. I was just telling you."

She shook her head, "No, Morgan, you were just telling me in hopes that it would make me feel bad. I get it. I'm a shitty friend."

It was my turn now to get defensive. I threw my hands up and laughed.

"What the hell is your problem? I said I was just telling you how I felt. I was fucking alone all the time, and you and Bailey were out making new best friends and forgetting about me."

Neither of us said anything until Allie eventually heaved a heavy sigh.

"I missed you too, okay? But you were a little exhausting during our first semester. You were so sad all the time, and you always made me feel guilty for having fun. Bailey felt the same way."

I stared hard at Allie. My fears that they were living a life without me were confirmed.

"You and Bailey talked about me?" I asked.

"Oh please, like you and Bailey never talked about me."

I shook my head, "Never."

The color drained from Allie's face, and she turned back

to the television.

"I'm sorry you were lonely," she started, "but you expected too much from us. We couldn't help you. We were so far away."

"That shouldn't have mattered."

"Maybe, but we were all dealing with our own stuff. We all had adjusting to do. Just because we were having fun, that doesn't mean it was easy."

When I'd dropped out of school, the therapist my mom made me go see shared a statistic with me about college freshmen. Apparently, thirty percent of freshmen dropped out after their first year.

"How many gave up after their first semester?" I'd asked her.

"Is that what you think? You gave up?" she asked back.

I looked at Allie now, extremely jealous that she had been able to fight through the loneliness, the pressure, the uncertainty. Something I had failed at.

"Where are the boys?" I asked, hoping a subject change would lighten the mood. I'd said what I had been wanting to say, and though there was no resolution to it, it was out in the open. What Allie did with the knowledge from here on out was her call.

She shrugged, "I'm not their keeper."

I noticed Allie was reverting back to her ways of high school. Instead of addressing conflict head on, she was so high on the defensive charts that saying anything else to her would be nearly impossible. Her eyes are focused now on the television show. I walked towards the back door and, in a lapse of maturity, looked at Allie.

"They don't win the money. They never figure out their perfect matches," I said before opening the back door and walking onto the deck.

When I settled into my chair, I saw Noah, Ethan, and Ryder all standing around a fire they built on the beach. They stood in a circle around it, laughing and smiling. There's absolutely no trace of any resentment between the three of them. And, God, Ethan even punched Ryder just a few hours ago.

But they're fine. Smiling. Laughing. Happy, even. I hated that Allie and I were struggling to get there. We'd been on an up and down since she arrived. One minute, we're silent. The next minute, we're allies. It's draining. I wished I didn't feel like I was going to battle whenever I talked to her. I turned around and looked through the glass door. She is glued to the television set now, but I'm not sure if it was out of entertainment or just because it was something to pass the time. She looked like a stranger to me. I hoped that the fireworks show tomorrow for July 4th would give us something to call a truce to, but, with Allie, I never knew.

Noah walked up to the deck and sat down next to me.

"How do you guys do it?" I asked.

Noah tilted his head, and I pointed to him, Ethan, and Ryder.

"They were literally punching each other earlier, and now everything is fine? Meanwhile, Allie acts like I killed her puppy, but I didn't even do anything to her."

Ethan and Ryder walked up to the deck. Ethan had a football in his hand that I didn't see earlier. He pulled his arm back and tossed the football to Ryder as they walked.

"Be careful around the windows, please," Noah groaned.

"Didn't we tell you that the house looks fine? How would your dad even know we were here?" Ethan asked.

"He didn't hire the cleaning crew to come this weekend because he didn't think anyone would be here. If the next guests check-in and the house isn't clean, and they complain, he'll know something happened."

Ryder tossed the football back to Ethan, who pretended to chuck it at the window. Ryder and I laughed, but Noah just stared at him.

"Bud, calm down, I'm just messing," Ethan said. He threw the football again with too much force for how close he and Ryder were to each other. Ryder ducked down and dodged it, and we all watched in horror as it slammed into the glass table to the right of us, which instantly shattered.

"Is this a joke?" Noah said. We all turned and stared at him, and I was shocked to see him so calm as he stood up and walked to the table.

"Why did you throw it so hard?" Ryder asked Ethan.

"Why didn't you catch it?" Ethan asked back.

The back door slid open, and Allie stood in the doorway. She looked from us to the football to the shattered table. She said nothing, just let out a laugh and shut the door again.

"Is today over yet?" Noah asked. Ethan ran inside and came back seconds later with the broom and dustpan. He bent down and picked up the larger pieces of glass and tossed them into the garbage can Ryder had hauled over from the side of the house. The three of them worked without talking to each other as they cleaned it up. Noah took the broom and swept the entire deck, telling us that the glass could have traveled, and the last thing he needed was one of us tracking blood into the house.

"Okay, Dad, thanks," Ryder joked. Ethan snorted out a laugh.

Noah glared at both of them, "Someone get on Craigslist and find a replacement table."

The three continued on, arguing over who would find the best table, and I felt my phone vibrate in my pocket. I pulled it out, expecting to see a text message from my mom, but instead saw my e-mail had a notification. I opened the e-mail app and saw the email address of my advisor at Flagler, Dr. Foley. The subject line read: Checking in. I opened the e-mail and read it.

Dear Morgan,

I wanted to check in and say hello and see how you are doing. I know that your first semester at Flagler ended unexpectedly due to personal issues, but I wanted to let you know that your admission decision to Flagler still stands. While you'd have to repeat some courses from your first semester, we could work with you to get you on track to graduate with your class. At our last advising meeting in the fall, you seemed very interested in marine biology. Is this still something you're thinking about? Please let me know if you'd like to chat. If Flagler is no longer in your future, I wish you the best on your endeavors.

Take care, Dr. Foley

I scanned the e-mail a few more times. I'd talked about marine biology to get Dr. Foley off my back. She always had great advice to give me and had been kind when I'd told her I was leaving. She'd understood, she said and had emailed me one other time before this to check in. I hadn't thought about returning to Flagler. It was too muddled with my bad memories and my loneliness. I looked around the back deck, realizing that the boys had gone inside while I was buried in my e-mail.

I was faced with a huge decision.

And I was alone.

Chapter 12

Last Fall

Me, 3:37 PM: How's everyone's day?
Bailey, 6:03 PM: Long.

At the end of the summer, I got an email from Flagler College with my roommate assignment. Rebecca wanted to be a teacher. She was tall with short blonde hair and a friendly smile. The first time we video-chatted, we talked about how lucky we were to get one of the few rooms on our floor that had its own bathroom. We decided we didn't need to make our beds into bunk beds, and we both agreed that posters on the wall would be tacky. She seemed like she would be a good friend to have.

Now it was October, and I'd been living in my small but comfortable dorm room with Rebecca for two months, coexisting peacefully. I went to lunch every day with classmates from my biology class. I didn't want to call them friends just yet. We weren't there yet.

One Friday night, I sat outside on the West Lawn of Flagler College, a large common space located right outside my all-female dorm building. Groups of students huddled together as they enjoyed the cool weather. I sat on a blanket with my psychology book open on my lap. I had failed the last quiz, and I knew that if I didn't want to have to retake the class, I needed to get serious.

I was distracted, though. I pulled out my phone and opened the group text thread with Allie and Bailey. My birthday was tomorrow, and neither of them had said anything about it. Sure, we weren't within walking distance anymore, but it wasn't too far a drive for anyone. Even if we just met up for lunch.

My Toyota Corolla still had a full tank of gas from when I had moved in. With everything in walking distance of campus, I felt like I'd been living in my own little bubble, never having to drive around for anything. I could even walk to the coffee shop where I worked part-time. Since getting to Flagler, I had been itching to get in my car and drive the two hours to Allie in Gainesville or the three to Bailey in Tallahassee.

But I hadn't.

Bailey had suggested we all try to adjust to our new lives for a few months before we met back up, and everyone had agreed. I should have voiced my opinion then: I didn't need more friends. We all still talked every day, but not like we used to. Ryder and I had planned to visit each other every weekend, but our workloads made it impossible. I was in a long-distance relationship, and even if that distance was only an hour drive, it still felt like we wouldn't make it to sophomore year.

The last time I had video-chatted with Bailey and Allie, I brought up my feelings. Not seeing Ryder every day was hard, especially since we'd spent the last five years seeing each other nearly every day. Each time we talked, it felt like we had less and less to say, and it troubled me.

"It's only a matter of time before Ryder meets someone

new and forgets about me," I'd told Bailey and Allie.

What hurt worse than the thought of that was that they didn't try to convince me otherwise. They seemed to be of the mindset that our lives before college didn't matter anymore, as proven by Bailey's pictures on Instagram with her roommate Marissa and Allie's mention of a new boy we had yet to see a picture of.

I scrolled to Ryder's name in my phone and tapped it. He answered after a few rings.

"Hey," he said breathlessly.

"Did I interrupt something?" I asked.

"Ethan and I just got back from a run."

"You run now?"

"How was your lit exam?" he asked, changing the subject.

Frowning, I strained to hear voices in the background. "Really hard, but I think I studied enough, so we'll see, I guess. You know, I was —"

"Morgan? Can I call you back later? Sorry, I'm just...I need to focus on something right now."

I tried not to let my world collapse in on me as we said goodbye. I tried not to think about how Noah had told me that they hung out frequently with the girls who lived across the hall from them. I tried not to sound desperate or jealous as I mused to myself that all my friends had moved on from me. Didn't they remember our summer together?

I folded up the blanket I was sitting on and stuffed it in my bag, slipped my shoes back on, and smoothed down my jeans. I walked through the front door of the dorms and avoided eye contact with everyone I passed.

As I unlocked my door, I was reminded again of how alone I was. Rebecca had gone home for the weekend for her grandparents' anniversary or something like that, and though she had left me a birthday card and we'd shared a cupcake the night before, the reality that I would be spending my nineteenth birthday alone was beginning to really set in.

Then I smelled it. A mix of floral and musk that sounded like it should smell horrible but somehow didn't. Allie's perfume.

I walked around my dorm room, trying to figure out where it was coming from. Our open floor plan allowed no room to hide. It was just our beds, our desks, and our shared closet. Not finding anything, I walked to the bathroom and opened the door. I almost screamed when I saw Allie and Bailey huddled in the shower, their faces red from trying not to laugh.

"Surprise!" they both yelled and jumped out of where they were in the shower. I was stunned as they wrapped their arms around me, and the three of us stood embracing each other.

"Happy birthday!" Bailey said. Next thing I knew, Bailey and Allie were pulling me out of my dorm room and down the hallway.

"What are you guys doing here? Wait, where are we going?" I asked as we ran through the halls of the dorm. Bailey flew past the elevator, and we ran down three flights of stairs. When we exited the dorms onto the West Lawn, I appreciated the beauty of Flagler's campus for the first time. The historical architecture, the gold-and-maroon molding, the fountain in the middle of the lawn that was now lit up, and the pure ambience of living in the oldest city in the country. Tonight, they were all breathtaking.

Standing on the other side of the lawn, all dressed in short-sleeved shirts and flip-flops, were Ryder, Ethan, and Noah. Ethan held a bouquet of balloons, and as soon as they saw us, all three started to sing "Happy Birthday." Ryder broke away from the group and walked up to me, wrapping his arms around me and kissing me.

"We would never let you celebrate your birthday alone!" Noah said.

"Now, let's go," Allie said, leading the way through the main campus gates.

I didn't question where we were going as I was shuffled into the front seat of Bailey's Volkswagen.

We pulled up to Flagler Beach fifteen minutes later. Noah backed his truck onto the beach, jumping out once he had stopped. He spread a blanket out in the bed of the truck and perched coolers delicately on the tailgate. Ethan grabbed a bag from Bailey's back seat as we climbed out and joined them on the beach.

"Party time!" Ethan handed us each a party hat. Noah cut the headlights. From the bed of the truck, Ryder reached down and pulled me up. Bailey and Allie followed.

Ryder handed me a drink. I noticed that the boys all drank beer with a casualness they'd never used before. We had never been big partiers in high school, so watching them drink beer as if they did it every day was something new. When everyone had something to drink, Noah looked around at all of us.

He held up his can. "Happy birthday, Morgan." I smiled as everyone cheered, and we took a drink together.

By midnight, Bailey and I found ourselves on the sand, giggling from the buzz we had from the "slightly spiked seltzer." In the bed of the truck, Ethan balanced on the railing, urging Ryder to try to join him. Allie and Noah cheered Ethan on from the bed of the truck. Bailey looked at them from where we sat.

"Ethan is so cute," she whispered.

I scoffed. "I thought you stopped hooking up with him

when you left for FSU?"

She took a sip of her drink and nodded. "So? That doesn't mean I can't still think he's cute."

"Please, Bailey, you're telling me you're still hung up on him when you have a world of possibilities at FSU?"

"You have a world of possibilities at Flagler."

Not this again. I wished Bailey would see the difference. Ryder was more than a crush. Plus, my feelings for Ryder were reciprocated, unlike hers for Ethan. I'd seen how Ethan treated dating. Like everything else, he thought of it as a competition, and Ethan hated to lose.

Then I thought about how he had always treated Bailey differently. Even before I knew they were hooking up, he'd favored Bailey over everyone. They had the same playful spirit, and Ethan always made sure Bailey was okay.

As I looked over at the truck, I couldn't help but wonder if I was jealous. Bailey and Ethan were heating up just as Ryder and I were starting to fall apart.

Bailey took a sip from her water bottle. "Have you made friends at Flagler yet?"

"Of course."

"Why were you about to spend your birthday alone, then?"

I pushed myself up out of the sand. "Your life at college is much better than mine. I get it."

"That's not what I meant, Morgan. I just worry about you." Bailey stood to join me. "We're all having such a good time, learning so much, growing. I know it takes time to adjust, but are you even trying?"

"I don't know why you want to replace me so badly."

"Oh my God, come on. I'm not replacing you!"

"You and Ryder both are. He takes forever to respond to my texts now, and you and Marissa might as well go get each other's names tattooed across your faces."

"Don't clump me in with Ryder. If you two are having problems, address them with him. I'm just trying to get the most out of college. I wish you'd at least try."

"I can't help it. I think of you at lunch tables with new friends and Allie running the show among all the other freshman premed students, and I am so embarrassed that I'm so alone." I sat back down in the sand, needing the ground's stability. "Plus, all I can think about is all the girls in Orlando talking about how to get invited to Ryder, Ethan, and Noah's apartment, and it's so stupid."

Bailey sat down next to me. She dropped her head against my shoulder. "I didn't know you felt that way."

It wasn't until that moment that I fully realized I did feel that way.

"Just leave me alone, okay?" I went on the defensive, but it was easier to think I could push everyone away so it wouldn't hurt as much when we all fell apart. I just wanted us to go back to our summers together.

Bailey stood up without a word and walked up to the truck. She conveniently sandwiched herself between Allie and Ethan.

Chapter 13

Me, 2:46 p.m.: The 4th of July festival is all set up. There's even an ice cream tent.
Me, 2:47 p.m.: We've got three more days here. Even more reason for you to come.

When the black SUV pulled into the driveway, I knew we had a problem. There was already something daunting about black SUVs, but when they carried the face of the same realtor who was plastered on the For Sale sign that decorated the front yard... well, that was very daunting indeed.

I leaned over the railing of the top deck. A woman who looked to be about my mom's age slid out of the SUV, wearing black jeans and a nice blouse, her blonde hair pulled back into a tight ponytail. She took out her phone and snapped a picture of the For Sale sign before smiling up at the house.

She started when she spotted me. "Oh, Daniel didn't say there would be a family here. I'm so sorry. My name is Maggie Milton. I'm selling the house for Daniel. We got good news today, so I came to take the sign down!" She pulled a large red Sold plaque out of the front seat of the SUV. Peeling off the backing, she stuck it over the For Sale sign.

"He sold the house?" I asked.

She nodded. "To some new-money young couple who wants to rent the thing on Airbnb. They said they could make a killing, and they're right."

Maggie walked closer to the house, shading her eyes with one hand and giving me another smile. "Are you enjoying your stay? I could have sworn the dates were blacked out for this week, but it's a busy time, so my calendar could be a mess!"

Footsteps sounded on the spiral staircase. Glancing back, I saw Noah stop as he reached the top.

"Noah? Is that you?" Maggie asked.

Noah stared at me, eyes wide. How on Earth did this woman know Noah? Noah closed his eyes and whispered, "Busted." He walked to the railing and looked down.

"Maggie? What's up?" His voice was filled with genuine shock.

"Your father didn't tell me you guys were here," she said.

"He's not here," Noah started.

Maggie smiled. "Well, good. I thought for a second there he was standing me up. That's nice. Just a trip with your friends, then? I'll tell him you guys are alive and well. I've got great news to deliver."

"What is going on?" I asked.

Noah looked at me. "This is Maggie. My dad's realtor and...girlfriend."

"Your dad is sleeping with the realtor?" I asked, my voice a whisper.

"Don't look so amused. We're about to get busted," he said.

We both looked down at Maggie, who was picking up a piece of trash that had blown into the yard and tossing it into the trash can. Noah jerked his head toward the stairs, and we ran down the spiral staircase.

We took the steps two at a time. "What's the plan?" I asked.

"No clue," he said, just as we met toe-to-toe with Maggie at the front gate. She smiled.

"Maggie, this is my cousin Morgan," Noah said. Maggie smiled and shook my hand.

"I've heard a lot about you, Morgan!" Maggie said.

"Hi," I said.

"All right," Noah said. "Let's just call a spade a spade. My dad doesn't know we're here."

"What?" Maggie asked.

"He thinks we're—"

"Taking a summer intensive class," Maggie said. "Yeah, he told me. Noah, what's going on? Is everything okay?" She leaned against the front gate and stared at Noah, concerned.

"Well, yes. And no. See, we came here, all of us, to try to, uh…"

"Fix our friendship," I said, jumping in.

Maggie looked between Noah and me and had an Aha! moment, as if she'd heard the stories of how we all fell apart.

"Well, Noah, I can't keep this from your father," Maggie started.

"I'm not asking you to. But maybe…just let me tell him? I'll call him right now, I promise. He's not going to be mad—"

"He's going to be pissed," I said.

"Yeah. Yeah, he's going to be pretty mad, so it's better that I just get it over with. You know, the lying and the coming here even though he told us summers at The Highview were over, blah, blah, blah."

Noah smiled at Maggie. She crossed her arms over her chest.

"Call him, Noah. I'll pretend I was never here. But if I drive the three hours to his house right now and I get there, and he doesn't know yet, then it's my turn to talk. Got it?"

Noah nodded. "Thanks."

She stared up at the house. "Well, live it up, I guess."

Noah smiled as they exchanged goodbyes, and Maggie walked back to her SUV. She got in and reversed out of the driveway. She stopped the SUV in the middle of the road and rolled down the window.

"Call your dad," she yelled and, with a wave of her perfectly manicured hand, was off.

Noah and I stood in the driveway, staring at the Sold sign in front of the house. "Now what?" I asked.

"Now, I call my dad."

After Maggie left, Noah and I went inside and called a house meeting.

"We're busted," Noah said as Ryder, Ethan, and Allie settled around the living room. We all tried to think of a plan or an excuse, everything ranging from Ryder's idea of "It was a spur of the moment thing" to Ethan's suggestion of alien abduction. In the end, Allie convinced Noah to just tell the truth.

Now, Allie, Ethan, Ryder, and I sat inside, staring out at the back deck where Noah paced, his phone pressed to his ear. He was on minute eight of the phone call and was nodding, periodically opening his mouth to speak, only to instantly close it, as if Uncle Daniel was telling him to "Save it, son."

"We should've gone with the alien abduction," Allie said

as Noah held the phone away from his ear. We all winced.

"I knew he was going to be mad," I added, "but this seems really mad."

We all turned our attention back to Noah, who was now hanging up the phone. He stared out at the beach before turning around and walking in.

"Well?" Ethan asked, handing Noah the open beer he had prepared for him for after the phone call.

"My dad had a lot to say. Mostly, he's mad at us for lying about where we were." Noah took a long sip of the beer. "He had some choice words, but he ended by saying he knows how much The Highview means to all of us and that he's proud of us for sticking together." Noah smiled. "Oh, and that he's on his way."

"He's coming here?" Allie asked.

"He's probably getting in the car as we speak. He said he doesn't want us here alone, that there's too much on the line, what with the house being sold and all."

"Well," I said, "we definitely need to do a ten-second tidy. This place is trashed."

Ethan stood and grabbed a roll of paper towels off the kitchen counter. He opened the cabinet underneath the sink and grabbed the disinfectant spray. "I'll do the bathroom."

Ryder grabbed trash and stuffed it into bags. Allie walked to the kitchen and turned on the faucet, eyeing the pile of dishes. I gathered all the rogue beach towels as Noah swept the sand that had fallen off them.

No one talked about the fight from the night before. Instead, Ryder tiptoed around Ethan and me. I put my phone in the drawer beside my bed, deciding to keep it there, at least until things settled down some more. As I looked around the house and saw that we had made it look pretty close to perfect, I felt comforted.

Four hours later, on the dot, we heard Uncle Daniel's SUV pull into the driveway. Noah walked outside, and we watched from the windows as Uncle Daniel pulled him into a hug. They exchanged words, Uncle Daniel nodding as they spoke, and then both paused and stared at the house. Uncle Daniel's eyes wandered to the Sold sign that had replaced the For Sale sign and looked away quickly. He walked up the stairs with Noah trailing, and suddenly, we were kids again, entering The Highview for the first time.

"Well, well, well," Uncle Daniel said, staring at each of us as he opened the door. He gave a small smile. "Glad to see classes are going so well." He kicked his shoes off and grabbed the pile of junk mail that had accumulated on the counter. He looked around the living room, where we all sat.

"It's good to see you, Daniel," Ethan started.

"Save it, dude," Uncle Daniel said. "I just got off the phone with your parents. I bet they'll be calling any minute."

Allie indicated the bag that Uncle Daniel had left by the front door. "Why the duffel bag?"

Daniel gave a hearty laugh. "As they say in the movies, Allie, 'the jig is up.' I'm staying here with you guys," he said. "And better yet, I'm not lifting a damn finger in that kitchen."

"Well, you're just in time for the fireworks! They start at seven," Ryder said.

Uncle Daniel looked at him. "Ryder, I appreciate you not lying to your parents. When I called them, they said they knew where you were."

"I'm an honest guy," Ryder said.

"They knew the rest of you little rats were lying though,"

"Well, in their defense, I'm an only child and an angel, as we've established, so I'm not sure they know how to handle lying teenagers."

Uncle Daniel cracked a smile at that. Ethan and Allie both looked up at the sound of a vibrating cell phone on the counter.

"Is that mine?" Allie asked.

I looked over at the counter to see my iPhone lit up.

"Mine," I said, and Allie and Ethan both let out a sigh of relief.

"Why'd you tell my mom? Can't you be my adult?" I asked Uncle Daniel as I walked over to the counter. I picked up my phone and hit the answer button. Before I could even say hello, my mom started talking at me.

"I trusted you, Morgan! Don't you know how dangerous what you are doing is?" she started with. I pressed my phone against my ear and walked to the back deck, closing the sliding glass door behind me. I looked out at the beach where tents were getting set up for the annual 4th of July fireworks show. From where I stood, I could see our favorite ice cream shoppe had set up a tent, along with the restaurant down the road that served Endless Shrimp every Wednesday night.

"Morgan? Talk to me, please," my mom said.

"What do you want me to say? I'm sorry I did it?" I asked.

She sighed, "I'm calling Dr. Mackintosh. This is not like you, Morgan," she said.

"Who?" I asked.

My mom was silent on the other end.

"Oh, Jesus. I'm going to kill your cousin," she finally said.

Neither of us said anything else for a few moments as I watched the bustle on the beach continue.

"The fireworks are tonight," I said.

"Great."

"Look, you can't be mad at me. I'm an adult," I argued.

My mom laughed on the other line, one of those 'what are you even talking about' laughs, "I can be mad at you, my dear, for lying and for putting yourself in danger. God, what was Noah thinking going back to that damn house?"

"It's been helpful," I said. I felt defeated. I wanted to tell my mom it took a lot of courage for me to even agree to come here. It took a lot to face Ethan, Ryder, and Allie. It took everything I had in me to not completely lose it as the days ticked away, and Bailey still didn't show up.

"How helpful can it be if you're still texting Bailey?" my mom started, "You don't need a summer vacation, Morgan, you need a God damn reality check."

On the other end, my mom gasped and exhaled with so much force I could almost feel her warm breath against my ear.

"I'm sorry, honey, I…" She stopped, "I'm going to come, okay?"

"You don't have to do that, Mom," I said. I picked at a frayed piece of denim on my shorts.

"It's fine," she said, but her voice was strained and tired. A sure sign that she thought this was anything but fine. We talked for a few more moments, forced pleasantries about her 4th of July plans and whether or not we'd been eating enough before I hung up. I stood on the back deck and put my phone back in my pocket. The beach was starting to fill up quickly, and I saw tents spread well down the shore. I walked to the back door and slid it open. Inside, everyone sat silently, the tension again so high I thought the windows would break. Allie stood at the kitchen island, talking in a hushed voice to Ryder. I didn't have the energy to figure out what they were whispering about now, but I had a pretty good feeling it was probably about me. Ethan looked up from the couch just as his phone started to vibrate in his hand.

"Let's go down to the beach, Morg," Noah said as he walked out of Uncle Daniel's room. He grabbed his portable speaker off the kitchen island and passed by me, walking towards the sand.

Noah and I walked straight down from the back deck to the beach to claim a spot big enough for all of us. I dropped the three chairs that I had while Noah spread out the large blanket we always used on the beach. Allie and Ethan were still inside, getting reamed out by their parents. When we walked by Ethan on the back deck, we heard his mother in tears, repeating that she couldn't believe her son didn't trust her enough to tell her where he really was.

"Don't you think they're all over-reacting?" I asked Noah as he put our flip-flops on the corners of the blanket to weigh it down. He shook his head.

"They're definitely not over-reacting," he said.

"It's not like we're in any grave danger," I said.

"Let's just enjoy the last few days," Noah said. He sat down on the blanket and looked out at the ocean. He checked his watch — I felt like my cousin was the only person left who wore a watch to strictly tell the time — and then turned around to look at the house.

"Just tell me something," he started, "has being here helped? Or was this a straight up waste?"

I thought about it for a moment. Surely, being together had helped my mood. Though I knew we weren't back to being one hundred percent, I at least could enter a room where Allie was and not want to puke. Ryder and I could look at each other again. I had hoped that Ethan and I would get there eventually. But now, as our days at The Highview were coming to a permanent end, I wondered how Bailey and I would ever get back to normal. I was scared that at the end of this if she still didn't show up, I would have to move on. Give up. Get over it.

"I just miss how we all used to be," I finally decided to tell Noah. Maybe it wasn't the answer he wanted, though, because he looked away so quickly as if I'd slapped him and did the weird, twisty thing he always did with his mouth when he was trying not to show how upset he was.

"I really tried. We all did," Noah said.

Before I could say anything else, I heard Allie, Ethan, and Ryder walking down the beach. Ryder was holding a shopping bag of snacks that Uncle Daniel had made him go to the store and get while we were all dealing with our parents.

"That was brutal, dude. My mom cried so much," Ethan said. He sat down in one of the chairs that I'd set up.

"Because you lied to her?" Allie asked.

"Not even because I lied. She just rambled a lot about the house and all of us being back together."

"My mom said that I am, gee, how did she word it, a 'spoiled little brat sometimes,'" Allie said, "She's mostly upset that I wasn't actually taking free courses that would knock off some of the debt I'm going to be in after we graduate."

Ryder laughed, "See you guys? Let this be a lesson. Telling the truth always works. Now I get to enjoy these fireworks guilt-free, and my parents can rest easy tonight knowing that they raised an angel."

We all settled down in our respective seats, each of us murmuring some sort of insult directed at Ryder. Ryder looked around the beach.

"Holy shit, Jay's Crab Shack is here? Endless Shrimp, thank

God," he said. He stood up and ran over to the stand, tripping over himself as he made his way to the line. He turned around and yelled at us, "Anyone else want anything?" Noah and Ethan stood up and jogged over to the line, and joined him.

Allie leaned back on her hands and looked up at the darkening sky.

"I know it's bad luck to talk about rain right before a firework show, but this looks daunting," she said.

"Why would you acknowledge the bad luck and then still bring it up?" I laughed.

After a moment, I took a breath. "My advisor from Flagler emailed me. She said I could go back in the fall if I wanted."

Allie peeked over her sunglasses at me, "Morgan, that's great. Are you going to?"

I shrugged, "I honestly hadn't thought too much about it."

"Well, I've been thinking, and you know, Flagler is actually pretty close to UF. And everyone says that sophomore year is easier because you're settled and everything. I could drive and come visit you. We could..." Allie paused, "We could have been better about that in the fall. And I'm sorry."

"Allie, I didn't need an apology —" I started. She held up her hand.

"But you deserved one," she said.

The simplicity of her statement shook me. Allie never apologized. She was notoriously stubborn. In fact, in 8th grade, she accidentally hit Miranda Simpson in the face with a kickball. Instead of apologizing, she had vehemently argued that she hadn't been the one to throw the ball. Allie and Miranda never spoke to each other again.

Allie gave me a small smile. "I can't take back what I did or what I said, but I can try to be better in the future."

I reached over and squeezed her hand, both of us choosing not to acknowledge that we both had tears in our eyes. That was probably for the best. The only thing Allie hated more than apologizing was crying.

Allie stood up and held her hand out for me to join her. She led us to the ice cream stand, where we got in line behind a family with yelling kids and frustrated parents. Allie did nothing to hide her disgust at the loudness of the children. I offered a sympathetic smile to the parents, though I knew nothing about what they were dealing with.

In the distance, a rumble of thunder echoed across the sky. Allie and I both looked at each other. The radio station that hosted the fireworks show yearly was set up under a tent, blasting top 40s hits, seemingly unfazed by the incoming storm. Around us, crowds of people gathered, all talking about whether or not the fireworks would still be able to go up if there was rain. Maybe they'll go early, someone suggested. Maybe they'll postpone to tomorrow, someone else offered up. Allie and I were too focused on getting our ice cream to really care about what that meant for the fireworks. Still, each time the thunder boomed, something deep in my core twisted. Allie must have noticed because she looked at me with an alarmed stare.

"You okay?" she asked.

I shook my head, "I don't know."

She gently placed her hand on my arm and led me forward as the line moved, clearly thinking that ice cream would fix whatever it was I was feeling. And normally, it did, but for some reason, being here with Allie as a storm circled around us, I couldn't shake the feeling that there was something much bigger that was wrong with today.

I felt alone. I felt like it was my first semester at Flagler again when I'd struggled to even get out of bed because of how lonely I was. I thought back to the days that were good at Flagler and how I'd felt guilty if I'd laugh with someone else or enjoy my classes. I'd felt so guilty for trying to start a new chapter in my life, just like my friends were, and I'd get so mad that they didn't seem to be feeling that guilty.

I was so alone. They left me so alone.

In the distance, the fireworks started. Ethan, Ryder, and Noah went back to our area with paper trays filled with fried shrimp. Uncle Daniel, who had set up camp when we'd all gone to look for food, took a tray from Noah. Allie handed me an ice cream cone — cookies and cream with rainbow sprinkles, just like she knew I liked — as I stood underneath the tent, holding up the line.

"Morgan? You there?" Allie asked as she nudged me to walk.

In the sky, the fireworks exploded. The sound of them exploding, the colors spreading across the horizon, as spectators "ooohhhhed" and "awwwwweeed." Families relaxed. Friends clapped. Locals and tourists alike celebrated.

My brain clouded. My chest constricted. My stomach churned.

I'm standing alone in the rain, screaming.

Chapter 14

Past
December

Morgan, 1:03 PM: My Fridays are the best. I'm done with class so early.
Bailey, 7:35 AM: Sorry, forgot to respond yesterday.

"Hey, it's just me. Can you call me back, please? I feel like we haven't talked in a million years," I paused with my phone against my ear and focused on making my voice sound cheery, "Anyway, I'm so busy too, but just wanted to say hi."

I hit the end call button on my phone screen and tossed my phone to the foot of my bed. I sat back and stared up at the ceiling. Though we were just one week away from winter break, it felt like the days were dragging by slower than ever before. I hadn't heard from Bailey or Allie all day, which was unusual. Even if it was a quick text message about not sleeping well or forgetting to study for a test, we always talked. It was dinner time now, and it had been a full day without any response from either of them.

I could call Ryder, I figured, but lately, he and I had been off as well. We'd video chat every night, share stories about our days, but it just felt forced. We used to be able to sit next to each other and talk for hours on end, laughing and scheming, but now our calls were silent and borderline painful.

I got off of my bed and put my shoes on. I grabbed my student ID off of my desk and walked out of my dorm, locking the door behind me. I wandered down the hallway to the elevator and pushed the button for the dining hall. As I stood in the elevator, I realized I left my phone in my room but made no moves to go back and get it. When the elevator stopped and the doors opened, I walked out and headed towards the dining hall. Since it was about to close, it was practically empty, except for the Flagler athletes who were getting out of late practices. The table in the corner was filled with guys all in workout clothes, laughing loudly. Their table was filled with plates and cups. The rest of the dining hall was empty, and as I got in line to grab a sandwich, I felt a phantom vibration of my phone.

God, I missed Bailey and Allie.

I couldn't wait for New Year's Eve when we would be back together at The Highview.

I wanted to be home. Everyone said that Flagler would start to feel like home, but every Friday, it took everything in me to not get into my car and drive home, even if it was just for a night to find the familiarity of my bed.

"Are you waiting in line?" a voice asked.

I turned around and saw a guy I'd never seen before standing behind me at the sandwich station. I realized I was standing in the middle of the walkway, blocking most of the line.

"No, sorry," I said, "I'm a little out of it."

My distractions were getting the best of me.

No, my loneliness was getting the best of me.

He laughed, "Too much partying, I get it. I remember

freshman year."

He looked me up and down, and I was suddenly self-conscious of my leggings and baggy sweatshirt. The girls that were sitting at the table with the guys were all in jeans and boxy sweaters that somehow fit perfectly.

I looked over at the table.

They were laughing, smiling, joking.

That used to be me. I used to be at the table where everyone would look at and think what I was thinking now: they are having the time of their lives.

In high school, Ethan's jokes would command the room. At lunch, Bailey would say hi to everyone as she walked over to where we sat. Girls would tell me all the time how jealous they were of Ryder and me. How cute we were. Noah was Mr. Space Coast High, friendly with everyone and ready to solve a problem. Allie was the queen.

We were those kids who had their whole lives ahead of them to be as happy as we were then.

Now, I was alone.

I scooped some salad onto my plate and made a sandwich before walking to a table in the corner of the cafeteria and sitting down. I kept my eyes down and took small bites of my food. I stared out the dining hall windows and watched the sunset.

"Hey, Morgan," a voice behind me said. I looked over my shoulder and saw a guy from my World History class standing there. He sat next to me during every class and would smile whenever he passed me the attendance sign-in. When I didn't respond to—was his name Tyler?—, he looked at me with a questioning look.

"Morgan, right? I'm Dylan. We sit next to each other in World History."

Dylan. Whatever.

"Hi."

Dylan nodded to the empty seat next to me.

"Can I sit there?" he asked. I looked at the seat and knew that I had no excuse.

"Yeah, sure," I decided.

Dylan sat down next to me, his body barely touching the seat before he was taking a bite of his chicken sandwich. I could smell the gallon of hot sauce that he poured on it, and he grabbed a napkin and wiped his face. He must have noticed me staring and laughed.

"Sorry, I'm a slob when I eat," he said.

"It's pretty good food for cafeteria cuisine," I said.

He laughed, "Right? None of my buds from back home believe me when I tell them that I eat like royalty."

He took a sip of his fountain drink, and I did the same. Out of the corner of my eye, I saw him tousle his blond hair as he silenced his vibrating phone. On the screen, I saw the name Taylor.

"My sister is blowing up my phone today," he said, sounding like he was apologizing.

"You should answer. It's not nice to ignore someone," I said. My tone sounded sharp and short, and he must have caught on.

"Noted. Morgan doesn't like to be ignored," he said.

"Does anyone like to be ignored?" I asked. I shifted in my seat.

"You alright?" he asked. For the first time in a long time, it sounded genuine. It sounded like someone was actually asking me, with pure concern, if I was okay. And here I was, pushing him away.

I shook my head, "No. Sorry, I…" I paused, "I've been trying all day to get a hold of my two best friends, and neither of them are answering me. Neither is my boyfriend."

Did I sound desperate? More importantly, did I care how I sounded? It was the truth, and if the only person who wanted to hear about it was Dylan, who may or may not have been trying to hit on me, was around to listen, then so be it. Dylan didn't answer right away, instead, he took a seemingly methodical bite of his sandwich.

"Forget about them," he finally said.

I laughed, "Great advice!"

He smiled and shrugged.

"Aren't we supposed to be selfish right now? It's college," he said.

This was a sentiment I never agreed with. Or understood. It shouldn't matter what time of day it was or if we were college freshmen or young professionals. When someone you loved needed you, you dropped everything to be there for them.

At least, that's what I thought. But I was starting to learn that maybe my friends didn't feel the same way. It was my turn to mull over the response, so I took a final bite of my salad and turned in my seat to face Dylan.

"We promised each other we'd always answer the phone," I said.

"Maybe they're busy."

"What if I was dying on the side of the road, and they're just ignoring me?"

Dylan gave me a smile, "You aren't dying on the side of the road. You're just lonely."

I stared at him. I couldn't remember the last time that someone had acknowledged how I was feeling. After getting home from our month at The Highview, we all went into such overdrive about worrying about our own dorms or fall schedules that we never stopped to ask each other how we were feeling. At our combined going away party, I had plastered on a smile so no one would notice that the fear that I had felt on graduation night was amplified now by a thousand. I had been terrified to leave behind the life I knew in Cocoa Beach, but it looked like I was the only one. So I never said anything.

Now, I spend Saturday nights eating alone. Or, in the case of this Saturday night, as a sympathy case for someone who very clearly was enjoying his time here. I looked away from Dylan, and with my eyes cast down at the table, I nodded.

"You're right. I'm really lonely," I admitted.

"My girlfriend and I broke up the first night of summer," he said, "she moved out of state for school."

"I'm sorry."

Dylan shrugged, "It was fine. We were together all of senior year. You and your boyfriend might be the only couple I know who stayed together."

I thought of Ryder. I thought of his eyes as he looked off his phone screen whenever we would FaceTime. I thought of how he never asked me questions about how I was doing, or when he did, he would try to convince me to ask my roommate if she wanted to hang out. We were growing apart. Then I thought of how he'd sent me a Starbucks gift card on the morning of my first day of classes. I thought of how he'd FaceTimed me during a party he was at to "prove to the guys he had the most beautiful girlfriend." I thought of how when I'd called him my first Friday night here, crying, he instantly got in his car and drove to come to spend the night with me.

I was so conflicted about Ryder. And sitting next to Dylan,

who was caring and encouraging, I knew that was a dangerous place to be.

"There's a party off campus tonight," Dylan started, "Right down the road. You should come with me."

When I didn't answer right away, Dylan continued talking.

"There's this girl I'm kind of interested in. I think you would get along well," he finished, surely wanting to let me know this was strictly platonic.

"Kind of interested?" I prodded.

"Okay, totally interested."

"And what? She'll fall to her knees in love when she sees how you rescued the friendless girl and brought her along?" I asked.

Dylan smiled at me, "Friendless? What the hell am I?"

"You barely know me."

"So, let's change that. Meet me in the rotunda in an hour."

After finishing my dinner, I walked back to my dorm room. When I opened the door, I thought back to just two months ago when I came home to Allie and Bailey hiding in my bathroom shower. Tonight, it was just silence. When I sat down on my bed, I looked over at my phone. I tapped the screen so it would light up and display any notifications.

Except for an email from my English professor, there was nothing.

No phone calls. No text messages.

Nothing.

That didn't matter, I decided, and instead of wallowing in my loneliness, I pulled off my leggings and put on my favorite pair of jeans. I ran my fingers through the roots of my hair and walked into the bathroom. Bailey may have been the actress of the group, but as I looked at myself in the mirror, I vowed to do a damn well performance tonight, pretending that I was happy.

I met Dylan and a brunette girl he'd introduced to me as Natasha an hour later. Natasha complimented my eyeshadow and begged me to teach her how to do a smoky eye. We were off to a good start.

The three of us walked off campus, and I was thankful that Dylan was friendly and talkative. He led us to the downtown area, a quick five-minute walk from campus, with ease.

"So, Morgan, what's your major?" Natasha asked. Okay, so she was super friendly, but of course, she led with that question. Every single person you met in college led with that question.

"Still undecided," I started, "Though leaning a little bit towards marine biology. I really loved science in high school," I said.

"Like saving the whales?" Natasha asked.

"Sure. But, other things too," I said.

"Well, good for you. Science makes me queasy," Natasha said, and we all laughed. A polite, somewhat strained laugh, but still, a laugh.

"Um, what about you?" I asked.

"Graphic design," she replied.

Luckily, before we had to struggle through more small talk, Dylan stopped in front of a bar and held his arms out.

"We have arrived!"

"You didn't say it was at a bar," I started, "how are we supposed to get in?"

Dylan looked at me with a smug smile, "You really think that I would lead you astray? The bouncer is my cousin. Come on," he said.

We walked up to the front of the bar, where a guy who looked just like Dylan sat. The group in front of us flashed IDs as they talked with each other. He waved them through. Dylan turned to us.

"The deal is, show your ID, lay low. He'll just wave us in, okay?"

Natasha and I both nodded. I pulled my ID out of my small purse that hung on my shoulder. We followed Dylan's lead and, before we knew it, were walking up to the bar.

After choking down two beers, I started to like Natasha and Dylan even more. We'd met up with some of their other friends, and though I didn't remember any of their names, I was still having a good time. Now, Natasha and I sat at a table, both of us laughing at everything as she babbled on about how cute she thought Dylan was.

"He reminds me of the type of guy who would stop traffic to help a baby turtle cross," Natasha said. She stared at where Dylan stood with two other guys, one of them I recognized from our class.

"He's like if you crossed Noah Centineo with a Nobel Peace Prize Winner," she said again.

"Wait, what?"

She looked at me with her mouth open, "Hot and nice, Morgan. Come on, get with me here."

I laughed, "My boyfriend is hot and nice. He just doesn't answer my texts anymore," I said.

Natasha held her arms out, motioning around the bar.

"I know your type just by looking at you. The Florida surfer boy with a nice heart. Look around. They're everywhere here."

I shook my head, "I have Ryder."

I took another sip of my beer. Did I, though? As if he was reading my mind, my phone vibrated. I looked at the screen and saw that it was him calling. I held it up so Natasha could read his name.

"See?" I said. She smiled as I walked out to the back deck of the bar, where there were less people and way less noise. I pressed the green phone icon on my screen.

"Well, well, well, Ryder Matthews," I said, a hiccup between each 'well' I said to him. He laughed.

"Are you okay?" he asked.

"I don't know, Ryder, am I? Maybe the better question is are you okay?"

He sighed, "Exhausted. I started my new job at the university bookstore. Didn't I tell you that?"

I fell silent. Maybe he did, but maybe he didn't. Maybe neither of us listened to the other anymore. Maybe Ryder wasn't the only one to blame for us feeling like we were falling apart.

"Oh. I forgot," I admitted.

He laughed, "That's okay. What are you up to?"

I smiled even though he couldn't see me, "I went out with some new friends."

"Morgan, that's amazing."

"Allie and Bailey hate me. They're hanging out without me," I said.

Until I admitted this to Ryder, I hadn't realized I felt this way. I had no evidence to believe that they were together, just a deeply rooted dread in my stomach that they had forgotten about me.

"Well, FSU played UF today," Ryder said, "Didn't they plan on getting together for the game?"

I felt my stomach tighten. It felt like someone reached into my belly button and squeezed on my intestines. I felt like I was going to puke.

"But they didn't invite me," I said, unsure if it was a question to Ryder as to why they didn't or if it was my realization.

"That sucks, Morg, I'm sorry. Hey, I'm getting in the car to go pick up food. Go have fun, okay?"

I'm sure we exchanged goodbyes, but I didn't remember them as I stood alone on the bar patio, my phone still in my hand.

Chapter 15

Me, 8:37 p.m.: Are you just going to pretend I don't exist anymore, or what?

Allie sat next to me on the couch as we stared out at the rain pelting down against the porch railings. It had started raining shortly after the fireworks started, and the usual late afternoon storm had turned into something much more. Luckily, we were able to use the rain as an excuse to pack up. No one noticed when I stumbled back to my seat. Allie said nothing as I threw away a barely touched ice cream cone as we walked back up to the house. On-lookers for the fireworks show cleared out quickly as the storm picked up. I counted to five in my head, and with perfect timing, lightning cracked down the middle of the sky.

"It'll probably stop by next summer," Uncle Daniel said as he walked in from the back porch. He placed the plate of grilled hamburgers he was carrying on the counter and then grabbed a towel and wiped off the rain that had sprayed his face.

"I can't believe you were grilling in the rain," Allie said.

Uncle Daniel raised his eyebrows at Allie. "These burgers

weren't going to grill themselves."

I stood and walked to the kitchen to help set up plates for everyone.

"Where are those knuckleheads?" Uncle Daniel asked. Reaching behind me, he grabbed the hamburger buns and tore open the package.

As if the wafting scent of the burgers had worked magic, voices filled the hallway, and Noah, Ethan, and Ryder walked straight into the kitchen and grabbed plates. Just as we were sitting down in the living room, lightning cracked again, sending a blast of light across the sky, followed instantly by thunder that shook the windows. The lights flickered, and within twenty seconds, the house was dark. Another crack of lightning illuminated the house momentarily, just long enough for all of us to find a place to set our plates. I tried to remember where the flashlights were and hoped they had batteries.

"It should come back on," Uncle Daniel said. "It's probably just a surge." When he opened the sliding door, though, all the other houses on the street were dark as well.

We sat in darkness for three hours. In that time, we managed half a game of candlelight Monopoly before we all decided to throw in the towel, mostly because Allie was getting too competitive over the requirements for building a hotel. With the electricity showing no sign of coming back on and the storm showing no sign of mercy, we continued to sit in the darkness. The rain continued to pound against the back deck, and there was a distant sound of the wind whipping the ocean water around. Who knew what kind of wreckage we'd wake up to in the morning? The forecasts on our phones streamed that this storm could very well be the official start of an otherwise dormant hurricane season.

Eventually, Uncle Daniel headed for the bedroom hallway. "I think I'm ready to call it a night." He paused and turned to face us. "Just because I sleep like the dead, that doesn't give you guys an excuse to act stupid. Don't you dare go out in that storm. Do you understand me?" We all nodded.

Outside, the sun had completely set, and the clouds covered the moon. Other than the weak flames of the candle and the spotlight cast by the flashlight Ethan had hung from the ceiling fan, we were surrounded by darkness.

"It's getting hot in here." Ethan stood up and made a feeble attempt to manually spin the ceiling fan. His efforts did absolutely nothing for any of us, and we all just laughed.

"Wow, what a breeze." Ryder reclined back in the loveseat next to me. Ethan stopped and checked his watch. It was barely ten, but between the heat and just plain boredom, I could tell that everyone was ready to join Uncle Daniel in calling it a night.

Allie stood and untied the flashlight from the ceiling fan. "I'll put this in the bathroom. I'm going to bed."

"I'll probably stay out here," I said. "I'm not really tired."

Mostly, I wasn't ready to be alone with my thoughts as I stared up at the ceiling, hoping to fall asleep.

"Me either," Ryder chimed in. Everyone stared at us.

"That's going to be interesting." Noah stood and followed Allie down the hall. He paused before he reached the boy's bedroom and turned around. "Come on, Ethan." Ethan stared at us and smirked before following behind Noah.

The candle flame flickered as the wick dwindled to the bottom of the wax. Soon, we'd be in complete darkness.

Ryder shifted in his seat, doing his best to look at me. "So…"

"So," I echoed.

I stretched my back against the couch. Ryder kept his eyes on me, his expression too similar to looks he'd given me in the past. I shifted in my seat and looked away.

"I was really scared at the fireworks show," I admitted.

Ryder shifted in his seat. "Why?"

I shook my head, "I don't know yet. It was just loud. And I felt really alone."

"You weren't alone. We all were there. We would've kept you safe," he said.

It didn't feel like that, though. It felt as if I was standing in the middle of a storm, screaming for someone to help me. I hated that I felt that way. I wasn't used to it.

"I'm sorry we had to break up." The words tumbled suddenly out of my mouth as if I had spent the last six months trying to choke them back. Maybe I had.

"I am, too."

"I wish you would get mad at me," I said quietly.

He laughed. "Mad at you for how you feel? What good would that do, Morgan?"

A few days ago, I had wanted him to walk in through the front door and not even make eye contact with me. I'd wanted to overhear him tell stories to Ethan and Noah about different girls he'd gone on dates with or a cute blonde who'd sat next to him in Psychology. Maybe he would tell them the girls were usually boring and unfulfilling, but he was finally living a life free of me, so he didn't care.

Instead, he sat perfectly still and told me it was fine and he wasn't lying. He didn't think I deserved his anger, much like I felt I didn't deserve his love.

"It does suck, but I understand why it had to happen." He

shrugged. "You know, I used to think I could hold out for you. That the only thing that mattered was that we loved each other."

I shifted in my seat. He gave me a sad smile, his lips pursed, and his eyes darted away from me.

"Being here, though, I know it's over. I need to just move on."

Just move on, like it was that easy. As though we could make it happen by just holding a flashlight to our relationship and revealing all the reasons why we should just move on. We couldn't just do anything; it wasn't that simple. In that moment, I knew the next girl Ryder loved would be the luckiest girl in the world, and I hated that it couldn't be me.

But man, did I love him.

Ryder started again. "We were always easy, you know? Like rock paper scissors."

"What happens if you win?" I asked.

"I don't think it works like that anymore."

My heart dropped into my stomach.

He smiled, a mix of yearning and regret plastered across his face. I looked away from him, unable to see the hazel in his eyes or the small dimple on his left cheek. I had Ryder memorized. It didn't matter that it was dark or that we hadn't been this close to each other in months. I could see Ryder's face when I closed my eyes. Feel a phantom touch when he'd walk by me, purposely avoiding me. I missed him. I looked back over at him, and his eyes glazed over as he looked back at me. With a deep inhale, he leaned forward and he brushed his thumb against my cheek. And he pressed his lips against mine.

It was nothing like the kisses I used to get from Ryder. Usually, he kissed me with a gentle urgency. In the past, he would wrap his arms around my waist or hold the nape of my neck in his hands. Now, he was distant. It felt empty. He pulled away, still leaving a mere inch between our lips. The kiss had been everything we hadn't been able to say over the last 173 days. It was our goodbye.

I remained on the couch as he stood up. He walked to the sliding glass door. There, he smoothed his curly hair back and turned to look at me.

"It's really over, then, huh?"

"I just don't know if anything is enough anymore," I said. Our breakup had not come completely out of left field, but it had left unanswered questions, questions I was still struggling with myself.

Ryder didn't say anything else, so I stood up and walked to him. "I still need to figure out what happened with Bailey."

"What happened with Bailey? Morgan, what about what happened with us?"

Lightning struck outside and illuminated the inside of the house for a brief second — long enough for me to see the pain on Ryder's face. Long enough for him to see the regret on mine.

"I loved you, Morgan."

Thunder exploded in the distance, turning the silence and space between us deafening. Ryder recoiled from the strike of thunder, but I didn't budge.

"What do you mean, what happened with us?" I asked, my voice soft. My brain was spinning as the words landed.

"My life got turned upside down, too. I think you forget that." Ryder shook his head. "I miss Bailey too. But she's gone, Morgan."

What did he mean, Bailey was gone? If I could just get her on the phone, we could clear the air. What I needed were answers about what had happened with Bailey. I needed to be alone.

Outside, the rain was slowing, and though thunder and lightning seemed to be striking right overhead, my only option for being alone seemed to be going outside. I pulled away from Ryder and slid open the door.

"Morgan, where are you going? It's raining." Ryder's voice was soft.

Ignoring his question, I stepped out on the deck. The sand that had collected there pooled at my feet, floating in the few inches of water that had accumulated. My toes pressed into the damp sand as I walked to the end of the deck. I couldn't see beyond a foot in front of me, the darkness surrounding me thoroughly even though the storm seemed to be ending. I stared at the house. The inside of it illuminated as the power kicked back on. With the lights on, the house looked out of place in the darkness. I turned away from the house and faced the ocean, expecting to be startled by the darkness.

I stood in the middle of the sand, with the sound of waves fading in the distance as the tide slowed. There was a gentle lapping—in and out, in and out. Everyone always talked about the calm before the storm, but no one ever talked about the calm after. But maybe it was not a calmness; maybe it existed just because it had to. It had no choice but to be messy and weathered.

I took my cell phone from my back pocket, knowing what I had to do. I opened the phone icon and scrolled to Bailey's name at the bottom of my recent call log. I tapped it.

I pressed the phone against my ear and listened to the echo of the wind in the earpiece. It rang—two times, three times, four times, five times—and then it stopped.

"The number you are trying to reach has been disconnected. Please hang up and try again."

Redial. My hands shook as I pressed her name again.

It rang—two times, three times, four times, five times—and stopped.

"The number you are trying to reach has been disconnected. Please hang up and try again."

"Come on, Bailey," I said. My voice shook.

I needed to hear her voice. I needed to hear that we could work this out. I needed to hear that even though she had lied and I had overreacted and torn us all apart, we could go back to the calm before the storm. I didn't want the mess anymore. I wanted the tangled legs squeezing into the bottom bunk because I was too scared to sleep on the top. I wanted the midnight giggles as she painted her toenails a different color for the third time that night. I wanted the feeling of undying love because we couldn't imagine our lives without each other, even if there were some days that the most exciting thing we did was an early-morning drive-through trip to get iced coffee and donuts.

I wanted Bailey back.

"Please answer," I said into the phone as it rang a fifth time.

"The number you are trying to reach has been disconnected. Please hang up and try again."

Ryder ran up to me. "Morgan, who are you calling?"

I looked back at him as horror settled across his face. "I need to talk to Bailey."

Ryder shook his head. "That's not going to happen. You have to know that."

"It has to; she has to answer," I pleaded as if he could change the outcome. He walked up to me and gently tried to take the phone out of my hand.

I pulled my arm back. "Stop."

He inhaled. "Morgan, please tell me this is all an act. Please tell me you know what is actually happening."

My whole body shook now.

"Bailey is not going to answer, Morgan," he added softly.

I dropped my head. Sobs ripped through my body. Ryder walked closer and placed both hands gently on my shoulders. I sank into him, feeling the familiarity of my cheek against his chest and his chin on top of my head. My body went limp.

"She has to answer," I cried, my voice breaking and cracking.

"She's not going to."

I pulled away and glared at him. "You're just jealous, Ryder. You've always been jealous of her." I scrolled through my phone again. Ryder reached forward and grabbed it. "Give it back!" I yelled.

"She's dead, Morgan. Jesus Christ, she's dead. You were there. We all were. Please tell me you've been playing a game."

We stared at each other through the rain. My heart raced, and my knees buckled underneath me. My chest tightened. Sweat pricked the nape of my neck.

"Where's Allie?" I screamed. "Go get her."

Ryder kept his voice calm. "Allie's inside. She's sleeping."

"Well, wake her up," I argued.

I pulled away again as Ryder reached for me. I walked to the door and barreled through the doorway to where Allie was sleeping. She was curled up on her bed, her breathing steady. Even when she slept, she looked perfect.

"You knew!" I accused, flipping on the light and waiting for her to stir. She did, rubbing her eyes, and stared at me. Then she sat up and glanced at the clock next to her bed.

"You knew Bailey wasn't ever going to answer me," I continued, "but you let me keep trying. You knew she was dead."

Allie stared at me, her face paling as she got out of bed. In the hallway, I heard Uncle Daniel arrive, followed by Noah, Ethan, and Ryder.

"What happened?" Uncle Daniel asked Ryder. I didn't hear Ryder's response.

"Morgan, come sit down." Noah placed his arm gently on my forearm, but I didn't budge.

I stared at Allie. "Was this fun and games for you? Sitting back and watching me so desperately think…"

I stopped.

"Think what?" Allie challenged me. We stared at each other. "I don't fucking believe this," she whispered. She sat up fully. "This is my fault now? Because I didn't tie you down and slap you back into reality?" She looked at Noah. "I told you this was a stupid idea. A dangerous idea."

She turned to Uncle Daniel. "And why didn't you stop this?" When he didn't respond, she stood up and looked at me.

"I've been on your side, Morgan. You need a serious shaking back into reality, and a trip to this stupid house isn't going to do it. I hate this place. I never wanted to come back here again, yet you all dragged me here with your stupid agenda and this stupid complex that you'd be able to change things—"

She stopped, took a deep breath, and shook her head. "Unless you can take us back to January, nothing is ever going to be the same."

Suddenly, I was back there. Back to this room, New Year's Eve, staring at Bailey in her black jumper, jealous of the natural waves in her hair, butterflies in my stomach from seeing Ryder again, champagne coursing through my veins, all while Noah and Ethan laughed obnoxiously outside the window.

You're a liar.

Chapter 16

Me, 10: 03 AM: I'm leaving now! Want anything from Dunkin'
Bailey, 10:03 AM: My usual pleasssssse. And HURRY. I'm so
effing bored.

Bailey stood in the driveway of her house, jumping up and down
and waving as I pulled in. I put the car in park, opened my door,
and got out, running to hug her.

"You're finally here. Oh my god, I thought I was going
to die of boredom." As she spoke, her voice was muffled by my
hair. She wore jeans that were cut off above the ankle and a solid-
colored maroon V-neck, and her hair fell straight instead of in
its usual beachy waves. She still looked like my best friend but
older.

Bailey pulled out of the hug and gave me a once-over. Did
I look the same? Besides my new haircut (and bangs, which I still
hated), not much about me had changed. I still dressed casually,
opting for flat sneakers and jeans most days.

I hoped Bailey couldn't sense the sadness that had settled over me during the semester at Flagler. I'd ended the semester with a perfect GPA, mostly because all I did was study to pass the time, as I had yet to make friends I wanted to hang out with. There had been Dylan and Natasha, but the second they started dating, I wasn't of much interest to them anymore. I'd spent the semester scooting by, saying hello to my dorm neighbors, and going out for dinner with my roommate once a week, but it had been hard. I felt as if I were breaking allegiance whenever I remotely enjoyed someone else's company.

Bailey picked her bag up from the driveway and walked to my car. I popped the trunk, and she placed it in before running to the passenger side and climbing in.

As I turned on the car, Bailey started messing with the playlist I had cued up on my phone. "Feel free to change the music," I said. "I've been in sort of a mood."

"Yeah, what the hell, Morgan? Why are these songs so depressing? Taylor Swift, sure, but the sad songs? Ew, your depressing country playlist?" She stopped scrolling and looked at me. "Are things okay with Ryder?"

I let out a long sigh.

"Oh, no. Morgan…"

"I don't know. We seem so distant. We saw each other the night we both got back into town, and it was like we were struggling to even have a conversation."

I thought back to three nights ago when Ryder had picked me up from my mom's house. We went to Scoops to get ice cream and sat at our normal table for less than an hour. Most of the time was spent in silence. Did we really have nothing to talk about?

Bailey nodded knowingly as I turned my car onto the highway. "Well, just think. You guys have the entire weekend to spend together! God, it's going to be so fun."

I knew she was trying her best to amp me up. As usual, she was right, and I felt a wave of excitement wash over me as I thought about the days ahead and how Ethan, Noah, and Ryder were already waiting for us at the house.

~*~

Three hours later, Ryder ran down the spiral staircase the second he saw us turn onto Shoreview Drive. He was in the driveway by the time we pulled in and picking me up in a tight embrace shortly afterward.

"Bailey!" He let go of me to give her a hug.

"Hey, dude," she said, hugging him back.

"You might want to buy new jeans; those don't seem to cover your whole leg." He pointed to her bare ankles.

"Good one, Dad," she said, and Ryder smiled. He grabbed our bags, and we all walked inside. Ethan and Noah were sitting on the couch, each holding a beer. All the windows were open, letting in a cool ocean breeze. The temperature was in the low seventies, perfect weather to fire up the firepit on the back deck once the sun had completely set.

Bailey looked out at the ocean. "How cold is the water?"

"We took the kayaks out," Ethan said, "but I don't recommend it. It's pretty cold."

"You're also a wuss, so…" Bailey turned and smiled at him.

"I'll remember that."

~*~

After eating enough pizza to satisfy a week's worth of calories, Bailey and I climbed the spiral staircase and wrapped ourselves in blankets as we sat on the top deck. I could always tell when she had something on her mind. Her gaze would grow gentle, her lips would curl under as if making a cartoon frown, and if I looked hard enough, I could see the wheels in her brain turning.

Now, as we sat together, each wearing a sweatshirt from our new college lives, I knew something was on her mind. Below us, the fire began to die down, and Noah poked at it with a tree branch Ethan had ripped down. Ethan, Noah, and Ryder stood around the fire, talking, their voices and laughter echoing through the night.

"I've been thinking about leaving Florida State," she said suddenly, turning to look at me. My eyes grew wide. "Not like dropping out of college, but...I don't know, maybe transferring somewhere else. I did get accepted to UCF, you know. I could transfer there in a heartbeat." She pulled her knees to her chest and rested her chin on them.

"Bails, what's up?" I asked.

She shrugged, her hair fanning out over her shoulders. "I don't know, Morgan. I feel like I don't belong. Do you ever feel that way?" She looked at me. "Like you're living somewhere or doing something you just don't belong in?"

I nodded. "Sure, but it's only been a few months. You could just need more time to adjust!" I hoped the spirit with which I spoke would help her. The truth was, I was constantly homesick at Flagler. I disliked almost everything about it.

Really, I just missed my friends here. I missed who I was here.

"What I mean is, we weren't put on this Earth to just work, pay bills, and die, Morgan. You have to do what makes you happy." She spoke with a finality that let me know she was done talking about it. But I wasn't done talking about it. All this time, I'd been suffering, thinking that there was something wrong with me because I couldn't seem to adjust to Flagler. But now, Bailey was telling me she'd felt the same way? It felt like a slap in the face. I'd expressed to her more than once that I was struggling, and she'd always made me feel bad about it.

"That doesn't make any sense, Bailey," I started, "You're eighteen. No one is telling you that you have to work, pay bills, and die."

She looked at me, "That's what my dad said."

"You told your parents?"

She shrugged, "We were talking about my living arrangements for next year."

"It's only December! We still have a whole semester left."

"You have to plan for those things," she said.

"Why didn't you tell me that you were upset?" I asked.

She looked away, "I wasn't upset. I just…Maybe UCF has something that FSU doesn't."

There was something she wasn't telling me, and I knew it. But suddenly, I didn't care to dig into it anymore. I wanted tonight to be fun for us, and forcing her to talk about this was the exact opposite of that.

~*~

The last bit of light stretched across the sky the following night, and with that, we felt it was time for the party to really start. Even though we weren't going anywhere, Bailey and I still spent an hour making sure our hair was perfect and putting on outfits we had bought earlier that day at the mall in Port Charlotte, forty-five minutes away. Bailey fluttered around in a black jumper that had yellow and purple floral patterns on it, as I zipped up a short navy dress that dipped in the back, showing off the seashell tattoo on my shoulder that I got as part of a matching set with Bailey and Allie at the end of last summer.

"You look cute," I said.

"Thanks. You never know who you'll meet on New Year's Eve." There was a certain sparkle in her eyes that I hadn't seen in a while. "I'll be outside," she called over her shoulder as she walked out of the room.

I heard the music start — a playlist of Top 40 remixes — and I looked in the mirror one last time. After running my fingers through my loose waves and dabbing light pink lipstick on — a color Allie had once said looked repulsive, but Bailey had said "could work" — I quickly joined everyone else outside.

I walked out to the back deck and grabbed a handful of chips from the open bag on the table. Noah walked up to me and flashed his phone in my face. "Did you see the picture Allie posted from her cruise?" In the picture, Allie and her mother stood cheek to cheek, smiling, with a large You Must Be This Tall to Drink sign in the back.

"Looks like she's having fun," Ethan offered.

"I don't care if she's having fun. She ditched us," Noah said.

We laughed. "Well, there's no way she's having more fun than us." Bailey handed everyone a flute of champagne.

"Where did you get that?" I asked.

Bailey winked at me. "I'll never reveal my secrets."

"My dad got it for us," Noah said. "He said he'd rather have us drinking here where he knows we're safe."

Bailey rolled her eyes and shot him a glance. He gave her an apologetic shrug and a small smile. Bailey held up her glass and looked around at all of us, waiting for us to catch on that she wanted to make a toast.

"To a perfect ending to a great year," Bailey said. We all clinked glasses before taking a sip.

~*~

Bailey yawned and threw a sideways glance at the clock.

"Why can I stay up until three a.m. watching reality shows about finding love, but on a night when it's tradition to stay up, I'm ready for bed by ten thirty?" She took another sip from her water bottle.

Noah nudged one of his beers toward Bailey. "Maybe if you drank something other than water, you'd be more excited about midnight."

Bailey shook her head. "Someone has to be in the right state of mind in case of an emergency. What if a hurricane shows up and wipes the place out? You guys wouldn't know right from left."

She stretched out on the chair, her dress rising slightly to reveal more of her legs. Ethan looked over and then snapped his attention back to the game of beer pong he and Ryder were playing. It was a smooth look that I'm sure he thought no one noticed.

"A national emergency on New Year's Eve would definitely mean that things could only go up from there." Ethan tossed a Ping-Pong ball into a cup on the other end of the table and nodded at Ryder to drink.

"Be careful what you wish for." Bailey stood and walked off the deck toward the ocean. "Morgan, come on. Let's go down to the beach."

I stood and followed her, pausing by Ryder to squeeze the back of his neck. "Yeah, it's kind of disheartening watching Ryder get killed in beer pong." I kicked off my shoes, leaving them on the edge of the deck, and ran through the sand to meet up with Bailey.

"Slow down. I have shorter legs than you." I giggled through the spiked seltzers I had been drinking all night.

Bailey plopped down into the sand and looked up at me. Though it was pitch dark and the only light reflecting from the moon was now hazed by storm clouds, I could tell she wanted to talk.

"Have you thought more about Florida State?" I asked.

"You mean since I told you about it last night?"

I smiled. She ran a hand through her wavy hair before looking back at the deck. Noah, Ethan, and Ryder exploded in a mix of laughter and screams as it appeared Ryder finally scored a point against Ethan.

"UCF does have a great English department," Bailey said again.

"So does Florida State."

"Let's talk about something else." She leaned back further until she was lying down in the sand. The storm clouds now completely covered the moon, the haze of the sky darkening with each second.

"I think Ryder and I are having trouble," I said. Saying it aloud to someone else for the first time felt like both a punch in the stomach and a relief at the same time.

Bailey propped herself up and stared at me. "Is it the distance, or is it something else? You're only, like, an hour away from each other."

"It's just hard to balance the relationship with schoolwork, plus trying to meet new people and not be a complete hermit. I just don't know how we're going to do this for three more years."

Bailey shifted next to me. "Believe me, I know," she said quietly.

"How?" I laughed. "You have no clue what it's like."

"I'm away from you and Allie."

"That's different."

"Are you finally admitting you love me more than you love Ryder?" Bailey joked.

I smirked. "Stop. It's a different love. But if I had to choose who to spend the rest of my life with—"

Bailey grabbed a handful of sand and tossed it on me. "Don't finish that sentence. Ryder loves you." We both giggled a little bit—me from the spiked seltzer, Bailey from her natural state of giggles—until we heard the clearing of a throat behind us. I turned around and saw Ryder standing there.

"Hi," I said, my voice a little too high-pitched as he stared down at me.

"I thought you'd want some water, but I guess someone else can handle that for you." His voice was deep and laced with hurt. He tossed the water bottle he was holding down into the sand and walked back up to the house.

"Shit," Bailey said.

I dropped my head. "You don't think he heard everything, do you?"

"If it looks like a duck and quacks like a duck…then yes, he heard you."

I stood up and walked after him, leaving Bailey in the sand. I ran up to the house, where Ethan and Noah sat in lounge chairs.

I looked around the deck. "Where's Ryder?" My voice was frantic, and Ethan and Noah instantly noticed.

"What's wrong?" Noah asked.

"It's stupid, but Bailey and I were talking about how I'd spend my life with her and Allie instead of Ryder. It's so dumb. He didn't hear the whole conversation, and then he came down, and now I can't find him." Tears rose in my eyes, and my throat throbbed as it constricted.

"Damn, that's harsh," Ethan said. We all turned as the sliding glass door opened. Ryder stood in the doorway, another beer in his hand as he stared at me.

He walked out onto the deck. "Where's the love of your life?"

I walked toward him. "Stop. Let's go talk. It's not like that." I put my hand on his chest, and he backed away.

"Isn't it, though? You know what's funny? Bailey is a liar, yet you'd choose her over me."

Ryder and I had never had anything more than a disagreement, and I felt myself shrink as he stared at me. He was so upset.

"What?" I asked.

"Sorry, maybe not lying, because you can't lie to someone if you just aren't telling them what you're really up to. She hasn't told you that she spends one weekend a month driving to Orlando to hang out with Ethan. And when she's not doing that, he's driving to her."

"What?" I repeated.

"You heard exactly what I said."

I turned and looked at Ethan. "Ethan?" He shrugged.

"It's almost midnight," Noah interrupted, and we all fell back into silence. In the distance, we could hear Bailey walking up the steps to the back deck.

"I'd go back down to the water if I were you," Ethan said quietly.

"Why?" she asked.

I turned to face her. "You and Ethan?"

Her hair was windblown as she bent down and brushed sand off her jeans. She stood up straight and stared at me. "What about Ethan?"

"You'll drive five hours to go hook up with Ethan, yet whenever we try to organize something with Allie, you're 'so busy,' or the drive is 'so nuts'? Are you fucking kidding me, Bailey?"

Bailey stared at me as she stood next to the outside shower, and I had to laugh. Months ago, we'd had this same conversation about how she'd kept her fling with Ethan secret. I had to give it to her; she was good at being a two-faced liar.

"Morgan, it's..."

She paused and looked to Ethan for help. He stared at her with a gentleness in his blue eyes, but he showed his true colors by cracking a joke. "Should we download some dating app for Noah really quick and try to find him some Englewood babe for midnight?"

Bailey furrowed her eyebrows and looked back at me. "It's not just some stupid fling, is what I was going to say."

I scoffed. "What is it, then?"

"Morgan, does it matter?" Ryder asked. "The point here is, you think your friendship with Bailey and Allie is so important, but you're the one stuck in the past, thinking that things are never going to change, and they have to. They already did! This is just proof of that."

I turned and stared at him. "You're just jealous of them. You always have been."

He laughed. "Whatever, Morgan. Happy New Year."

He tossed a small box onto the table with the same carelessness he'd used to toss a water bottle into the sand five minutes ago. I walked over, picked it up, and opened it. Staring back at me was a framed picture of all of us covered in paint, the memory of our last day of high school when we'd left our handprints on the wall of the cafeteria.

When I glanced back up at Ryder, he was still staring at me. "I knew how hard it's been for you to adjust this semester. I wanted to remind you that even if it feels different, we'd always love you."

The picture was only a few months old, but we looked so different. Had that much really changed in our months living apart? Everyone had always told us that college would change things, but I hadn't realized the changes would be so visible. So touchable.

I looked up at Ryder. "I do love you."

He shrugged. "Are you about to dump me in front of all our friends?"

"What? God no. No. I drank too much, I think." I turned to Bailey. "And you've been lying to me."

She shook her head. "That's not fair."

"You'll drive to go have sex with Ethan, but—"

"I love Ethan." Bailey didn't look away from me as she said it.

I recoiled a little. "You what?"

"What?" Ethan echoed, his voice hitching in his throat as he stood up.

Bailey looked at all of us. "And you know what, guys, thanks so much for taking something that was finally mine—just mine—and making it all about you." She walked closer to me. "You guys always do this. You're so fucking suffocating. What if I told you we could be friends and not have to tell each other whenever we breathe?" Her voice fluctuated as she spoke. "This isn't how I wanted this to happen, obviously, but as usual, Morgan doesn't know how to handle things that aren't all about her."

"Bailey, it was my fault. I—" Ryder fell silent and stared at her. Then he glanced between her and Ethan. "I'm sorry."

"Yeah," Bailey said. "So now I get to stand here like an idiot while I confess my love for Ethan, who, as we are all very aware, said nothing in return. But god, Ryder, I hope you got what you wanted. I hope you feel better."

She pushed past us and walked inside the house. I followed her.

"You can't be mad at me for caring about you."

She turned and stared at me. "Caring about me? Morgan, right now, you're suffocating me. I love you, you're my best friend, but you never let me live my own life. We're always in each other's shadows; don't you realize that? We've been the same person for so long, and going away to different colleges meant that we could create our own identities, but you aren't letting that happen!"

"You're the one obviously stuck in the past," I spat, "still hooking up with Ethan."

Bailey laughed. "You're just mad we've all been lying to you. It wasn't just me. Everyone knew." She spoke with a meanness I didn't know could exist in her voice, her eyes piercing into me. I turned and walked away, instinctively heading for the front door—maybe just so I could slam it behind me.

My brain was clouded as I marched out the front door, and I flinched as it slammed closed.

"Morgan, wait," I heard Bailey yell, but it was too little, too late.

I was the laughingstock of the night, the only person kept in the dark about Bailey and Ethan. I always told Bailey everything. I had spent every waking moment during the semester responding to endless text messages and nights apart, filling her with confidence boosters of "Who cares about him?" anecdotes, and she hadn't even needed them. At the end of last summer, I'd stood next to her as she admitted that it was a mistake, and there had been sadness in her eyes as she admitted that blurring the lines of friendship hadn't worked for Ethan and her like it had for Ryder and me.

Yet here we were, nearly half a year later. Apparently, it had worked. All those weekends she'd texted back. Sorry, been so busy! she'd actually been in her car driving to Orlando, spending every waking moment with Ethan.

The worst part: everyone knew but me.

Bailey ran out the front door after me and down the stairs, giving small yelps as she ran barefoot over loose pebbles. I hated that she never wore shoes.

"Morg, come on," she pleaded. She caught up to me and grabbed my shoulder. I paused but didn't turn around to look at her.

"Why didn't you just tell me?"

It was a simple enough question, but I was learning that nothing in Bailey's life could ever be simple. I turned around to stare at her, and she shrugged. The rain started then, small drizzles falling on us as we stood under a flickering streetlight. Her hair was matting to her cheeks already.

"It was something just for me. I'm always doing stuff for other people, Morgan. People just always unload their problems onto me, but the second I want to talk or have something to say, it's like I don't exist. It wasn't like that with Ethan; I could escape it." I turned away from Bailey and kept walking away. She followed. "I don't know, Morgan. He made me feel like I was interesting. Like I had stuff to say, and that stuff I was saying was important."

I swallowed. "But he doesn't love you, Bailey."

Hurt spread across her face. It was as if I'd slapped her, but not really because she didn't move. She stayed planted under the streetlight as I turned and walked farther away from the house.

"Bailey, can we talk?" Ethan called from behind both of us.

I heard her footsteps behind me. "I need to get to Morgan."

I didn't want to see her. Didn't want to look at her. I didn't want to hear her.

"Stop running away from me," she said, hurt now dripping from her words.

I laughed and kept walking. "You're delusional if you believe that Ethan actually loves you. And you're a liar. You know what, Bailey? I'm glad you're hurt right now. I'm fucking glad you're embarrassed—that at midnight when you were expecting Ethan to kiss you and profess his love for you, he was silent." Rage and hurt filled my voice.

"We talked about it. We wanted to talk to you about it tonight, and I tried. Look, Morgan, I don't owe you anything. It's my life, it's my choice, and if I love him—"

"There you go again, talking about loving him. What's it like to be with someone who clearly doesn't feel the same? If he really loved you, Bailey, he wouldn't have convinced you to keep this a secret for the last six months."

She stopped walking and forced out a laugh. "I was the one who wanted to keep it a secret. From you. I don't know why you think I owe you every second of my life."

I stopped then. I felt her eyes staring at my back as the rain picked up. We were near the bridge, where we could either turn around and go back home, or we could keep walking.

"Is that why you want to leave FSU? You want to go to UCF to be with him?"

She just stared at me. Her silence told me everything I needed to know.

The thing that was craziest to me, with the innate amounts of realization that came from standing drunk in the rain, was that I was the fool here. Bailey was so aware of what she was doing with Ethan; I was the one standing in the rain, an idiot because I'd been wrong about all my relationships.

"I thought I was your best friend?" I did nothing to disguise that I was past the anger stage and now was just downright sad as I stood at the base of the bridge.

"You are. I feel horrible, Morgan. Please, just come back to the house," she pleaded.

I craved an explanation, but as Bailey's voice showed no sign of her expanding on her answer, I knew I wasn't going to get it. I kept walking.

"You're a damn liar, Bailey," I said, pushing forward and going up the bridge. "You deserve this."

I heard her stop, and I heard her breath pick up and hitch in her throat as she cried. I knew what I'd said had crossed a line. Bailey and I had never fought before, ever, so I didn't know how to navigate this. But I did know that tomorrow when the seltzer wore off for me and the rejection from Ethan wore off for her, we could have a civil conversation. Right now, though, I just wanted to get away from her.

The rain was picking up, and I knew it was a matter of minutes before the sky opened to a torrential downpour. I turned around when I got to the top of the bridge and saw Bailey had turned around, too. She was walking back toward the house, her shoulders slumped.

Good.

I paused at the top of the bridge and thought about last

summer when we'd all jumped off it. We'd made a pact — friends forever — as we held hands and jumped. It had been a symbol of us jumping into the unknown together, never knowing what the future held for us. Or something like that. Right now, the memory just seemed to be a symbol of an ending.

I sighed, picked a pebble off the ground, and tossed it into the water. Through the darkness, I waited for the plop of the pebble hitting the water and felt a small satisfaction when I did hear it.

A single streetlight stood above me, shining down on me like a spotlight or a halo, but more light quickly illuminated me as the headlights of a truck spread across the bridge. I looked over my shoulder and barely had time to blink before I heard Bailey scream.

"Morgan, watch out!"

She had followed me up here, her gut no doubt feeling the same as mine, that it didn't feel right to be fighting. Not tonight. I looked up as the truck barreled toward me, the driver apparently having no plans of swerving as they veered off the road. I heard Bailey yell again as I stood frozen, unable to think about what to do. Move! I yelled to myself. Swerve! I yelled to the driver.

Neither of those things happened.

"Morgan, move!" Bailey yelled again, running toward me. Her hand reached my arm, and I felt her push me away from the edge just as the truck barreled into the railing.

The only thing louder than the crash of metal as the truck collided with the side of the bridge, breaking through the barrier and teetering over the edge, was the sound of my scream as I realized Bailey was flying through the air and into the water, right along with the old blue truck.

~*~

Noah found me first, sitting on the bridge, the rain pounding against my body. The dark bridge was now illuminated by the flashing lights of emergency vehicles. The sounds of rescuers drifted from below, on the bank in dive suits and on boats with flashlights. The blue truck was floating on the surface of the water, and the driver had been pulled out and was now sitting in the back of a police car.

"Morgan, where have you been?" Noah asked, running up to me. He ignored the shouts from a police officer that the bridge was closed. Ryder and Ethan trailed behind him, deep in conversation, Ethan nodding and contemplative, until they saw me. They broke into a sprint to reach my side.

"Morgan?" Ryder shouted. He grabbed me and pulled me into his chest, then took off his hoodie and wrapped me in it. I stared blankly at them.

"What happened?" Ethan asked. "Where's Bailey?"

"She's down there," I choked out. I pointed to where the bridge's barrier was broken, where pieces of glass covered the asphalt.

"Morgan, what happened?" Noah asked, his voice deep and scared. Ethan walked toward the edge. From where we sat, we could see everything he was seeing, due mostly to the now-missing chunk of the bridge. He stood on the edge but stumbled back as we all watched a diver pull Bailey's body out of the water. When he stumbled more, Noah stood to go meet him, and we watched in silent horror as the responders pressed on Bailey's chest.

Broken leg. Be careful of the rib cage. Collapsed lung. Not breathing. No pulse.

The words played through the air and repeated in my head like Bailey's favorite song.

No pulse.

I didn't realize I was screaming again until Ryder pulled me in closer, muffling my screams against his neck as I collapsed into his arms.

Chapter 17

Present

The tea Noah had brewed was cold now. I'd spent the last five minutes staring at the mug. There was a chip on the handle, and the words Cape Cod 2015 were fading along the side.

"Drink that," Noah said. I sipped it, letting my lips just sit with the liquid against them. I didn't let the tea into my mouth. I hadn't even known Noah knew how to make tea.

Past
New Year's Eve

"Drink that," Ryder said quietly, nudging the foam cup across the small table between us. I put the cup to my lips; it was hot. It felt good, slowly warming my chattering teeth.

I hadn't realized it was so cold out. The rain must have made it colder.

The lights overhead buzzed. We sat in an empty waiting room, waiting.

"She's dead, isn't she?" I asked. Ryder didn't respond.

It was still raining.

Present

"She's dead, isn't she?" I asked. Noah didn't respond.
It was still raining.

A memory:
Bailey sat on the edge of the back deck, sighing dramatically, her elbows resting on her knees, her chin resting in her hands. We were sixteen. It was our last day at The Highview for the summer, and though we knew we'd be back, the last day was always the hardest. Plus, Bailey really sucked at goodbyes. She looked at me over her shoulder and raised her eyebrows, her hazel eyes sparkling as the sun hit them.
"I can't believe summer is over."
"It's not over," I replied.
"Yeah, but it will never be the same again."
"Why?"
She shrugged. "Because once you leave your dream world and go back to reality, the truth starts to hit."
It was my turn to leave my dream world now. Time to leave behind unanswered messages to Bailey. Time to trade in sandy flip-flops for the dusty textbooks that have sat in my bedroom closet since February.
It was time to pretend that pretending didn't hurt.
For most of those days, Noah told me, I had pretended the truth wasn't what it actually was. Something would send me into a spin: a picture of Bailey and me, the sound of a car horn, and most recently, Uncle Daniel selling The Highview.
Some days were okay, Noah said. Some days, I would remember, and I would cry. But most days, I waited for a phone call that would never come.

Now, I lay in the twin sized bed with Allie pressed up against me. It was nearing two in the morning, and the commotion in the house finally died down. Once it hit me, it felt like I was experiencing Bailey's death all over again. With sadness and regret, I admitted to my friends that I think deep down, I always knew. I was just holding on to that one last ounce of hope.

Allie smoothed my hair and tugged at the blanket that we were huddled under. It felt safe to be close to Allie like this. It had been so long since we'd fallen into a bed, laughing. When we were still having sleepovers, I remembered how Allie, Bailey, and I would cram into one bed despite there being a guest room or an air mattress. It had always felt like we'd miss something if we weren't together all the time, and now it felt good to be here with Allie.

"I'm sorry I wasn't with you that night," Allie whispered, "And I'm sorry I abandoned you. I'm sorry because I wanted to be there for you, but I couldn't. I knew you couldn't be there for me, so I was mad, and I did nothing to try to pull you back in after pushing you away."

"It's not your fault," I said. I swallowed. My throat felt raw from screaming and crying. I wanted to block the last two hours out of my mind. Noah's face when he realized what I was realizing. Ryder yelling at me outside in the rain. Ethan refusing to be in the room when I'd finally stopped crying so Uncle Daniel could painfully go through what happened on New Year's Eve. Everyone hovered over me as they fought exhaustion, and I'd tried my best to convince them that it was fine to go to sleep. When Allie and I came back into this room, she got into bed with me without me having to ask, which was more important than anything else anyone could do for me tonight.

"Bailey would be so pissed at us for not sticking together,"

Allie said. The way her words choked, I could tell she was crying. My eyes felt heavy as I pulled the blanket up closer to my chin. My eyelids fluttered shut, and my breathing calmed.

Chapter 18

I stared at the television set in the corner of the hospital waiting room. Though we had muted it long ago, staring at it distracted me from what we should have been talking about. I didn't feel anything; I didn't acknowledge Ryder when he said that maybe we should go home and sleep.

"Beach Road Bridge is closed. There was an accident," someone said as they walked by the room.

"Probably someone drinking and driving," another voice responded.

That shook us all back to reality. Back to the white walls of the hospital waiting room, where we sat waiting for someone to tell us what we should do. We thought we were so grown up, but as we looked around the room, the stark reality that we were still just kids hit us.

When we had arrived at the emergency room, Noah had taken the lead and led us to the waiting room, where he had asked a passing nurse about Bailey.

"Where are her parents?" the nurse asked.

"They're on their way, but they're still a few hours away. Can you tell us anything?"

The nurse gave a grim apology and walked away. Someone would be by when her parents arrived.

After a paramedic pulled Bailey from the water, emergency services had said there was still a chance. We had watched them pump her chest as the doors to the ambulance slammed shut. But we all knew: Bailey was dead. If it had been good news they wanted to deliver, they would've told us. We would have been sitting next to Bailey, tearfully apologizing to each other for our stupid fight.

This was bad news they wanted to deliver.

Ryder placed his hand on top of my thigh. I was shaking. He pulled me under his arm, and my head found its automatic home: The same spot it had found the night we first kissed. The same spot it had found when we danced to our song at senior prom. The same spot it always found. I closed my eyes — it was nearly four in the morning — and felt myself start to drift.

"Can't they just call her parents and tell them what they need to tell them so we can know?" Ethan asked.

I opened my eyes to find him staring at me. I returned the stare. There was red around the rim of his eyes. He played nervously with his thumbs, twiddling them in circles around each other.

"We wanted to tell you, Morgan."

His voice was hoarse and filled with regret, but that didn't matter.

I didn't respond. It was too late. There was nothing to be done but sit back and know that this all could have been prevented.

We all turned as footsteps approached. We'd been in this

room for three hours now and had missed midnight.

Happy New Year.

"Morgan."

Bailey's mom and dad stood in the doorway.

"Hi," I choked out, standing up.

Bailey's mother, Sarah, wrapped her arms around me and smoothed back my hair. Her dark brown hair mixed with mine.

"What happened?" her father, Joe, asked. I shrugged, my eyes filling with tears, and I started to ramble.

"Ethan and we fought, and I said I loved Bailey more than I loved Ryder, and it rained, and a truck came, and she pushed me out of the way. But they pulled her out, so she might be okay. Please, please go find the doctor. Please. And tell her I'm sorry. I'm so sorry. Just go find the doctors, okay?"

I stumbled over my own words. The same nurse who had been checking in on us all night walked into the waiting room.

"Mr. and Mrs. Meyers," she said. She guided them out of the room and talked to them in a hushed voice in the doorway. We all looked on. Sarah grabbed Joe's shoulder and started to cry. They were led down the hallway with the nurse.

"Tell her I'm sorry, okay?" I called after them.

Chapter 19

The dress that draped over the footboard of my bed looked too short for a funeral. I stared down at my old middle school chorus shirt and favorite pajama pants that I was wearing. My phone buzzed from the nightstand—I had lost count of how many times it had buzzed—and I looked over as the screen lit up my dark room. A knock on my bedroom door.

"Yeah," I said, neither inviting the guest in nor asking them to go away. The door opened, and Noah walked in.

"Your mom said I could come in," he said.

He wore slacks and a button-down shirt and a dark blue tie. I'd never seen my cousin in a tie. His hair was perfectly styled. He looked so handsome. I caught my reflection in my full-length mirror. My eyes had dark circles underneath them, and my hair hung limp down my back.

"I'm not going. I have nothing to wear," I said. He exhaled.

"Morgan," he started, and I turned around.

"This is the only black dress I own, and it's too short. I don't need to look like a skank," I said and sat down next to him.

Neither of us said anything else.

Directly across me was my desk, which in its prime years had been crowded with textbooks and notebooks, but it was empty now. All of my textbooks and notebooks were sitting on my desk in my dorm room in Flagler. I should have been back at school this week, but it turns out your best friend's funeral delays your back-to-school travel plans. I stared at the framed picture of Allie, Bailey, and me the night after high school graduation when we'd skipped the school-wide lock-in and went and got matching tattoos instead. Our parents had lost their minds, but we had all smugly said to them that we were eighteen and graduated now.

When we'd taken that picture, we had the whole summer ahead of us.

When we'd taken that picture, we had our whole lives ahead of us.

"Ryder's been trying to get a hold of you," Noah said. I nodded a dull and slow nod. I didn't want to talk to Ryder.

"He and Ethan are going to meet us there. Allie, too."

"Noah, why don't you email me the itinerary for the day, okay?" I said. Noah chuckled.

"Wow, that was the first time I've laughed all year," he said.

The weight in his shoulders slumped forward. Despite being put together, his eyes looked tired. Like me, he looked like he was fighting to keep any sort of composure.

Noah stood up and picked the black dress up.

"This dress sucks, anyway," he said, and he tossed it into my dirty clothes bin. I looked over at him. Noah walked to my closet and pulled down a floral blouse. He put the blouse on my bed and walked to my dresser, where he took out a pair of black jeans.

"Wear this," he said, "Bailey liked that top. The floral and the black made you look cute, she used to say."

"I'm not wearing a floral top to a fucking funeral, Noah. Get a grip."

"Fine."

"Do you want me to leave?" he asked. I nodded.

"Fine."

He walked towards the door and paused, "Turn a light on in here, would you?"

"Noah?"

I didn't have to say anything else, just felt him wrap his arms around me as I sobbed against his shoulder.

"Everyone blames me," I said.

"No one blames you," he replied quietly, but I'm sure he was thinking, "You're God damn right we do." We sat for a few moments. He rubbed my back as I practiced the breathing techniques my new therapist, Dr. Mackintosh, taught me last night.

"You've witnessed a trauma," Dr. Mackintosh said, "of course you will need to find ways to cope that work for you."

After Noah helped me pick out grey wool tights to wear under my dress, he squeezed my shoulder and walked out of my room. I ran a brush through my hair. I changed into the dress. I stared at my phone on the desk. I put the phone in my desk drawer. Took it back out. I halfway acknowledged my mother when she knocked on my door and said it was time to go.

Uncle Daniel, my mom, Noah, and I rode in twenty minutes of silence to the church where the funeral was being held.

Bailey's funeral.

Every time I thought those words, a wave of nausea

overtook me. When we'd gotten in the car, Uncle Daniel offered to stop at Dunkin' Donuts for iced coffees.

"My treat," he'd said.

"It's not a damn party, Dan," my mom huffed from the front seat.

Now, Uncle Daniel turned his car into the parking lot. The church was located on A1A in Cocoa Beach and had a gravel parking lot that was packed to capacity. The church was beautiful, with a large oak tree in front that dipped down. On regular service days, kids could be seen climbing the tree, their dress pants and pressed skirts getting stuck in twigs and dirt. Today, no one touched the tree. It stood alone in the middle of the neatly trimmed lawn, reaching up to the sky. It wasn't until Bailey had died that I'd ever considered what happened to us when we died. In the last week, I'd yet to reach a conclusion, but I hoped that wherever Bailey was, she wasn't upset that no one was climbing that tree.

The church posted Bailey's funeral notice on their website.
Bailey Meyers- funeral and burial January 7th at 10:30 AM.
MAY THE SOULS OF THE FAITHFUL DEPARTED,
THROUGH THE MERCY OF GOD,
REST IN PEACE.

When I'd seen that, I threw my phone across the room, confused not only by what it meant but why it had to be up there in the first place.

Uncle Daniel and my mom got out of the car first. My uncle instantly put his arm around my mom, who was already crying. In the backseat, Noah put his hand on my shoulder and looked at me.

"I'm right here with you, okay?" he said.

I nodded. I hated how weak I was. I wasn't the only one

who was missing Bailey. I knew that, yet it still felt like this was the biggest loss to me. From the backseat, I saw Allie and her mom walk by. Allie looked in the car window and paused. She gave me a look that I took to mean, "Please get out and hug me. Please don't make me go in alone." Instead, I looked away. Guilt still stabbed me whenever I thought of Allie and how the minute her cruise ship docked two days after Bailey died, she'd texted in our group text, unaware of what had happened. When I closed my eyes, I could still picture the text thread.

Allie, January 3, 10:31 AM: Wow, gotta say, kind of pissed off at you guys for not surprising me at the port with balloons and champagne and presents. Did you not miss me??? ;)

None of us responded. I learned later that day that after receiving the text message, Noah called her and told her what happened. And then, he'd gotten in his car and drove to her mom's house and spent the day with her while she cried. Every time she tried to contact me in the last week, I'd ignored her.

I couldn't face her yet.

Noah got out of the car and walked over to Allie and her mom. Allie hugged him, and from the way her shoulders moved as Noah rubbed her back, I knew she was crying.

I sat alone in the backseat of the car, hoping that if I just didn't get out, maybe the funeral wouldn't happen. Maybe that wouldn't make it real.

My mom walked over to my door and opened it. She held out her hand for me, and I took it. We walked hand in hand to the front of the church, and I stared at the doors. If I walked in, that would make this real. My mom squeezed my hand as she took two pamphlets from the man who greeted us at the door. Uncle Daniel and Noah joined us, and Noah grabbed my other hand.

The air in the old church was stiff.

That was just one of many things on the list of what was wrong about today. The typo inside the pamphlet I was holding was another. My wool tights, ripped near my ankle by a twig that had snagged me on the way in, was pretty high on the list as well.

Bailey being dead, though—that was the number-one thing wrong about today.

Bailey May Meyers was etched in dark blue ink on the front of the pamphlet in my hand. The paper felt rough, and the crooked fold mismatched its two sides. Above the date was a picture I had taken only six months before as I'd helped Bailey move into her dorm room at Florida State University.

"Look at me and smile," I'd said.

"Why do you have to take pictures of everything?" Despite her protest, Bailey had stopped folding her running shorts and grinned. A genuine "happy to be alive," "happy to start a new life," "happy to be here in front of you" smile.

The picture now looked like it belonged to a different world. Bailey's light-brown hair was pulled into a ponytail, and her dark blue eyes were framed by lines that spoke of eighteen years of laughter. The picture didn't belong on the pamphlet. It didn't even belong in this room.

"Should we go sit?" asked Noah. He stood with me in the church's entryway. His voice was nearly lost amid the sound of the air conditioner that groaned as it worked to accommodate the fifty-plus people walking through the double doors.

I managed to shrug. Over the last seven days, my ability to speak felt like it had been taken from me, as if when Bailey had taken her last breath, she had taken my voice as well. Noah gently placed his hand on my forearm and walked me through the lobby. Old photographs hung on the water-stained wallpaper, and as we walked, I noted all the places where the wallpaper was peeling off.

God, couldn't they invest in ceiling fans here?

When we walked through the double doors, the first person I saw was Allie. She had a sunburn on her nose and her long blonde hair tied back in a tight ponytail. She shifted in her seat, staring at the same pamphlet I had been. The red rim of her eyes matched the burn on her nose.

She must've forgotten to wear sunscreen.

For the first time, I wondered what it must have been like for her to be completely oblivious to the horror happening at home while she was on international waters. I imagined her dancing the Cha-Cha Slide while the ball dropped.

Who am I kidding? Allie would never dance in public.

Noah and I slid into pews reserved for close friends and relatives — front-row VIP seats to a funeral when we'd all thought we would one day be front-row VIP at Bailey's Broadway debut. Allie said nothing to me, and I was thankful that Noah sat next to her.

"Where's everyone else?" she asked Noah.

"Ryder is picking up Ethan now. He didn't want to drive."

I focused my gaze ahead at the casket and the huge photograph of Bailey that stood next to it. It was wrong, all wrong. Why was Bailey wearing that light blue dress? She'd hated that dress. Didn't her mother know that? And the music that was playing: slow, painful organs that were so out of Bailey's style. I tried to give Sarah and Joe a pass. I'm sure they'd never thought to start planning for their daughter's funeral. They'd just planned her high school graduation party less than a year ago.

I looked away from the casket and scanned the room. Every adult wore the same expression, one that screamed, "Thank God it wasn't my child."

This is all wrong.

Just as I was going to stand up and walk out, Ryder and Ethan took a seat in our row. None of us looked at each other. Just a week ago, we could have all been found cracking up and taking digs at each other. Now, we looked like a row of strangers. I fought the urge to look at Ryder and Ethan, but I gave in. I needed to know that they were struggling just as much as me. When I looked at Ryder, he was staring at me. His usual loose curls were gelled back, and I imagined his dad instructing him to tidy himself up. Ethan looked like the walking dead as if at any moment he would be able to join Bailey in her casket. My stomach churned again.

The organs came to a painful stop as a priest I'd never seen before stood in front of us and began droning on about life. He wore all black and had skin that sagged around his eyes. This guy looked like he was one hundred years old, and here he was, about to eulogize a teenager.

The nausea in the pit of my stomach was making its way slowly up my chest, my vision blurred — not from tears but from the overwhelming dizziness the nausea brought with it — and my neck itched, a side effect I'd always suffered when I'd start to sweat.

Sweating in winter is an alarming phenomenon. Think on that, I told myself. Think of how unnatural it is to sweat when it's January, not of how unnatural it is to listen to a stranger talk about your dead best friend.

From the podium, the priest scanned each face in the pews. "Today, we look not at what the world has lost because she did not live but at what the world gained because she did."

Oh, shut up.

Before I could process what was going on, Bailey's dad was walking to the podium. He shook hands with the priest, and my eyes darted to Bailey's mother. She sat with tissues balled up in her lap and stared ahead at her husband with a dimpled frown.

The first time I'd met Bailey's dad, he had called me "kiddo" and insisted I call him Joe. He had cut the crust off my sandwich without me asking, something Bailey would later tell me she had instructed him to do in the minutes before I walked through their front door. We had only been kids then.

I couldn't hear what her father was saying because, as he stood at the podium, I noticed, for the first time, a projected collage of photographs. One stuck out to me. It was of Bailey, Allie, and me, hip to hip at senior prom. Bailey wore a dark blue dress, and her hair hung over her shoulders. She wore no makeup except for a dab of mascara. She had spent fifteen minutes getting ready. While Allie and I had blocked off the entire afternoon to get ready, Bailey had lounged on my bed, flipping through her Florida State acceptance package. Then I saw the other picture. The six of us on our last day of high school, paint smeared on our faces, standing in front of our handprints on the cafeteria wall.

"Bailey also loved her friends," Joe said. "She met Allie and Morgan in elementary school, adding some fine young men to the group throughout middle school. And though we were not thrilled to see her spending time with boys..." He paused as the crowd laughed. "We knew that her friends loved her as much as she loved them. We find comfort that her last night was spent surrounded by people who loved her."

He looked over at where we all sat and gave us a tearful smile. I thought back to seeing Bailey's parents the night she died, how they had hugged me to make sure I was okay before getting the news that their own daughter was not.

They didn't know. They had no clue what had happened at The Highview.

Next thing I knew, we were standing up, having been told we could now line up to say our final goodbyes to the casket as if we were back in high school lining up for a fire drill.

"I don't want to," I said quietly. Noah reached for my hand.

"You don't have to. It might help, though."

I stared up at him. "I'm out of here." I rubbed my pointer finger and my thumb together, something I'd been doing out of nerves lately.

I pushed against the crowd of people lining up at the front of the room. Cold air burst against my face as I stepped outside, and I felt able to inhale for the first time since the church came into view earlier today.

My shoes crunched on dead grass, a sure sign that, for maybe the first time ever, Florida was experiencing a season other than Hot, Really Hot, and Hot Again. Directly in front of me was the A1A, a highway that stretched along the coast, littered with convenience stores, discount beach chairs, and today, a police car preparing to stop traffic for a funeral procession. The parking lot was packed to capacity with cars, another sign that everyone Bailey had ever come into contact with loved her. I had to sit down.

"You okay?"

I turned to see Ryder standing behind me. I let the silence between us answer his question, yet he still walked over and sat down next to me on the stone bench. Before, the silence between us had been fine. We had been able to sit across from each other at the lunch table with nothing to say and still feel we were saying it all. Now, the silence was a reminder of all the dead space between us and what we had both done to cause it.

"I know you probably don't want to talk to me, Morgan, but—"

"So why are you trying?"

The doors of the church opened again, this time releasing everyone who had sat in the pews and mourned, pretending they'd known Bailey like I had. Pretending that their worlds had stopped moving when she died, though I knew the second they left the parking lot and had lunch at Frankie's Wings and Things down the street, they'd forget why they were even in black suits or high heels.

I saw Allie and Noah walking with my mom and Uncle Daniel in a tight circle. They moved as one, a school of fish swimming toward Ryder and me, and they picked up stragglers along the way, most notably Ethan. The only relief I felt in seeing them was how bad Ethan looked. His eyes were sunken, the blue that once sparkled was muted, and his skin was blotchy. His blond hair was disheveled as if the store had run out of that stupid hair gel he would run through his hair every morning to make it look styled yet "cool." He slouched, his shoulders drooping. Mr. All Star had been knocked down as far as I had been.

Misery loves company.

My nausea returned when a smile spread across his face as he looked down at Allie.

"What on earth could be funny right now?" I asked him as the group stopped in front of us.

"We were just talking about that time in junior year when Bailey almost got suspended for sneaking off campus to go get us milkshakes—"

"And that's funny how?"

Noah shifted uncomfortably and gave me a warning glance.

"Morgan, it's okay to be sad, but it's also okay to remember Bailey," my mom said.

"I don't want to remember Bailey. I want her to be here," I said.

"As usual, it's always about what Morgan wants," Allie said.

"Guys, come on," Noah pleaded.

But Allie continued on, "You aren't the only one who lost Bailey. At least you got to spend one last night with her." Allie wiped at a tear balancing on her cheek. "If I had been there, I could have convinced her of the truth: you weren't worth running after." She stormed off before anyone could reply.

My mother sat down next to me and wrapped her arm around my shoulders. "She doesn't mean that."

"Allie doesn't say things just to say them." I stood and walked away, reaching into my dress pocket for my cell phone. I scrolled down the list of unanswered messages: condolences from my roommate at Flagler College, an advertisement from Target about a sale on cozy socks, and questions from old classmates about Bailey's funeral.

I stopped on Bailey's name and the last text she'd sent.

Bailey, 12:37 AM: Where are you? I'm sorry, just come back to the house!!!!

I stared at it and began typing.

Allie is unbearable.

Send.

Chapter 20

Me, 3:37 PM: My dorm room is empty.

I pushed the last box of clothes into the back of my car and slammed the trunk door. The sleeve of my favorite sweater got caught, and I stared at the sleeve sticking out at the bottom. The simple solution would be to just open it back up, push the sweater in farther—it barely took up any space—and be on with my morning. Instead, I stared at it. Would the lace tear? If I just left it alone, what would it collect in the hour-and-a-half drive back home?

"Need help with that?" I heard from behind me. I turned to see Dylan standing with a smile on his face.

"No," I said.

He stuck his hands in his pockets.

"Going on a road trip?" he asked.

"No," I repeated.

"Off to save endangered sea turtles, then," he paused, "if you're not talking to me because I still use plastic straws, I can change."

He smiled, then must have noticed that I wasn't smiling. He walked closer to me and put his hand on my shoulder.

"I'm going to go break up with my boyfriend right now. I'm driving to his apartment in Orlando, breaking up with him, and then driving back to my mom's place in Cocoa Beach and moving back in with her. Dropping out of school. No one knows that yet, Dylan, except for you, because my best friend, Bailey, died on New Year's Eve, and since then, no one will talk to me, especially my other best friend, Allie—" I stopped and looked at him more closely. "Come to think of it, you are Allie's type. If I weren't about the throw away my entire life here at Flagler, I'd probably hook you guys up. She goes to UF. She's studying to be a doctor. Wait, are you and Natasha still dating?"

Dylan gave me a sympathetic look and stepped closer to me. He gently placed his hand on my shoulder. There were tears in my eyes.

"Is that why I haven't seen you around?" he asked, and I nodded. He held out his arms, offering a hug to me. I stepped into his embrace and lightly hugged him back. I pulled away almost instantly. It felt painful to be in anyone else's embrace. It felt like I didn't deserve his sympathy, either.

"Am I making a mistake, Dylan?" I asked, leaning against the back of my car. He leaned next to me.

"Maybe."

I inhaled, "It's my fault Bailey's dead," I said, "I still text her sometimes, hoping she'll respond."

"That's rough."

"I'm crazy."

He shook his head, "When my goldfish died, I still fed his empty fish bowl."

Despite everything, I cracked a small smile.

"That's a little different," I said.

"Very different, but that's to say that I get it. It fucking sucks," he said.

I looked over at him, and I instantly got angry with myself. I'd spent so much time at Flagler holding on to relationships that were growing without me when I could have had a great friendship right here with Dylan.

"I'm sorry your friend died," he offered.

"Me too."

We sat against the back of my car in silence for a moment. I looked at the time on my phone.

"Well, Dylan, I should get going. I've got a boyfriend to break up with," I said sadly.

Dylan looked down at me. "Good luck, Morgan."

I nodded. "Thanks. You too."

"I hope you decide to come back next year," he said.

He cupped my shoulder again and straightened to walk away. He paused and turned around. "Something is stuck in your trunk." He pointed at the sleeve that had made its home both inside and outside of my car.

"I know." I walked around to the driver's side and sat in the car.

I stared up at the castle-like dormitories I'd been living in since September. Flagler College used to be a hotel created by Henry Flagler in the oldest city in America. The design had inspired anyone who had ever stepped foot inside to contemplate becoming an architect in hopes of creating something so beautiful and long-lasting. Once home to eloquent dinners, it was now home to teenagers out on their own for the first time. A journey for anyone involved.

I turned the car on and pulled out of the student parking area, refusing to look at the beautiful buildings hanging out in my rearview mirror.

~*~

I drove in silence the entire way to Orlando, staring at my hands on the steering wheel. I should go get a manicure, I thought, maybe a nice light blue or a pale pink. Once I'd parked in the lot outside Ryder's apartment, I sat in more silence. The cold air from the vents blew on my face, and I wondered what it would be like to live somewhere that actually required heat in February.

I shut my car door and took in the sight of all my belongings shoved into my back seat and trunk. I walked to the stairway and decided to climb the six flights instead of taking the elevator. Anything to delay.

Ryder, Ethan, and Noah lived on the sixth floor of a seven-floor student apartment building. They shared one bathroom. Their neighbors, a set of twin brothers who both played for the University of Central Florida football team, were loud but really nice. When I helped Ryder move in and unpack, he'd slipped me a spare key to their apartment.

Despite having a key, I knocked because no one was expecting me.

Ethan opened the door. "Hi, Morgan." He wore old Nike shorts and a loose V-neck shirt, his blond hair disheveled. He didn't seem the least surprised to see me, and it was as if our shared grief in losing Bailey had connected us.

"You need to sleep," I told him and put my bag on the kitchen table. I look around their apartment. A pizza box sat open on the counter, an array of soda cans lined up next to it. Dishes littered the sink, and the garbage can overflowed — and that was just the kitchen.

"Where's Ryder?" I asked, my palms sweating and my heart beating dully. My head hurt, and I wondered if Ethan could tell that I was trying not to cry.

"Ryder," Ethan yelled, as he walked over to the couch and sat down, staring at the paused movie he had been watching. He didn't make a move to press play.

I heard the bedroom door open, and Ryder walked out.

"I told you, dude, I'll watch the movie with you—" He stopped when he saw me standing in the hallway.

"Hi, Morgan. What are you doing here? I mean, I'm glad to see you, but…" He walked over to me and kissed my cheek. My heart dropped some more, and I wondered exactly how glad he would be after I was done.

"Can we go outside and talk?" I asked. Ethan took that as a cue to press play and settled back into the couch. He didn't look at us as we crossed the living room to the balcony door.

I sat down immediately, needing the stability of the worn balcony furniture to ground me.

Ryder sat next to me. "What's going on, Morgan?"

"I packed up my dorm room today. I'm moving back home."

Ryder didn't react. Instead, he remained silent, waiting for me to continue. I inhaled and dropped my head.

"I just can't do it. It's too hard."

"It is hard, yeah. I feel that, too. I think we all do. But are you positive this is your best solution?"

I shrugged. "I don't know what else to do, Ryder. I don't want to believe it yet. I don't want to accept it, so for right now, I'm not going to."

He reached over and placed his hand on mine, rubbing his finger against my palm. "Are you still going to your therapy appointments? Talking about Bailey will help."

From the balcony, we had a perfect view of the college campus. The newly constructed buildings and the football stadium lights looked nothing like the grounds of Flagler. Flagler's campus was hundreds of years old compared to UCF's decades of history; somehow, this campus looked more ghostly, though. The bright lights and the city below — it all felt so empty as I sat on the balcony next to Ryder.

I turned to Ryder and mentally threw away the script I had rehearsed of "It's not you, it's me." I couldn't lie to him; if I was going to do this, he at least deserved the truth.

"We need to break up. I think, right now, I'm not deserving of anything good, not after what happened. And you're about as good as it gets. I want to be alone. I don't want anyone to talk to me, and I don't want anyone to try to change my mind."

Ryder leaned back in his chair but kept his eyes locked on me. That was when I should have apologized, told him I was sorry, and reminded him that I did love him. But I couldn't. As he stared at me, the color in his face draining to a lighter shade, I felt what remained of my heart start to collapse. I wondered how much grief and pain a nineteen-year-old heart could take before it just gave up. I wondered if it was possible to die from a broken heart.

Below us, horns blared on University Drive, students leaving campus to go to their apartments to cook dinner or study or to go to a yoga class or read a book. Above them, Ryder and I kissed our future goodbye. Our nights of using rock paper scissors to determine the simplest of things were gone, and though that might have been the smallest memory, it was what hurt the most. The simplicity and innocence of who we had been were overshadowed by the uncertainty that we would never recover from New Year's Eve. From Bailey. From this.

He didn't beg me to change my mind. He didn't tell me to take some time to think about it. He didn't remind me that he knew more about me than anyone else in the world. He didn't project anger onto me. Instead, he asked if I was okay to drive home. He offered me his bed to sleep in and iced coffee from the coffee shop down the road when I woke in the morning.

"I should go. I haven't really told my mom yet that I'm leaving Flagler."

"What are you going to do?" Ryder asked. I shrugged. I didn't have a plan.

"Well, you'll figure it out. You're smart."

I inhaled, and with that inhalation, something in me broke. I dropped my head into my hands and cried. Ryder's hand rubbed my back as I cried, my entire body shaking with sobs.

I pulled into my driveway, parked the car, and stared at the front door. My mom opened it right away and stood in the door, looking back at me. She walked towards my car and peered inside. She glanced over the boxes, probably noting how my car looked similar to how it did when she helped me move into my dorm room last fall. She gave me a small smile and opened my door. I unbuckled my seatbelt and got out. She wrapped her arms around me and smoothed my hair down as I sobbed into her shoulder.

My mom's solution to nearly everything has always been a large glass of water. When I'd fall as a kid and scrape up my knees, she'd meet me not with a Band-Aid but with a water bottle. Now, as we sat at the kitchen table, I wasn't sure how much water she thought she needed to comfort this. There was nothing to fix this.

"I'll get a job, I guess," I said, answering her question of, "Now what?" before she even had a chance to ask it. She sipped from a coffee cup. Never mind that it was nearly seven at night.

"Is this about Bailey?" my mom asked, "Because if it is, I have to think that she wouldn't want you throwing away your life like this."

I shook my head. This wasn't just about Bailey. It was about everything else, too. Like how Allie hadn't talked to me since the funeral. How Noah called me every day to check up on me like I was damaged goods. I was mad that Ethan was sad, too, but at least he could function. And then, Ryder. I didn't know how to put into words how I felt about him. On one hand, if he hadn't been jealous of Bailey...No. I couldn't let myself think that. It wasn't fair.

Bailey was dead. I was to blame.

The next morning, my mom arranged an emergency appointment with the therapist she'd found me since Bailey died. As I sat in the waiting room, I scrolled through my phone with little to nothing to do. Allie wasn't talking to me. Noah checked in, but that was nothing new. What could I say to Ryder? I felt a pang of sadness as I saw our old group thread, still pinned to my favorite conversations on my messaging app.

The door to the office opened, and Dr. Mackintosh stuck her head out. She smiled at me.

"Come on in, Morgan," she said.

I followed behind her begrudgingly. My mom swore that this would help me. Maybe Dr. Mackintosh could help me put things into perspective. I thought she was just secretly hoping that Dr. Mackintosh would convince me not to leave school just yet, not to give up on myself so easily. I sat down in my usual spot on the dark blue sofa. The first time I'd come here last month, I'd asked her if I had to lie down. Now, I curled my legs under me and sat crisscross, waiting for her to start firing away with "How have you been since we last spoke?" and "Your mom told me you're still texting your dead friend. What's up with that?"

"What's been going on, Morgan?" she asked. Typical. I shrugged.

"I'm sure my mom told you," I said. She smiled at me from across from where I sat.

"She mentioned some things when we spoke, but you're an adult. You can tell me yourself what's going on," she said.

"I quit school. Dumped Ryder."

She nodded. She stared down at the notepad she had next to her. She put down her pen and sat back. "Tell me more about that," she said.

I exhaled, blowing the air out of my mouth in what I knew was an overly dramatic sigh.

"There's not much to say. I'm a mess. Ryder deserves someone who isn't a mess."

She stared at me and smiled again. "Have you been doing the grounding exercises we talked about?"

"No."

"Morgan, I can't force you to do anything we discuss here. But it would be a real shame if you threw away your future—"

I shook my head, cutting her off before she had the chance to go on. She spoke the same speech my mom did last night, and I had to wonder if they'd strategized this. Dr. Mackintosh cocked her head.

"When was the last time you texted Bailey's old number?" she asked.

I shrugged.

"You really don't recall, or you don't want to tell me?"

"This morning," I admitted.

"Grief is hard, Morgan, but we have discussed some healthy coping mechanisms," she said. I looked at her diplomas hanging on the wall. I searched around the room for any family pictures. I looked at her hand to see if she had a wedding band.

"Do you believe in soulmates?" I asked. She leaned back as if to say, 'Now we're talking!'

"There's a story in Greek mythology that said humans were originally created with four arms, four legs, and two faces," she started, "Zeus split them in half because he was scared humans would be too powerful. It forced them to spend the rest of their lives searching for their other halves."

"That doesn't answer my question," I said. She smiled.

"I believe that we all have the ability to love someone so deeply that we cannot imagine what life would look like should we be cut in half, figuratively speaking. Is that how you felt about Ryder?" she asked.

"That's how I felt about Bailey. And Allie."

"It must be really hard for you right now, then, to know that you will never talk to Bailey again. And to have Allie mad at you."

I stared at her. "Am I crazy for thinking that Bailey will answer me?"

"I don't use the word crazy in my office."

I rolled my eyes, "What am I then?"

She looked at me for a long time before sliding her box of tissues over to me. I hadn't realized I was crying.

"You're sad, Morgan. You're heartbroken. You're grieving," she paused, "You went through a very traumatic experience, and it's barely been a full month since that happened. The trauma from that event, well, it's causing you great stress still. I'll admit the texting is unusual, and it does worry me. But, off the record, I don't blame you."

I looked at her with confusion.

"Sometimes it's easier to be in denial. But that's what I'm here for."

She stood up and walked over to a cabinet next to her desk, and pulled out a small notebook. She handed it to me.

"I want you to actively try to record whenever you text Bailey. This way, we can try to find a common thread. If I had to guess, the texting would be your stress response. You were so used to going to Bailey for everything, you are still holding on to that relationship. Bailey was your rock, and now that she's gone, you're a little lost."

"And what? The journal is supposed to make me not miss her?"

Dr. Mackintosh looked at me. She had light gray hairs speckled throughout her blonde ponytail. She wore glasses. God, could she be any more of a cliché?

"You've been through so much. School, Bailey, Ryder. All of your friends, really. I want to make sure you're taking care of yourself," she said.

I walked out of Dr. Mackintosh's office with my purse slung over my shoulder and the journal in my hand. As I opened the door to the parking lot, I walked by a trash can and dropped the journal into it. I pulled my phone out of my back pocket and scrolled through my messaging app. I clicked on Bailey's name. I added Allie to the thread as well.

Me, 10:47 AM: My mom has lost it with this therapy shit.

Chapter 21

I stared down at my bright yellow toenail polish.

I'm running. No, sprinting up the stairs. Rain splashed down next to me. I didn't see anything but my toenail polish.

"Morgan, wait."

Bailey's voice. She sounded far away. Then she sounded underwater. I saw the beach now, and I realized I'm standing on the top deck. It's raining harder. As I looked over the ledge of the deck, I noticed the house below crumbling. The roof was ripped off, and rain poured into each room. I looked closer and saw Ryder swimming in the flooded house. He reached out a hand, called my name. Someone touched my shoulder, and then I'm falling off the top deck.

Falling into the flood.

Screaming.

Tossing.

The last thing I see before I hit the ground is Bailey standing on the top deck. She called down to me: "Now you know how it felt."

When I shot up in bed, it felt like I had been asleep for five minutes. Allie was still next to me, her breathing calm and even. My heart pounded against my chest as I pushed the blanket off of me and climbed out of the bed, careful to not budge Allie. She groaned lightly and rolled over, blissfully unaware of the terror that I'd just experienced. I walked out of the room and into the kitchen. Uncle Daniel stood at the counter with the coffee pot brewing. He looked at me.

"Good, you slept in," he said. He poured coffee into a mug and passed it to me across the kitchen island.

"Slept in? It's barely light out," I said.

He winked, "That's sleeping in for you."

I took a sip of the coffee to make room to add plenty of creamer. I gagged, which caused Uncle Daniel to laugh.

"I had a nightmare," I admitted.

"That doesn't surprise me."

I paused, "I've had the nightmare before. Lots of times. I never knew what it meant."

"How do you feel?" he asked.

I thought about it for a moment, "Empty."

The terms Uncle Daniel shared with me were starting to blend together as he sat next to me on the back porch. Uncle Daniel had used words such as grief, bereavement, post-traumatic stress disorder, and—the icing on the cake—complicated grief. In my hand, I held a coffee mug so tightly that I could see the coffee ripple as I shook. Uncle Daniel had a bagel in front of him, from which he picked off pieces in between words. He'd turned some music on like he did every morning, and colliding with the sound of the crashing waves, Bob Dylan crooned about what the world needed in order to change for the better, posing questions about what we could do to help.

This morning, I'd looked back at my text messages.

In January, I sent an average of fifteen text messages a week to Bailey. By February, that number grew to twenty. In March, it dwindled, picked back up in April when it would have been her birthday, and was an embarrassing thirty-plus a week in May. Each one was left undelivered, the usually blue bubble turning a shocking green. It reminded me of ninth grade when Bailey's older cousin Leah had told us that the new fad in dating was to just block someone's number. She had sat with her long-term boyfriend, telling us horror stories of their friends from college and how they had handled dating, even telling us that their friends had coined a rhyme for whenever one of them went on a bad date.

"If it's green, Cupid won't intervene," she had joked, hinting that if the bubble wasn't that soft blue, then there was no chance of a reply.

I wondered if Leah had been at Bailey's funeral.

Uncle Daniel hummed along to the music playing and looked at me.

"Your mom is going to come; she'll be here later today."

I remained quiet for a while, then swallowed hard. "Are you guys mad at us?"

He waved his hand as if to say what we'd done was old news now. My mom and him had always been proud that Noah and I were as close as we were, "thick as thieves," they used to joke, so maybe it helped that at least we did this together.

The song that was playing ended, and it changed to the next song on the playlist.

Well, it ain't no use to sit and wonder why, babe…

The sound of Bob Dylan's harmonica filled the air. I thought back to the video my mom had of Noah and me as five-year-olds singing to this song while we were playing, blissfully unaware of how heartbreaking it actually was.

"Did I ever tell you about the time your Nana and Papa caught your mom and me sneaking back into the house after seeing Bob Dylan in concert?"

I shook my head.

He smirked. "Man, we must've been sixteen or seventeen. He was playing right down the road from where we lived at the time, some venue in Tampa that was pretty lax about checking IDs." He paused and looked at me. "Your mom is going to kill me for telling you this story."

"My lips are sealed."

He laughed. "We told your Nana and Papa that we were going to an overnight lock-in at school for physics. We even made fake permission slips for them to sign. We packed an overnight bag and made a plan to actually sleep under the stars after the concert."

He laughed. "Anyway, it was the eighties, right? People didn't really give a shit about teenagers going to concerts, but we were so certain Nana and Papa would have said no if we'd asked. So we just went. It was the most amazing concert I've ever seen, still to this day. Your mom and I left as soon as he finished, and as we were walking out to the car, you know who we saw?"

I shrugged.

"Nana and Papa. Your Papa even had a cigarette dangling from his lips." Uncle Daniel was laughing now, hard, wiping a tear from his eye.

"Did you get in trouble?" I asked.

"No!" he said with a smile. "They were actually proud of us for going. They said everyone should see Dylan in concert once in their lives." He paused.

"Do I wish you guys hadn't lied about coming here? Sure, every parent wants to believe their kids are doing the right thing and making good choices, but I trust Noah. Hell, I trust him more than I trust myself sometimes. He thought this was the right choice, so I can't be mad at the kid."

"Was it the right choice?"

He inhaled, his lips pursing together.

"Probably not." His expression turned pained. "But after watching your mother take you to countless therapy sessions and grief counseling, just for you to shut down—I don't blame anyone for thinking it would be a last-ditch effort to help you. It's good to talk about the memories, Morgan. That's what I'm trying to say."

I had been living in denial. Denial with a heart-shaped bow on top. I had spent the last seven months convincing myself that Bailey was going to come back to me. I had myself absolutely believing that if I had a chance to talk to her, I could make it right.

Dr. Mackintosh had told my mother to give it time, while my mother had told me to give it space, but in the end, neither had worked. The nights I had spent staring at my phone screen; the mornings I had spent sitting on the old leather couch in my living room while my friends went off to college, finished their semester, and made plans to move off campus for sophomore year—it all added up to the singular moment of realization. The moment everyone had waited for me to take a bow as if I'd been playing them all along, and this was my greatest performance to date.

I thought of Noah, who had never given up on me. I remembered him coming to my mom's house and sitting with me on the couch. We would chat cautiously at the beginning. If I was having a Remembering Day, as he referred to the days on which I remembered Bailey's death, we would ease into plans for my future. He was adamant about me going back to school. He even had an email out to an admissions counselor at UCF, with plans of us moving in together if I transferred there. If it was a day on which I didn't remember, he would sit quietly while I stared at the television or asked about Bailey.

Now, the reality was settled in.

Bailey was dead. I was crazy.

"Being back in the house changed things for you, I think," Uncle Daniel said. "I'm no expert, but I think it probably brought you back to the truth on a lot of things."

"Like?"

"Like the truth behind your relationships. You guys are growing and changing. It's not supposed to stay the same." Uncle Daniel took a bite of his bagel as I loosened my grip on my coffee cup.

"But the same is comforting," I said quietly.

He nodded. "After Noah's mom left and we moved to Cocoa Beach, I was so scared of messing up. You might understand that one day: what it feels like to have an entire person to take care of besides yourself, and exactly how terrifying it is to know that one wrong move can ruin them for life."

He leaned back in his chair.

"I had the same feeling when I brought Noah to this house for the first time as I did when we brought him home from the hospital. There was so much hope. I hated that his mom and I hadn't worked it out, but I knew he'd be fine because he's the greatest dude alive, right? Plus, he had you. And he found his tribe quickly. You know, Bailey was the first friend of his I remember meeting? Because she was the only one who didn't call me 'Noah's dad.'"

I laughed, "That sounds like Bailey."

Uncle Daniel had bags under his eyes that mirrored mine, a deep-rooted sadness that made itself at home in the deepest part of our stomachs.

"I shouldn't have let you guys come here on New Year's Eve. We wouldn't be here right now if I hadn't."

We sat together in silence for a few more moments, watching as families started to crowd the beach. We were at the halfway point of the season with the impossibility of permanently freckled shoulders and icy lemonade on flowing refill at the front of everyone's mind. In less than two months, everyone would be back in their cities — back in school, back in practice, back in reality. Dream worlds had to end, even if it was just a summer vacation.

Worse than that: in four days, we would be leaving The Highview and for the last time.

"I can't believe you're selling the house," I said quietly. At least that was something we could all agree to be in denial about this summer, our last summer at The Highview. I looked over at Uncle Daniel, trying to see if there was any trace in his expression of him changing his mind, but he remained stoic.

Until he didn't anymore.

"I always thought Noah would bring his kids here one day. A generational thing, you know? Noah was a little boy down in the dirt next to me when I bought the place, digging through soil and trying to plant a garden but having no clue what the hell I was doing. Very symbolic of life, I guess."

He paused. After I watched him swallow down tears, he continued, "I thought I'd sit on this very porch and look out at our growing family: you kids with families of your own, tracking new sand into the house and sitting your wet bathing suits on my damn couch."

His voice trailed off. When he spoke again, his words were hushed.

"It feels wrong to wish for that now. This house ruined so many lives back in January that, of course, I had to sell it." He sipped his own coffee and picked at his bagel again.

I thought of the picture-perfect plans we had created for our lives: happiness draped in beach towels and post-beach naps, surrounded by dinners filled with laughter and rainy afternoons we could crawl into. As summer turned to fall, which eventually circled back to the summer after chilly mornings and wet Aprils, we ticked away at an invisible checklist, hoping for a healthy and long life. This didn't feel like something a nineteen-year-old should know so deeply, yet here I was, settling into a life that proved we were all in a race against the clock.

If I knew anything from the last twenty-four hours of my life, it was that there was no point in holding onto hope against the inevitable.

The back door slid open, and Allie walked out onto the deck. She held a water bottle that was dripping in condensation and a bowl of fruit. She sat down in the chair across from me and sighed.

"How are you feeling?" she asked.

I appreciated it, but I wondered how many times I was going to get asked that same question today. I shrugged.

"I slept like shit," Allie laughed as she popped a strawberry into her mouth. Uncle Daniel smiled.

"It's good beach weather today," he said, "maybe I'll wake the dudes up, and you guys can go paddle boarding."

Allie looked at me.

"Morgan and I need to go buy our anklets before we go

home," she said. I smiled at her.

We were the first customers in The Barefoot Trader. At the counter, the two employees working were already drinking from cold bottles of soda, their own version of the same caffeine high that coffee gave Allie and me. One of them waved at us, and they went back to their conversation. Allie and I had walked here, the short half-mile stroll filled mostly with comfortable silence, especially when Allie led us the longer way that wouldn't bring us by the bridge.

We walked over to the rack where the various jewelry hung. I turned it until the side filled with anklets was directly in front of us. I scanned the rows, looking for one that would stick out. Next to me, Allie laughed. She bent down to the very bottom row and picked up an anklet. She turned it around so I could see it.

A gaudy anklet filled with seashells and dangling turtle charms.

"I'll do anything if you let me get this anklet."

"God, I wish we hadn't promised her we'd get this anklet this summer," Allie said. She stared at it.

"It really is the ugliest thing I've ever seen," I said.

Allie shrugged, "A promise is a promise."

She grabbed three off the rack.

"Maybe we can go put it at her tombstone when we get home," she said. I swallowed back tears and just nodded. Allie squeezed my arm and walked over to the counter. At the register, the same cashier Bailey had joked with last summer was. He smiled at us. Surely, he didn't remember us, he saw thousands of customers a year, but he still felt like a connection to our last summer together. Allie swiped her debit card and smiled.

"Thanks, Owen," she said. He smiled back at her.

Allie and I walked out of the store and stopped at the bench outside. I put my foot up on it, and she bent down, and, like always, tied my anklet on for me. We both looked at the dangling turtles and obnoxious turtles that now decorated our anklets.

"It's so ugly," Allie said.

"The worst thing that's ever been on my body," I agreed. She chuckled and looked at me.

"I love you, Morg. We'll get through this. Together, okay?" I nodded, "Love you."

Chapter 22

When Allie and I got back to The Highview, the first thing we noticed was my mom's car in the driveway. We opened the front door, and she was standing in the kitchen cooking rows of bacon on a large skillet. She turned at the sound of the door and stared at us. She dropped her spatula and walked over, wrapped her arms around me, and hugged me.

"My girl," she said. She held me with a tightness I'd never recalled, not even when I was eight, and flipped off my handlebars when my pool towel got stuck in my bike wheel. Allie sidestepped us and sat down at the kitchen island. She picked a piece of cooked bacon off a plate. Noah walked out of the bedroom and sat down next to her, and my mom finally pulled away. She had tears streaked down her face.

"Hey, Aunt Em," Noah said. She turned and looked at him with a faux expression of anger. Noah smiled at her.

"Did your dad already ream your ass out?" she asked.

"Several times."

"Great. Then I'll save my breath."

I looked at Noah and then back at my mom, "Noah did

keep his promise, though. He told you he'd take care of me, and he did."

Noah smiled at me and nodded, a nod that I took to mean, "I'd do it all over again, too."

My mom looked down and wiped a tear away from her eye. "Where are the others?" she asked. She walked around the kitchen island and gave Allie and Noah both a hug.

"Ethan went for a run. Ryder's rolling out of bed," Noah said. My mom walked back to the stove and turned her back to us as she flipped the bacon.

"Breakfast will be ready soon," she started, "Well. Lunch, I guess. You lazies slept until almost noon," she said.

"That's probably my fault," I joked.

An uncomfortable laugh filled the room as Uncle Daniel walked inside. He looked at us.

"You're telling me you're going to sneak here, and you don't even head down to the beach? Get moving," he said.

"Dad, we just woke up," Noah whined.

Uncle Daniel shrugged, "Put your swimsuits on and go."

After scarfing down food, Noah convinced Ethan and Ryder to go kayaking with him. Allie and I had a different plan, though. The top deck had always been our favorite part of The Highview. It was where we'd go to escape moments like this when, in the awkward years of adolescence, we feared that any sort of comment from my mom or Uncle Daniel could ruin our lives.

Allie was leaning against the railing when I made it to the top. Without turning around, she laughed. "I forgot how weird your mom and uncle are together. I swear, your mom snorting when she laughs is still the most unexpected thing about her. It surprises me every single time."

I rested my forearms against the thick railing and laughed, too.

"There are too many memories here," Allie said quietly. She was staring out at the beach, where the waves crashed against the shore. In the distance, we saw three girls, who looked like they were barely teenagers, collecting seashells. Allie must have seen them at the same time I did because she smiled.

Then I remembered. We'd been together, grocery shopping with my mom for a barbecue for my eleventh birthday. Allie had had her first crush — on Noah.

"If I make this, you both have to give me five bucks," Bailey said.

"If you throw it in like that, you're going to break the jar," Allie said.

"Shut up, Allie. Live a little. I'll definitely make it in."

Bailey took a step back and tossed the glass jar of pickle slices into the cart. But Allie was right. The jar hit the corner of the cart, sending it onto the floor, where it shattered, pickle juice splashing up and spraying all three of us. We looked at each other in horror and then down at the floor, where pickle juice pooled.

"Now I'm going to smell like your disgusting pickles when I see Noah!" Allie shrieked.

"Morgan?" Allie called. I shook my head and blinked to see Allie staring at me in concern. "Where'd you go?"

"You used to have a crush on Noah. And we smelled like pickle juice because Bailey broke the jar…"

Allie smiled. "Being eleven was the absolute worst."

We stared at the girls again. Allie walked away from the rail and sat down in one of the Adirondack chairs.

"I used to wish I could go back to being eight years old and convince you to never sit down next to Bailey," she said sadly.

Allie paused.

"Eight years old, and we knew that we needed her. Remember?" She shook her head. "You and I had gotten into a fight because you told me that purple nail polish was for you and you alone. So, at lunch that day, you went and sat down next to Bailey instead of me. Of course, I still followed. Now look where we are."

"Now you wouldn't be seen in public with purple nail polish," I joked.

Allie laughed. After a moment, she looked over at me. "I kept thinking that if only we had never met her, we wouldn't be so heartbroken right now. Was I really willing to give up ten years of the greatest moments of my life just to get over this pain?"

"I know how you feel."

What was hardest for me was that one day, Allie and I would run out of memories of Bailey because they weren't indefinite. Allie and I could keep making memories together, but with Bailey, we had to preserve them in a capsule. One day, we'd forget the weird perfume she had that smelled different when each of us wore it. We'd forget the sound of her voice when she sang along to the radio. We'd forget the feel of her legs rubbing against ours when she'd beg us to tell her how soft her skin was.

"Right after she died, in my mind, it felt like it would have been easier to throw away the good just so the bad went with it." She stopped and stared at me.

"It doesn't work that way, though," I said. "You can't take the good without the ugly, I guess. Or something like that."

I thought about that. If I could go back in time and have someone look me in the eye on the day I met Bailey, tell me, "This is going to end, and it's going to hurt so badly," but then show me a slideshow of what I'd get that didn't hurt, I'd make the choice over and over again to sit down next to her at the lunch table.

Was that love? Was loving someone deeper than what the movies made it out to be? Love wasn't just romantic. Love was taking someone for all they had to offer, all they could be, and knowing there were going to be days that just downright sucked. I realized now that there were going to be days when it felt like I was left in pieces on the floor with recovery miles down the road, and I'd give anything to have one more day with Bailey and Allie, the three of us all together.

But then I thought back to the 3 a.m. phone calls after a fight with my mom. A six-hour drive on my birthday just to spend a few hours together. A goodbye on a balcony, even though Ryder wanted to fight to stay. We'd been through hell together. All of us had. And though the last few months had felt like I would never recover, at the end of the darkness, I still had people willing to help me find light.

Love was Noah, who, even though he was hurting too, had never given up on helping me get better. Ethan, who had swallowed his own pain to be here with us. Allie, who had dragged herself to the place she now hated the most with no promise that things would ever be okay. Love was Ryder, who had given me my space but still found the energy to check in with me on days he must have known were bad.

And Bailey, who had brought us all together — for good.

"Are we ever going to be able to get over this?" I asked.

Allie moved closer and dropped her head on my shoulder. After a minute, she stood up straight. "No one said we had to get over it."

"But it hurts so much. We're never going to see her again," I said. I pursed my lips together, not ready to cry.

"It doesn't feel like we lost her, though. You know what I mean? We still have each other. That means something."

I nodded. I knew, but damn, it was hard to really accept. From the top deck, we saw the boys running up from the ocean. They were laughing as they chased each other with buckets filled with ocean water. Ryder tackled Ethan and poured the bucket over his head. They laughed even louder. Allie looked over at me.

"You know, you don't have to punish yourself," she said.

"What do you mean?" I asked.

"If you and Ryder still love each other, you should be together."

I looked at her and smiled, "When did you become such a romantic?"

She shrugged and gave me a sly smile, "I'm just saying, I know you, and I know Ryder, and I don't think that this is the end for you two."

"I haven't accepted the fact that it's over between us."

"Maybe you don't have to."

I thought of the months I'd spent ignoring Ryder's text messages. Even though I'd dumped him, he'd tried to remain loyal. He'd checked in on me from time to time. When he stopped, it had devastated me in a way I hadn't expected.

I wanted to believe that Ryder had never stopped loving me, but we'd both felt it last night when we'd kissed. That had been goodbye.

Right?

I shook my head and looked at Allie, "I'll be right back."

I ran down the spiral staircase to the main deck by the front door. I peered inside, catching a glance of Noah and Ethan piling leftovers onto a plate. I could hear my mom and Uncle

Daniel laughing. No sign of Ryder, but I knew where he was.

During our first year at The Highview together as boyfriend and girlfriend, Ryder and I had spent our downtime together in a hammock we had installed, our own private getaway, despite being out in the open in the side yard. We'd go there to lie together, the hammock barely rocking back and forth in a stagnant Florida breeze. It was where we'd go to escape the loudness. We'd lie in the hammock, me reading whatever newest book I was devouring, him looking at videos of the Miami Dolphins, taking notes on each play as if he could present the coaching team with a winning game plan. It became a place of solitude for anyone who needed it. When the noise got overwhelming, or we just wanted a break from each other, the hammock became a popular spot. As I turned the corner from the back deck, I hoped that I'd find Ryder there.

And there he was, his legs up and his arms folded behind his head as he stared up at the sky. I kept my eyes on him, even though I didn't need to look at him to see him perfectly in my head: His brown hair and eyes, both growing a shade lighter whenever the sun hit. The small scar on his nose from when he was surfing one summer and sliced it on a broken seashell. The rare trace of stubble.

He sat up partially when he heard me. "How'd you know I'd be here?"

"Who says I was looking for you?" I replied with a small smile.

He laughed. "Fair."

"It's our spot. Everything else has changed, but I'd hoped this would stay the same."

He nodded. "Everyone keeps saying that: 'Everything else has changed'."

"Hasn't it, though?"

He shrugged. "Not everything."

"Mostly everything."

We fell silent for a long moment. Then I opened my mouth to say something, at the same time Ryder did, and we both stopped.

"You go first," I said.

"I came here with the hope we could get back together," Ryder said. "Then I got here, and I realized exactly how important it was for you to get better. That became the priority. After the first night here, I told Noah that was more important, so I kind of pushed it out of my head that we might ever be together again."

A warm breeze pushed the hammock, and Ryder swayed slowly. He blew the gum he'd been chewing into a bubble.

"So?" I finally asked.

"When we kissed last night, it was the best thing that's happened to me since January."

Ryder sat up in the hammock. "I didn't want to spend the rest of my life thinking I'd never get any closure over us. I couldn't wait around in hopes that we'd get back together or things would suddenly be okay, but I also couldn't act like we didn't have a great life together. I don't care if we were young or if people said we were just kids in love, I know that what we had was real."

He looked at his feet. My cheeks burned, and a small lump settled in my throat.

"We used to talk about forever," he added, "but we had no clue what forever actually meant. Not until Bailey died. And after she died, I still had hope that we'd have forever. I think I still do, maybe."

Tears blurred my vision. I didn't want to say goodbye to

Ryder. Not again.

"Please, can we start over?" I asked.

He peered at me. "We can't start over. If we started over, we'd be pretending that the last six years didn't happen. I don't want to do that."

"We can't do that," I agreed.

We stared at each other.

"I'd like to think we'll be in love again one day, Morgan. But until then, I'll be here as your friend. For whatever you need."

I nodded. "Thanks, Ryder."

He moved over in the hammock to make room for me, and I lay down next to him. We stared up at the sky, and I felt his finger brush against mine.

Chapter 23

Present

Noah jogged over to where Allie and I sat on the beach. He bent over and put his hands on his knees. Inhaling deeply, he reached for a water bottle sitting on top of the cooler. He stood up straight, opened the bottle, and took several big gulps.

Allie briefly looked up from her beach towel. "Are you having an asthma attack?"

"Five miles…on the beach…with Ethan," he said between labored inhales and shaky exhales.

"Like, running?" Allie asked. Noah nodded.

"Honestly, is this beach even five miles long?" I asked. Noah looked up and glared at us.

"I thought you hated running," Allie said.

Noah nodded and took another sip of water. "I do. I was trying to take a nap, but Ethan woke me up and asked me if I wanted to go fishing. When I met him downstairs, he had sneakers waiting for me and told me it was time to run."

"You could've said no," Allie said. "You do know that, right?"

Noah sat down in a nearby chair. "Yeah, why didn't I? The

crazy part is that Ethan is still running. He kept going."

Allie and Noah continued talking as I stared up at the completely clear sky. Yesterday, Ryder and I had lain in the hammock for most of the afternoon. He'd told me stories of his second semester at UCF, and I'd told him about the string of reality shows I'd gotten hooked on. He'd joked that I needed a television detox, to which I retorted that after hearing some of his stories, I thought he probably needed an alcohol detox.

He'd confided in me that he missed Bailey. I hadn't had to say anything in return.

Today was a new day. Allie and I had woken up early and gotten iced coffee. She'd huffed over my ordering coffee with more flavoring than actual coffee while I'd given her shit for straightening her hair just to go to the beach. It was closer to normal than we'd been five days before.

Last night, my mom had said a therapy appointment could be scheduled with Dr. Mackintosh as soon as we got back home.

Everyone was making plans for me, but I still felt clouded. I still felt as if, at any minute, I could slip away again. I needed to make a conscious effort to stay grounded. Lucid.

I wondered if everyone thought that now we were at this place, things could start going back to normal, our "new normal," we'd proudly tout. I would reenroll in school—sure, a semester behind everyone, but I could always take summer classes. I could move back to St. Augustine and finish up my dream program at my dream college, and I'd look back at this time in my life as a bad dream.

"I've been thinking," Allie started. "What if we could convince your dad to not sell the house?"

Noah laughed. "Do you have some trust fund we don't know about, Al? 'Cause I'm pretty sure he's already got a plan for that money."

"It's not about the money," Allie said. "It's about the memories. Your dad thinks this house is tainted with bad memories now. What if we show him there can be good memories again?"

"Are you going to propose to me?" Noah joked.

Allie rolled her eyes, blushing slightly. "Let's have a memorial service. For Bailey."

Noah, visibly shaken, started. "Oh, Allie, I don't know…"

"We love her. We miss her, of course. Let's celebrate her."

I looked at Noah, who was digging a hole in the sand with his feet. "What if it doesn't work?"

Noah shook his head. "It won't work. He's still going to sell the house."

"Don't you get it, Noah? It's not about the house." Allie shook her head. "It never has been. It's about who we are when we're at the house. The Highview isn't the reason we're friends, it's not the reason Morgan and Ryder fell in love, and it's definitely not the reason Bailey died. It's just a house."

I knew my best friend. Whenever she was fired up about a plan, she always saw it through. Like in high school, when she single-handedly swayed our senior class to choose a Taylor Swift song for our graduation song. Allie was good at convincing people.

"So wait, it's not about the house, but we want to keep the house?" Noah pointed out.

Allie shook her head, "Will you listen to me? If we can get him to see that we don't blame the house, then we can get him to see how we can move on and still keep the house. It's all part of my brilliant plan."

Noah and I looked at each other. Allie looked over her

shoulder at the house.

"It's just a stupid house, but it's our stupid house."

Allie sat back in her chair, and we knew it was the last she'd talk about it. She was already planning her next steps.

~*~

A few hours later, Allie stood at the end of the picnic table on the back deck and placed both hands on the table. She looked like a detective interrogating a suspect as she opened her mouth to speak.

"I hope everyone is enjoying their turkey sandwiches and cold pizza." Allie paused and looked at each of us. "We did a really wonderful job this week of making sure there would be no leftovers to deal with come Sunday morning when we leave."

She smiled, and her demeanor shifted from detective to politician as she stood up straighter.

Uncle Daniel looked around the deck. Allie had filled the others in on her plan, but we weren't exactly sure what she would say to convince them of the memorial.

"What the hell is this?" Uncle Daniel demanded though he had a smug smile on his face.

"Let her talk, Daniel," my mom said, elbowing him.

"This, Daniel, is a proposition for how to spend our final day in The Highview."

Allie picked up a book that had been resting next to her and put it down on the table: the guest book. I stared at the familiar worn cover. I could picture the lined pages filled with messy cursive, block print, and even stick-figure drawings.

Each summer, we would spend our first night at the house reading the guest book entries from the months before. Some were wildly romantic recounts of blissful weekends in paradise, while others seemed to come straight out of a corny Nicholas Sparks novel, filled with fancy wording and play-by-play accounts of the visitors' vacations. We would read aloud our favorite entries in dramatic voices through fits of laughter as we made up stories to go along with the entries.

At the end of each week, Bailey would do the honors of writing an over-the-top message in hopes that readers after us would get the same joy we did.

Allie held the book now and flipped through its pages. She kept flipping until she'd landed on whatever entry she was looking for. She stared down at it.

"December 31…"

She stopped reading and pursed her lips together. With an encouraging nod from Noah, she continued on.

"It's strange to be on the beach during the winter, even though it's Florida and not that cold. The usual bustle of the street is quiet now, smaller. There's no ice cream truck going up and down the road, no kites suspended in midair advertising Jet Ski rentals, no cover band set up outside Jay's Surf Shack. Being here tonight has made me realize you don't need it to be summer for The Highview to be magical. I'm here with my best friends."

Allie stopped reading again and looked up at us. She smiled. "And then in parentheses, it says, 'Allie, when it's July and you read this, just remember that you ditched us for a cruise!'"

We all laughed at that. Allie's eyes brimmed with tears. Around the table, I could see everyone's face: My mother, sitting next to Ethan with a hand on his shoulder. Ethan staring stone-faced at the table, though a smile flickered across his face every few seconds. Noah looking up at Allie. Ryder, next to me. Uncle Daniel, sitting with tears openly in his eyes. I tuned back into Allie's reading.

"It's like magic, coming back to a place you've known

so well, for so long. Even after things have changed, you like to believe that you can still go home. Yet, being here—it's like nothing has changed. It's as if we were stuck in a time capsule, in which I still wear one-piece bathing suits, and Morgan still doesn't know how to French-braid hair.

"It's New Year's Eve, which, historically, means it's time to make a wish for our future. But I can't think of what I would wish for to make this life more perfect than it already is. Here's to another night at The Highview. Be back soon."

Allie stopped one more time before inhaling deeply.

"Love always, Bailey."

Allie stared at the page a long time before running her finger along the ink as if she were touching Bailey. She looked up at us.

"We're throwing Bailey a party tomorrow. I hope you'll all be in attendance." She closed the guest book and sat back down.

"A party?" my mother asked. She looked at me with worry.

"A party, yeah," I said. "A goodbye party."

"I don't think that's a good idea," Uncle Daniel said.

"Dad," Noah interjected. "I know you think The Highview was to blame. Just like Morgan thinks she was to blame. Or how Ryder thinks that if he had never stirred the pot, it wouldn't have happened. Or how Ethan thinks that if he had yelled at Bailey that he loved her, it would've changed the timeline. Everyone thinks they're to blame. And the shitty truth is, Bailey and Morgan were in the unlucky path of a bad driver, and there was absolutely nothing any of us could have done to change that."

Hearing Noah talk so openly about the blame and guilt we were all feeling felt like exactly what we needed. All of us had spent this entire week sitting around, not mentioning what we needed to talk about the most: forgiveness. Forgiveness for each other but also for ourselves. We had been through hell. Now, we needed each other.

And Noah was right: there was nothing anyone could have done. And man, that sucked.

"Instead of leaving The Highview with one horrible memory," Allie added, "we're going to spend tomorrow remembering the best memories. And making one final memory together. For Bailey."

We were all quiet.

"Well, make a grocery list," Uncle Daniel finally said. He stood up and walked toward the beach. My mom got up and followed him.

"Was that a yes?" Ethan asked once Uncle Daniel was out of earshot. We all looked at Noah, who was staring after his father as he walked away.

"That was a hell yes," Noah said.

Chapter 24

The next morning, I woke to Noah standing over my bed with a plate of bacon. "Time to get up!"

"I don't wanna," I groaned, rolling over. I picked up my phone from the bedside table and saw that it was nearly nine—the latest I'd slept in all week.

Noah sat on the edge of my bed. "Come on. Your mom made those delicious pancakes that she swears are gluten-free but really aren't."

I stretched my arms above my head. I looked around the room and noticed it was empty. "Where's Allie?"

He glanced away from me. "She's down on the beach already."

I slowly sat up. "Do you have a thing for Allie?"

Noah furrowed his eyebrows and forced out a nervous laugh. "A thing for Allie? What? No." He laughed again, and I smirked. "Don't give me that face." He grabbed a pillow and threw it at my head. "Get up."

As he walked out, I rubbed my forehead and took a deep breath. I got out of bed and put on my favorite purple bathing suit and a white sundress over it. I didn't bother running a brush through my hair; I just pulled at some messy strands with my fingers and walked out onto the back deck, where Ethan, Ryder, and Noah were sitting. The sun was already high and beating down on bare shoulders and permanently red noses as I sat down in the chair next to Ryder's.

"What's the argument about today?" I motioned toward Ethan and Noah, who was shaking his head while Ethan rambled on.

Ryder grinned. "Ethan says Noah's snoring has kept him up all night. Noah says it's actually Ethan who's snoring and waking himself up. They've fought about this our whole friendship, and the best part is, it's always me who's snoring."

"They'll never learn, huh?" I smiled as Ethan finally gave up and walked away.

At that same moment, Allie came up the walkway with a bag full of seashells. She took her sunglasses off and stared at us. "Is anyone going to do anything, or am I going to have to get everything ready?"

We looked at each other.

"No, we'll help...but..."

"But what, Ryder?" Allie asked.

"Someone's in trouble." Ethan laughed and tossed a half-eaten croissant at Allie's head.

"Really mature, Ethan. Now get up. We've got food to cook and decorations to hang."

"Al," Ryder cut in, "we are all obviously very excited about this, and it's going to be so good to remember Bailey, but don't you think...I don't know. I'm going to sound like an asshole, but don't you think that going this extravagant is a little much?"

He clenched his jaw as he waited for her response.

Allie smiled. "You guys think I'd go through all this just for you? God, no." She pulled her phone out of the back pocket of her jean shorts. "You haven't checked Facebook, have you?"

She held her phone out toward us. We all stood and crowded around it. The screen displayed a Facebook event page. The event listed today's date, the address of The Highview, and RSVPs from nearly thirty people. The list comprised Englewood locals whom we had grown to know and love over our years here, plus friends from back home and Bailey's family.

I looked up at Allie.

"Bailey deserves it," Allie said. "If we're going to say goodbye to the house, then we need to say goodbye to what it meant to be here with Bailey. And we need to do that big. Plus, I'm sick of you guys. I need new people to talk to." She pocketed her phone and walked inside, leaving us all on the porch quietly staring at each other.

~*~

It shouldn't have surprised me that so many people would be willing and ready to make the three-hour drive from our hometown to The Highview. Yet, hours later, I still found myself shocked by the guests who walked through the door. Girls who Bailey had sat next to in history, guys who had all come out of the woodwork after graduation to say they should've asked her out on a date in math class, her cousins, even her old drama teacher she had remained in contact with throughout her first semester at Florida State. The Highview, the beach, and the deck were all filled with people.

But when I saw the familiar Volkswagen park on the side of the road, which was already lined with cars overflowing from the packed driveway, I felt true sadness settle in. Mostly because I knew — and even accepted — that it would not be Bailey getting out of that car.

For Bailey's seventeenth birthday (and a combination of a few Christmases and even graduation), her parents had gifted her a used Volkswagen. Within the first week of owning the car — her first car — Bailey had decorated the back window with bumper stickers, hung a pineapple-scented air freshener from the rearview mirror, and bought hot-pink floor mats. She had loved that car, despite the fact that it overheated at stop lights and the back driver's side tire would go flat every other week.

I watched as the Volkswagen's doors opened, and her mother and father got out. Bailey had always had a striking resemblance to her mother; they both had the same light-brown hair and eyes. However, Bailey had gotten her height from her father, who stood taller than six feet. He towered over her mother, and I watched as he gently reached for her hand, and they walked up to the house. I ran down the spiral staircase from where I had been on the top deck with Ethan and Allie and met them at the front gate.

"Hi," I said. The nerves in my stomach were overwhelming.

"Hi, Morgan." Sarah pulled me into a hug and held me there for a few moments as Joe gave my shoulder a pat.

"It's so good to see you," she said when she finally pulled back from the embrace. "And to see you healthy." There were tears in her eyes as she stared at me and smiled, and I felt like my heart was being crushed. I had thought I'd never see Bailey's smile again, but there it was, reflected in Sarah's face as she smiled at me. My chest hurt.

"You too," I said.

My mom must have also seen them pull in because, soon enough, she was standing next to us, talking with Sarah. I stayed standing there while they exchanged pleasantries until

Sarah gave my mom a warm hug, and my mom hurried away to "attend to guests," with a wink to me.

"Morgan, we wanted to give you something," Sarah said.

She walked over to some chairs we had put out on the front porch. She sat down, and I sat next to her. She reached into her purse and pulled out a small box. Opening it, I found inside the charm bracelet I had given Bailey on her tenth birthday. For each subsequent birthday, I'd buy her a new charm. It was decorated with silver flip-flops, a dark blue B, and a seashell. There was also a music note from the year she had dedicated to teaching herself the violin, an etched book, and the one I had gotten her for graduation: an infinity sign.

I ran my fingers over the charms and looked at her parents. "For me?"

"It's too small for my wrist," Sarah joked and gave me a small smile. We sat side by side in silence for a few seconds. I slipped the bracelet on my wrist and ran my thumb over the charms.

"We miss her so much, Morgan," Joe said.

"I do, too. I'm so sorry. It's all my fault." I avoided Sarah's gaze as she tried to meet my eyes.

"Morgan, no one thinks that," Sarah said. "Nothing about her death was your fault."

"If I hadn't been on that bridge, she never would have come after me. I overreacted and was so dramatic, and now everything is different, and Bailey's dead. It wasn't worth it. I got so mad for no reason."

Sarah gave me a small, sad smile.

Joe looked down at me from where he stood. "We miss her too, Morgan, but at the end of it all, we got a wonderful eighteen years with her. The most wonderful girl in the world. Think of it that way, okay? Think of what you gained with Bailey, not about everything you feel like you've lost."

Sarah smiled up at her husband. I suddenly thought of all the stories we'd heard about the early years of their relationship. Bailey would tell us fairy tales about how her parents had met in college while her father was studying English and her mother was studying education. After graduation, they had both accepted jobs on Florida's Space Coast, where they settled down and lived a fairy-tale life. A fairy-tale life that led them to a beautiful little girl, but their fairy tale wasn't over. Tragedy didn't look like it would ruin their love.

"It's just not fair," I said.

"We've thought the same thing every day," Joe started, "but you can't stop living because of it."

"We were mad, Morgan. But not at you. Never at you. And I promise, we aren't just saying that," Sarah said. "We believe it."

I nodded. I needed to learn to believe that I wasn't to blame. I knew it would take some time.

"Now, did your mom make her delicious deviled eggs?" Joe asked.

I laughed, feeling tears I hadn't realized had formed roll down my cheeks as Sarah wrapped me in a hug.

~*~

As the afternoon progressed, I started to feel the exhaustion from the week sneaking up on me. I knew that this was worth it, though. I'd talked with Bailey's parents and mingled with some of Bailey's friends from drama club, but it was the vaguely familiar brunette who was walking towards me now that really caught my eye.

"You're Morgan," she said to me. She held her hands out to me as if wanting to hug me and seemed as shocked as if she was running into her favorite celebrity on the street.

"I am," I said. I hoped my uncertainty wasn't too obvious, but I truly had no clue who she was. But then I stared at her a second longer.

"You're Marissa," I added. Of course, she looked familiar. Bailey's semester at Florida State University was filled with stories about and pictures of Marissa. Marissa smiled at me now, and we both hugged each other, lingering just a second too long. She was a part of Bailey I never really got a chance to know, and now, I wanted to absorb everything she could tell me.

"Allie found me on Instagram and messaged me," Marissa started, "I live kind of nearby in Tampa, and I'm home for the summer, so, of course, I couldn't miss this."

She smiled again and looked around the back deck some more. We'd spread out blankets in the sand and lined the actual deck with chairs, coolers, and tables. The family that was staying in the house next door brought over some of their lawn furniture as well, so that overflowed into the sand.

"Bailey talked about this house all the time. And you, God, I think she thought you hung the moon," Marissa said. She pushed a piece of her hair back and grinned.

"Really?" I asked, hopefully not sounding too desperate.

Marissa nodded, "She had so many pictures of you guys all up on her side of the dorm room. It made me feel like a weirdo because when I graduated high school, none of my friends and I kept in touch."

I smiled. I swallowed.

"Come meet everyone else," I offered.

Marissa smiled, "I did already, thank you. I was just waiting to talk to you. I just wanted to tell you I'm sorry about what happened." She paused, "Bailey was really special. She made me feel special. I can only imagine how you must feel."

"It sucks," I said.

Marissa laughed, a beautiful, full laugh that seemed to spread through her whole body.

"Take care of yourself, okay? And good luck."

I nodded, "You too. Thank you for coming by."

She gave me another hug, and we stood like that for just a second. I wished Bailey could be here to see her worlds collide.

Regret filled me again as Marissa walked away, and I thought back to all the days during our first semester when I was sure Bailey had replaced me. Really, though, it was never about replacing someone. It was about having so much room in your heart that there was space for more than one person. Bailey was my best friend, but I never once gave her the space to explore life without me. When she found out that a life like that existed, she'd still chosen to stay with me. I'd just never seen it that way. I noticed now that the majority of the crowd was gone. The last few people were making their rounds and saying goodbye. I turned around and saw Ryder, Ethan, Allie, and Noah spread out on one of the blankets on the sand. Ryder held his hand up and waved me over. When I walked across the back deck, Ryder met me at the edge of it with a can of Diet Dr. Pepper.

I smiled, "Thanks."

He placed his hand gently on my shoulder, a touch from him I hadn't realized I'd been craving. I sat down in the space next to Allie. I put my head on her shoulder as she took a sip from her drink.

"I can't believe so many people ended up coming," I said.

"I can," Ethan said.

"Did you see the pictures my dad hung up?" Noah asked.

He pointed toward a string of twinkle lights that illuminated hanging photographs. We all stood up and walked over to where they hung right along the entryway of the back of the house. It was like stepping into a time machine, back through our years at The Highview. From candid pictures taken on digital cameras to selfie-styled pictures taken on iPhones, it was a journey through the years we'd spent together. It was photographic proof that we had been there. Our footsteps in the sand would wash away, the doorframe where we had carved our initials would get painted over, and the locks would be changed. But we had been here. We had grown up here, fallen in love here, suffered loss here. We had lived here.

I stared at the pictures of tan lines and laugh lines. We had all been so happy together, and though we were painfully different now, we could be so happy together again. I exhaled a breath of relief and felt in my gut that we would be okay. It would take time, and maybe we would never fully heal, but we would be okay.

The last picture that caught my eye was one I'd never seen before. We were fifteen years old, maybe even fourteen. I was standing on a paddleboard in between Allie and Bailey. We were laughing and trying to balance. Bailey had her head thrown back, her hair dripping salt water down her back. Allie was gripping my arm for dear life, and in the middle of the chaos, I was frozen in time with a smile on my face. Looking closer, I could see Noah in the background, his hands on the paddleboard in an attempt to flip us off. Ryder and Ethan were on either side of the board, each offering a thumbs up. Ethan stared up at Bailey, and Ryder was using his other hand to grab at my leg.

I took the picture down and held it in my hand.

Ryder laughed. "Damn, I remember that day."

Noah leaned over to stare at the picture. He took it from

my hands and examined it, then held it up for Ethan to see.

"I can't believe we've made it this whole week without someone flipping me off a paddleboard," Allie said as she stood on her tiptoes to see over Ethan's shoulder.

"We've still got time," Noah said. Allie glared at him.

"Remember how pissed Bailey would get on the paddleboards?" Ryder asked.

"Yeah, cause her balance sucked," I laughed.

Noah joined in, "But she was too determined to let anyone beat her in any sort of game or activity."

"I secretly think she would get up early and practice while we were still sleeping. She woke up weirdly early all the time," Ethan said.

I laughed at that, imagining Bailey lugging down the seven-foot-long paddleboard to the ocean just to prove a point. It was very feasible. I hung the picture back up and let my eyes wander over the row of photographs one more time.

"God, I miss her," Ethan said quietly. Ryder placed his hand on Ethan's shoulder.

"We're going to be okay," I said.

"What do you mean?" Allie asked.

I looked at everyone, "All of us. We're going to be okay."

"And if we're not?" Ethan asked.

"Then we have each other," Allie said.

"Allie," Noah said, "you're walking proof that good therapy can help even the coldest hearts." Allie threw an empty sparkling water can at his head.

"What I mean is, I'd rather be not okay with you guys than perfectly fine with anyone else," I said.

"Same," Noah said.

Suddenly, it was clear: the goal of life wasn't to always be okay; it was to be with people who understood when you weren't and would still choose to stay.

Chapter 25

Uncle Daniel tossed the last of the recyclables into the bin and sat down with us on the back porch.

"You always do that, Dan," my mom said. "You tell the kids they can do something, but you give them a stipulation, and then you don't enforce it."

"What do you mean?" he asked.

Ethan lowered his voice an octave in a mocking tone. "You kids can have the party, but I'm not lifting a finger to help you clean up after."

Uncle Daniel smiled. "All right, wise ass. Watch out."

The last of the guests had cleared out about an hour before, leaving us with more leftovers than we could ever need and memories that overflowed. It had been a somber celebration at the start, people tiptoeing around each other, unsure of what they could say or how they could react. It hadn't even been a full year since Bailey had died, and it was obvious the wounds were still very fresh. After we all started to settle, though, the day got slightly easier. It turned quickly into something that Bailey would have approved of. Music played on the speaker, laughter filled the empty spaces between songs, and now we were ready for a beautiful sunset: our final sunset together at The Highview.

Uncle Daniel looked around the back deck and out to the beach.

"This is it," he said to no one in particular.

"When do you surrender the keys?" Noah asked.

Uncle Daniel took a sip of the coffee he was drinking, despite it being nearly eight at night. "I sign the papers on Monday."

"Still?" Allie asked.

"What do you mean, 'still'?" Uncle Daniel asked.

"I told you guys. He wasn't going to change his mind," Noah said.

Uncle Daniel nodded. "There will be other houses, son. New memories to make. New things to overcome. We aren't a family because of this house. I want you all to remember that." No one had anything to say to that.

I couldn't believe it. This would really be the last night at The Highview. I'd spent every year since I was a kid counting down until the summertime when we'd be at the house again. My best memories were in this house, on this beach. But also, my best memories were because of these people.

Ethan took a sip of his drink and stared at the hanging pictures again. Bailey. The house. Our friendships and relationships over the years. They all were framed in those pictures, solid proof that what Uncle Daniel was saying was true. We'd never go back to who we were, but we could remember. We could create something new from what we were leaving behind.

"I'd hoped this summer would change your mind," Noah said. "It worked with Morgan. I was hoping you'd see that, and that would be enough to keep the house."

"I'll be forever grateful for this house, Noah. But this is my decision. And it's been made."

"You know we don't blame you for letting us use the house on New Year's Eve, right?" Noah said. "We don't blame the house for what happened. You shouldn't either."

"Noah, sweetie—"

Noah shook his head, interrupting my mom. "It's not fair. This is what we had when Mom left; it's where everything made sense. My whole life was here, Dad, and you're choosing to say goodbye to it."

"Noah, I'm not choosing—"

"But you are. You already did. You already made the choice long before any of us had a say in it."

Uncle Daniel sighed. "Noah, you have grown into a great man. You teach me something new every day, but dude, this is my lesson to you. It's a lesson in moving on." Uncle Daniel stopped. "You kids know better than anyone that life is a scary place to not have people who love you in it. Focus on that. Not on the house."

"This is so unfair," Noah said.

"You're right on that one." Uncle Daniel cupped his hand around Noah's shoulder, and Noah let that settle in.

"Why don't you guys finish cleaning up?" my mom asked. She and Daniel stood up and walked inside the house, shutting the door behind them.

Once the door was shut, Noah looked at us. "Who's ready for one final epic idea?"

~*~

As the sun started to set, Noah led us up to the top deck. Allie was the last to climb the spiral staircase, and we all stood in silent awe as the sun began to set over the ocean. Noah reached into his pocket and pulled out his car keys. Ryder looked at him, confused. I, however, knew exactly what Noah was up to.

He walked to the end of the top deck and placed a hand on the corner of the wooden ledge. The first night after Uncle Daniel had finished building the top deck, Noah and I had snuck up here. At ten years old, we had giggled as we carved our initials into the wood. They were still there.

"I'm sorry my plan didn't work," Noah said to us.

"Dude, what are you talking about?" Ryder said. "This week has been unbelievable."

Noah shrugged. "I really thought he'd change his mind." He looked at where our initials were carved. "But...obviously, I had a backup plan."

He placed his key against the wood and started carefully carving. After a few moments, he stepped back. I peered over his shoulder at the jagged script that now sat next to our initials.

Love always, Bailey.

I smiled. Allie put her arm around my shoulder. Ethan and Ryder both hugged Noah. And we stood on the top deck one final time together. I thought of our last few days together here at The Highview. The awkward silences that melted away as the sun beamed down on us. The arguments that felt like they were dehydrating us. The laughs that came out of nowhere. The memories that protected me.

I thought of Bailey. On the bridge. In the rain.

I thought of Ethan. How he never got to tell her the truth. That he loved her, too.

I walked over to Ethan, who was now on the opposite end of the top deck. He looked down at me and smiled.

"That was a great party," he said.

I nodded.

"We need to go say goodbye," I said, so softly that I thought I'd have to repeat it.

Ethan looked away from me, down at the ocean.

"Will you go to the bridge with me?" I asked.

Chapter 26

Present

Bailey died on a Monday, which sucked because she actually loved Mondays. She had this whole speech every Monday morning when I'd complain as we drove to school.

"There are only 52 Mondays in the year," she'd claimed, "52 chances to start fresh."

I'd once joked it sounded like something that should be painted on an old piece of wood and hung up in a kitchen. She had agreed.

Now, a little over twenty-six Mondays after Bailey died, I was walking up the same bridge where she took her last breath. The breath she took after calling after me and yelling, "Morgan, move!"

I wished there was a way to make this moment so it wasn't just about me, but in the deepest and most selfish pits of my stomach, it was. It had to be. I'd spent twenty-six Mondays in bitter denial and in suffocating pain. I'd spent every sunrise this summer trying to make sense of anything. The times Ryder sat on his hands, waiting for me to get better. Every single moment Ethan looked at me, his eyes screaming that he wasn't sleeping either, and dear God, please remember.

It was fitting to be standing here with him. We were two people who loved Bailey and two people who had hurt her.

On this same bridge twenty-six Mondays ago, Bailey had run up after me, heartbroken because Ethan had stayed silent. Heartbroken because I had said she deserved it. That she was a liar.

She had followed me up this bridge to walk me home, but champagne had clouded my brain as she called after me.

A car. A horn. An ambulance.

When I replay it in my head, I change the ending. Instead, it went like this:

"Bailey, wait," Ethan called at the last minute. He didn't want to spend another second away from her. He did love her.

"I have to get Morgan. Can we talk when I get back?" she replied. In her mind, it was bad news he had wanted to deliver.

And I heard her devotion to me. And I heard how she loved someone, but we promised we'd always be there for each other, so she had to do that. I heard all of that, and I turned around. I told her I was mad. I wanted space. But we got back to the house and to safety. The next morning, we'd awkwardly laugh about it.

I wished she had stayed back with him. She never got to hear the words herself: Wow, I love you too.

Now, Ethan stuck his hands in his pockets. He stood next to me as a shell of perfection. He was a shell, and I was a void, both of us waiting for anyone or anything to fill us up again. To make us whole.

Out over the water, the sun was beginning to set, streaks of color crashing around us: Pink, like the color of the anklet Bailey had picked out last summer at the corner store. Red, like the color of her favorite sweatshirt, the one she had packed each summer for when she got ridiculously sunburned, and Allie and I would refuse to turn off the fan. Orange, like the color of her fingernails. Even the sunset was a reminder that everything in my life, for the rest of my life, would remind me of Bailey.

Cars drove past Ethan and me, and as we stood at the bottom of the bridge that had ruined our lives, yet somehow, something started to feel like it was stitching me back up again.

Bailey would never watch a sunset again. She'd never get another chance to go digging through coolers at a gas station, looking for a Coca-Cola bottle with her name on it. She'd never again be able to do the simple things, like get a haircut or go for a run on the beach, or smell that first wisp of salt air on a hot summer morning.

Bailey would never, would never, would never.

She'd never graduate college. She'd never start a career and then decide she hated it and would rather travel the world trying to find herself. She'd never live in a small studio apartment in New York City like she'd always wanted to. She'd never fall in love again. She'd never stand next to me at my wedding or over me, staring down at my future newborn baby.

Remember this moment, she used to say, smiling back over her freckled shoulders and pointing a finger at Allie or me.

She'd never do any of that again, but I could.

"What are you thinking about?" Ethan asked.

"What I want to eat for dinner," I joked. Ethan laughed.

We stopped at the top of the bridge and stared out at the water. He put an arm around my shoulders.

"Did you love her?" I asked.

Ethan looked taken aback by my question. "Isn't it obvious?"

I shrugged.

"Of course I did."

"But…why?" I asked. "What made her so special?"

Maybe if I heard him say it, we could figure it out together. We could figure out what we needed to do if we were ever going to be able to fill this void.

"Okay," he started and then laughed. "The first time I kissed her, she pulled away kind of quickly and told me to calm down, that we'd have the rest of our lives to ruin our friendship with a kiss."

"I feel so guilty that she felt like she couldn't tell me about you guys," I admitted.

"We felt guilty too. We just didn't know how to."

Ethan gazed out at the water, where a dolphin sight-seeing boat floated by. "I just keep thinking about how easy everything was with her. She did things like memorize my food orders, and in ninth grade, she swore she wouldn't tell you guys when I cried reading To Kill a Mockingbird in English."

"Oh, we knew about that. She told Allie and me the second we sat down at lunch that day."

Ethan laughed. "She cared about me. When she visited me in Orlando, she would always organize my desk. And it was such a small act, but it meant so much. I wish I had told her how much it meant to me."

He stopped talking. In our ten years of friendship, I had rarely seen Ethan cry. Looking at him now, I knew it was getting close to a second time.

"You know, I don't know if she was the love of my life, but I loved her. I think, even more important was the fact that she was my best friend. That's what can't be replaced."

I wondered how Bailey had felt about Ethan, and for what I knew would not be the last time in my life, I felt a pang of guilt that when she did tell me about them, my first response had been anger. My best friend, who had loved everyone so fiercely, had been in love, and I had looked the other way because I wasn't the first person she told.

"I think she really loved you too."

Ethan smiled. After a moment, he nudged me. "What about you and Ryder, though?"

"God, someone give that guy a medal for putting up with me."

Ethan laughed. "Do you want to get back together with him?"

"I wish I had an answer."

Ethan kicked at the sidewalk and let his eyes meet mine. "We've gotta get better, Morgan. For her. You know she wouldn't want this." His voice cracked, and tears spilled from his eyes. I shook my head as a lump formed in my throat.

We turned away from the bridge and started walking back toward The Highview. Twenty-six Mondays ago, the brightest person in my life had screamed my name as a car came barreling toward me. At the last minute, she had pushed me out of the way, and I had stood in the middle of the road as I watched that same car swerve and change my life forever. That was twenty-six Mondays, and I would do anything to go back to twenty-six Sundays ago and tell her we could talk it out. Instead of storming away, I'd follow her up the spiral staircase, and we'd giggle as the clock turned to midnight, and she told me what it was like to kiss Ethan and fall in love.

I would have given every Monday for the rest of my life if it meant I could go back to that Sunday.

~*~

Ethan and I took our time walking back to the house. When we got there, Ryder, Allie, and Noah were sitting in the driveway.

"There you are. We were just about to go to the beach and watch the sunset," Ryder said.

Allie wrapped her arm through mine. "How was it?" she asked.

Ethan and I looked at each other. How did we explain the moment when healing forced itself to begin on the same bridge that had caused the trauma in the first place? That was what was so tragic about it all: had it not happened, we would all be here. We weren't just missing Bailey. We missed the carefree way in which Ethan and Noah would race the kayaks. We longed for the stretched-out summer days that felt like they could go on forever. We mourned lost love in every aspect possible. We didn't just lose Bailey on New Year's Eve. We lost our childhood.

When neither of us responded, Allie squeezed Ethan's shoulder and smiled at me.

On previous evenings, we'd run down to the beach with the hope of catching the last glimpse of the sun before it set. But tonight, things were somber with the confirmation that The Highview wasn't ours anymore. I hoped that Uncle Daniel was right. It was just a house. We still had the memories.

Ryder, Ethan, and Noah eventually broke into a sprint. They pulled off their shirts, dropped their phones in the sand, and jumped into the ocean. Allie walked alongside my mom, telling her about the classes she'd loved over her first year of college.

Uncle Daniel walked next to me. "I love daylight. It gives me so much hope."

We walked closer to the water and stopped just as the tide broke at our ankles.

"Are you mad at me about the house, kiddo?" he asked.

I shrugged. "A little. But I think I finally understand it."

"Oh, yeah?"

"We've been putting too much pressure on the house to save us. To be perfect, so to speak. Kind of like we do for each other."

I stopped talking. I looked out at the ocean where Noah, Ryder, and Ethan were splashing.

"I thought I was better off grieving alone. I thought I was the only one hurt. I was so wrong; I needed people."

Uncle Daniel nodded. "You're a good one, Morgan." He patted my back and then put an arm around my shoulders.

I didn't know what the future held. I might wake up and still find it hard to get out of bed, but I knew my days of texting Bailey were done. Maybe I'd go back to college in August, a few credits behind but with a new sense of who I was. I could do all of those things that Bailey would never do. And I would do them for her, but for myself too.

Whatever happened, I knew that in the moments of darkness, I had people who would be there to always lead me back to daylight.

It was a simple life, intertwined with late nights on the top deck and mornings of pranks to pull each other out of bed.

It was a life characterized by love. One I would never forget.

The End

Acknowledgments

There are a handful of people that championed this book early on, and I'll forever be thankful: Brendan Kiely, David Yoo, Laura Williams McCaffrey, Olugbemisola Rhuday-Perkovich. To my lovely Solstice cohort, Jasmine, Martin, Monika, Betsy, and Renee: thank you for being early readers and loving these characters deeply.

This book simply wouldn't exist without Jenn and Jenna. I could write love stories about what your friendship has meant to me daily. Thank you for loving every version of me over the last 20 years.

Thank you Todd Tinker and the team at World Castle Publishing, for editorial guidance.

My stories are all based in relationships, and as this is my first published book, I need to take the time to thank those relationships in my life that make my writing better by making my life better.

My sisters, Rachel and Ryan, and my mom, for encouraging

me to turn everything into a story. Nene and Dede, for always asking if I'm happy. Sabina, Maddie, and Mara, thank you for reading this manuscript during lockdown. Mallory, Marisa, and Teddy who are the fiercest supporters of anything I do. Sammie, Jenae, and Devin, for the laughter and ghost tours. Kristin Morgan-Hughes, for our time in Colorado. To all of my babies: Jude, Owen, Emmy, Max, Bella, Gia, Liam, and Logan: I hope you don't mind that I'll be using your names in future novels.

And finally, Dustin Grinnell who listened with curiosity as I explained the premise that first night we met and has done so since for the last five years. I hope we get to watch Goosebumps together forever.

Samantha Cooke is a Florida native who writes stories close to her beachside roots. As a playwright, her work has appeared on stage at The Orlando International Fringe Festival, The University of Central Florida, and Rocky Mountain Theatre for Kids (Denver, CO). Her fiction has been published in various online journals. She holds an MFA in Creative Writing for Young Adults from The Solstice MFA Program. She now lives in the seaside town of Winthrop, MA, where she works as a communications manager for KIPP Massachusetts Public Charter Schools.

www.ingramcontent.com/pod-product-compliance
Lightning Source LLC
Chambersburg PA
CBHW050725180626
46814CB00002B/608